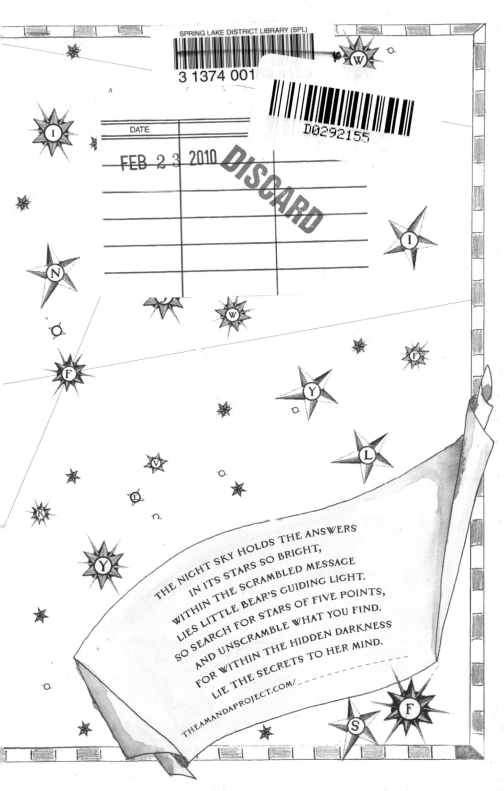

THE NIGHT SKY HOLDS THE ANSWERS
IN ITS STARS SO BRIGHT,
WITHIN THE SCRAMBLED MESSAGE
LIES LITTLE BEAR'S GUIDING LIGHT.
SO SEARCH FOR STARS OF FIVE POINTS,
AND UNSCRAMBLE WHAT YOU FIND.
FOR WITHIN THE HIDDEN DARKNESS
LIE THE SECRETS TO HER MIND.

THEAMANDAPROJECT.COM/_ _ _ _ _ _ _ _

THE AMANDA PROJECT

invisible i

BOOK ONE
BY MELISSA KANTOR

HARPER TEEN

An Imprint of HarperCollinsPublishers

FOURTH STORY MEDIA
NEW YORK

Fourth Story Media, 115 South Street, 4F, New York, NY 10038

Library of Congress Cataloging-in-Publication Data is available.
ISBN 978-0-06-174212-5
Book design by Polly Kanevsky and Dale Robbins
Interior illustrations by Brian Floca
09 10 11 12 13   CG/RRDH   10 9 8 7 6 5 4 3 2 1

First Edition

for jillellyn riley and lisa holton

"Every exit is an entrance somewhere else."

Tom Stoppard
Rosencrantz and Guildenstern Are Dead

CHAPTER ONE

Why is it that when you don't want to think about something, you can't stop thinking about it?

From the second I woke up, the scene Amanda had witnessed at my house yesterday kept playing over and over in my head like some kind of sick YouTube video on repeat. I'd thought about it while I was getting dressed, while I was riding my bike to school, and even while Kelli and I stood by her locker and she tried to recap the entire plot of the Reese Witherspoon movie she'd caught just the tail end of last night. Now I was sitting in history class, hearing not Mr. Randolph explaining the causes of World War I but my dad's voice in my head saying the same words over and over again while I tried to figure out what, exactly, Amanda had overheard. Everything, probably. The phone rang while I was upstairs looking for my Scribble Book, and since my dad was practically screaming into the receiver by the time I got back to the kitchen, the conversation had obviously begun a while back. I mean, considering how much she and I have talked, Amanda had obviously known *something* was going on. She knew more than anyone else at school did. But up until yesterday she hadn't known *everything*. She hadn't known the worst of it. She knew about my mom, but she didn't know about the money.

And now she did.

The crazy thing was, she hadn't seemed surprised. It was almost as if somehow she'd guessed a long time ago . . .

". . . Which is why, yes, the assassination of the Archduke *is* the catalyst but is not the cause *per se*." I'm usually kind of into Mr. Randolph's class even though I'm not exactly what you'd call a history buff. He's really nice and patient and he explains everything clearly, and he's one of the only teachers at Endeavor who actually prepares you for the test he's going to give. Still, there was no way I could concentrate on this morning's lesson.

I shook my head and straightened up in my chair, clicking some lead out of my mechanical pencil. Perhaps if I resembled an attentive student, I would become one.

"Did you all write that down? *Entangling alliances*. If you remember nothing else from today, remember that."

The board was covered in notes, but Mr. Randolph had found room to write *entangling alliances* in letters almost six inches high and he'd underlined "entangling" about fifty times. I rolled my eyes at myself as I began to copy down the crucial phrase. No doubt entangling alliances *was* the only thing I'd be remembering from today's class. Too bad I had no idea what they were or who had them.

Just as I started writing *alliances*, Lexa Booker, who was sitting next to me, slid a crumpled piece of paper across my notebook. I palmed it expertly—Heidi and I have had enough classes together that I can pretty much make a note from her disappear in a nanosecond—and finished the word, then carefully unfolded the paper.

I looked up. The desks in Mr. Randolph's room are in a big horseshoe, and Heidi was all the way on the other side of it, but her eyes met mine and she raised her exquisitely shaped eyebrows. I nodded almost imperceptibly, grateful to have something to think about besides Amanda knowing even more about my screwed-up family than she had last week. This Saturday's party was going to be amazing, and the I-Girls—Kelli, Heidi, Traci, and yours truly (okay, I briefly spelled my name with an "i," but not anymore!)—the reigning queens of the ninth grade, were going in green. That was cool—I have a dark green fitted T-shirt, and once when we all went to the movies I wore it. Lee was there, and he'd said my eyes looked really pretty when I wore green. Thinking about Lee, I felt my face go pink, which is what happens to redheaded Irish girls when we're embarrassed. Or scared. Or hot. Or just the slightest bit nervous or uncomfortable. Basically between twenty and a thousand times a day.

"Callista Leary?"

My head shot up at the sound of my full name. Had Mr. Randolph noticed the note going around the horseshoe? Some teachers, if they catch you passing a note, make you read it out loud to the class. Not that this was such an incriminating missive, but still. Then I realized it was a woman's voice that had said my name and Mr. Randolph wasn't even looking at me; he (along with everyone else in the room) had turned toward the door where one of the secretaries from the main office was standing.

"Um . . . that's me." Everyone was staring, and I could feel the heat spreading across my face and down my chest in a hard-core blush.

"You're wanted in the vice principal's office."

For a split second it was as though I'd just been addressed in a language other than English; I literally couldn't make sense of the words she'd spoken. "I'm . . . ?" I repeated stupidly.

"You can take your things," she added, bobbing her head with its tight bun. "You won't be coming back this period."

As if my befuddlement were written on my face, Mr. Randolph said, "You'll get the notes from someone tomorrow, Callie. Go with Mrs. Leong for now."

Suddenly I wasn't confused anymore, I was frightened.

4

Could this have something to do with my mom? I stood up fast, nearly toppling my desk. Then my backpack got twisted up in the chair and my shaking fingers couldn't work the zipper. I could practically hear everyone in the room pitying me.

As I passed her, Heidi whispered, "What happened?" Unlike Traci and Kelli, Heidi knew about my mom. She knew, but we never talked about it. Just like we never talked about anything else that happened that night. Ever.

I shook my head as a way of saying I had no idea, and as she reached out her hand to touch mine for a second, her lovely face wrinkled with concern, I had this really ugly thought. *Is she doing that because she's worried about me or because she wants it to look like she's worried about me?*

I seemed to be having those thoughts about Heidi a lot lately, but before I could turn back to check the expression on her face, I was outside the classroom with the door swinging shut behind me.

It was weird walking down the silent hallway. Normally I'm only in the corridors between classes, when there are a million other Endeavor students elbowing past one another to get to class. Now it was so silent I could actually feel the echo from the click of Mrs. Leong's chunky heels. I noticed a corner of an old homecoming banner had come loose, the heavy blue felt swaying in a breeze I couldn't feel. "The Endeavor Enders: We don't GOT spirit, we ARE spirits!" How had anyone ever thought having a ghost for a mascot was a good idea? And why did I have to be reminded of ghosts now, when for all I knew I was about to find out that my mom was . . .

Mrs. Leong pushed open the door to the main office. Here there was no hint of the silence of the hallways—a dozen phones seemed to be ringing at once, a Xerox machine was going about a hundred miles a minute and at least two other secretaries were busily typing away at their computers. It was like I was in the headquarters of a major corporation instead of the office of the Endeavor Unified Middle and High School.

Remembering Amanda's suggestion for a new school motto ("We don't stand a ghost of a chance!") momentarily held my anxiety at bay, but my stomach sank as Mrs. Leong gestured toward Vice Principal Thornhill's office. "Go in. He's expecting you." I had a second to consider the irony that it was Mr. Thornhill who was about to witness my getting the worst possible news about my mom. For no good reason, my dad totally hates him, yet it was in this man's office that he'd have to tell me the awful truth.

Heart pounding, I pushed open the door, sure the next sight I'd see would be my father's tear-stained face.

CHAPTER 2

But my dad wasn't even there.

Three chairs faced Mr. Thornhill's desk. The middle one was empty, while the other two were filled by Nia Rivera, the biggest freak in the ninth grade, and Hal Bennett, who I guess is what you could call a recovering loser. All through middle school, Hal was this bean pole who wore high-waisted, too-short pants and looked like his mom cut his hair by putting a bowl over his head and trimming around the base of it. But he must have spent his summer watching *Queer Eye for the Straight Guy* or something because when we got back to school in September, he had become über-cool. Now he wore vintage T-shirts and worn jeans that he totally filled out, if you know what I'm saying, and his dark blond hair had this whole shaggy-but-styled thing going on. Also, he was, like, an artistic genius. Maybe he always had been, but this year he'd done a devastating caricature of Thornhill in the school paper that created a buzz for a few days, and then he was chosen to go to New York to represent the entire state of Maryland in a contest that some big museum sponsored back in November. He'd even shown up on the I-Girls' radar—Kelli and Traci were talking at lunch last week about what a hottie Hal Bennett was becoming, and after years of being afraid that they would somehow find out that he and I had hung out together before I became an I-Girl, I suddenly wanted to tell them. I didn't say anything, though. I noticed that Heidi did not weigh in at all, and what if I told them about our once having been friends and then he somehow got re-dorkified?

"Have a seat, Callie," said Mr. Thornhill. Totally confused, I slipped into the empty chair. Clearly my being summoned here had nothing to do with my mother.

Mr. Thornhill had his hands folded under his chin, his index fingers touching the ends of his short, bristly moustache, forming a V around his mouth. The fluorescent light shone on his bald head, so shiny you'd have thought he spent his mornings polishing it.

No one was talking, and no one other than Mr. Thornhill acknowledged my entry. Since I'd never been in the vice principal's office before, I checked out the room. There wasn't a whole lot there, no diplomas or pictures of his family. One wall was covered in file cabinets with alphabetized labels, and in the center of the desk was a small pile of manila folders but nothing personal—no Endeavor mug to hold his pencils or a

#1 DAD paperweight. It was almost weird how blank the room was considering Mr. Thornhill had been the vice principal here since I started middle school.

The silence grew. I turned my head slightly to look first at Hal and then at Nia, but he was staring at the carpet, and her thick hair hung along the side of her face so I couldn't see her expression. As my eyes swept the room, Mr. Thornhill and I made eye contact for a second and his stare was so intense I had to look away. It was like he was . . . angry at me or something. For the first time, it occurred to me that I could be in trouble. I mean, he *was* the vice principal. I tried to think of a rule I might have broken recently, but it wasn't like I'd been smoking in the bathroom or not doing my homework or anything.

"Well," he announced finally, "I think you all know why you're here."

Okay, this was getting really weird. For the first time since Mrs. Leong had called my name, I actually started to find the whole thing funny. I imagined telling Heidi, Traci, and Kelli the story over lunch. *And then it was like he thought I'd done something. With Nia Rivera!* For the past two years, the words *Nia Rivera* had been a guaranteed punch line with the I-Girls, so I knew they'd crack up as soon as I uttered them.

As it happened, Nia was the first to break the silence. "Actually, I have no idea why I'm here." She swept her long brown hair over her shoulder, not flirtatiously, like an I-Girl would have, but impatiently, like it was annoying to have hair.

I was really surprised by how confident she sounded, as if

she wasn't afraid of the vice principal at all, and for a second I was reminded of the fact that she is Cisco Rivera's sister. Cisco is the coolest, most popular guy in the junior class. It's hard to believe two people who are such polar opposites could be even distantly related, much less siblings. It makes you think their parents performed some kind of social experiment on them when they were young.

Mr. Thornhill slammed his hand down on the desk so hard I jumped slightly, but I noticed Nia did not flinch. "Nia, I really don't have time for lies right now. This is potentially a very serious situation."

Like I said, I don't exactly spend a lot of time getting called into the vice principal's office, but I had heard him get mad before. Actually, the person I'd heard him getting mad at was Amanda—many times since she arrived in October, and most recently about a month ago. I'd come to the office to drop off the day's attendance slip for Mrs. Peabody, and his door was open and he was yelling at her. It was the day after the President's Day holiday, and the vice principal had opened the door to his office to discover a huge stuffed raven wearing a stovepipe hat sitting on his chair. I don't know how Thornhill figured out that Amanda had done it, and she'd never told me if he'd been right to accuse her or, if he had, how she'd gotten into the vice principal's office in the first place, but he was furious. And that was far from the only time, either. After the master clock in the

office was rigged to run fast so that school got out early two Fridays in a row, I could hear him yelling at her in his office while I was walking by in the hallway.

Now he sounded that mad. Mad like Nia had done something really, really terrible.

Whatever it was, I definitely didn't want to be associated with it. Or her. I cleared my throat. "Um, Mr. Thornhill, I think there's been some mistake. We don't even *know* one another." Sometimes the cluelessness of adults is nothing short of shocking. I mean, not to be snotty, but I'm an I-Girl and Nia's a social leper. Did Mr. Thornhill think we were friends or something?

"Callie, you've always been an excellent student with spotless behavior." Mr. Thornhill tapped the folders on his desk and I wondered if one of them had something to do with me. "I highly doubt you want to ruin such a stellar record by failing to tell me what you know." Was it my imagination, or did Mr. Thornhill emphasize the word *stellar*? Once again, I thought of my mother.

"Look, Mr. Thornhill, they're not lying," said Hal. "We really don't hang together." As he leaned forward, the small gold loop in his ear caught the light, and I remembered Traci had said something about his supposedly getting a tattoo somewhere on his body over the summer.

"No, *you* look, Hal. I am talking about a *serious* act of vandalism. I want you to tell me what you know and I want you to tell me *now*."

Mr. Thornhill was so angry a vein bulged on his neck. I

actually felt a little afraid of him. This time, when I glanced over at Nia, she was looking at me, and I knew the *What the hell?* look on her face was mirrored on my own.

"Why don't you tell us what *you* know?" said Hal. His voice was calm, soothing. Like he thought Mr. Thornhill was crazy or something.

Which, given the circumstances, didn't seem so impossible.

Mr. Thornhill leaned forward and jabbed his finger in Hal's direction. "Don't you condescend to me, Hal Bennett. You all *know* what Amanda Valentino did this morning. What I want to know is, why has she implicated the three of you in her crime?"

Okay, this was so weird. I mean, I'd *just* been thinking of Amanda when Mrs. Leong called me into Thornhill's office, and now he was mad at me for something she'd done. But still, what he was saying made no sense. I mean, Amanda and I were friends, but Amanda and Nia and Hal weren't. *Nobody* was friends with Nia, except maybe some of the other weirdos in Model Congress or Mock Trial or whatever lame clubs she belonged to. And as hot as Hal may have been, he still only hung out with a few other dorky guys whose names escaped me. But not Amanda.

"Look, obviously you're not going to believe us if we say we're innocent. So why don't you just ask her yourself? She'll tell you," said Nia, and the crazy thing was that now her confidence didn't remind me of Cisco so much as of Amanda, the only other person I knew who never backed down in the face of authority.

Vice Principal Thornhill got up and walked around to the front of his desk. Then he leaned back on it and crossed his arms, staring at each of us in turn.

"That's a lovely idea, Nia, and I'd be happy to comply. There's just one problem with your plan. As the three of you know perfectly well, Amanda Valentino has disappeared."

chapter 3

I felt as if Mr. Thornhill hadn't spoken so much as he'd just slammed me in the head with a piece of wood from my dad's workshop. Amanda had disappeared?

"But—" I was about to say that Amanda hadn't disappeared, that she'd just been over at my house yesterday, but before I could finish my sentence, Nia cut me off.

"But you don't seem to understand, Mr. Thornhill. None of us is even *friends* with Amanda Valentino."

I jerked my head to stare at her. On the one hand, I knew Nia was telling the truth. I *knew* it. How could Amanda have been friends with someone so . . . well, so weird? And she'd never even *mentioned* Nia, not once. Of *course* they weren't friends.

But there was something about the way Nia's face was whiter than the school mascot and how tightly she was clutching the arms of her chair that made it seem as if she were lying. Which would mean she and Amanda *were* friends. Only that was . . .

"Impossible, Nia," said Vice Principal Thornhill, and now he sounded almost tired. "That is simply not possible." He walked over to the window and opened the blind. "First of all: look."

The sky had cleared after last night's rain, and the bright sun on the wet pavement of the parking lot was nearly blinding. I squinted against its rays as the three of us stood up and went over to the window.

"What are we looking at?" asked Hal, and I realized I was so lost in my own thoughts I hadn't been looking for anything *to* look at.

"My car," said the vice principal.

As soon as he said it, I saw which car was his. Which car *had* to be his. Parked slightly off to one side of the faculty parking lot, it was the brightest thing in sight. Actually, it could have been the brightest thing in the entire world. Even from a distance, it seemed to throb with color—I couldn't decipher all the designs,

but there was a gigantic rainbow that extended from the front wheel to the back wheel and a huge peace sign covering most of the driver's side door. I could just make out what looked like a group of stars on the back door and a bright yellow sun on the hubcap below it.

The whole thing was so outrageous that I suddenly burst out laughing. I couldn't help myself—it was like the car was some huge joke of Amanda's. Only, once I started laughing, I couldn't stop. I was sure everyone else was going to laugh, too, but they didn't, and I started to get freaked out, like maybe I was getting hysterical or something. I almost wished someone would throw a glass of cold water in my face.

"I'm glad you find this funny, Callista," said Mr. Thornhill.

It wasn't a glass of cold water, but it worked like one. As if I had an on-off switch, I stopped laughing immediately. Mr. Thornhill left the blind up, walked back to his desk, and sat down. I wasn't sure if we were supposed to sit down also, but since neither Nia nor Hal made a move to go back to their chairs, I stayed with them by the window. I didn't look back at the car, though. I was afraid if I did I'd just start laughing again.

"Even if Amanda did paint all over your car," said Hal, "what makes you think we had something to do with it? Like Nia said, we aren't even, you know, friends with her."

I was about to open my mouth to correct Hal and tell Mr. Thornhill that I *was* friends with Amanda even though obviously Hal and Nia weren't, when Hal looked directly at me with his startlingly blue eyes and added, "We don't know her at all." Was it my imagination or was he trying to tell me something?

Or trying to tell me *not* to tell something?

"If you aren't friends with her," said Vice Principal Thornhill, "then why, in addition to vandalizing my car, did she spray-paint a symbol on each of your lockers?"

Amanda had spray-painted something on my *locker*? I was about to ask what, but before I could say anything, Mr. Thornhill continued.

"And perhaps you'd like to tell me if she left something *inside* your lockers?"

She'd gone in my locker? Why would he think she had gone in my locker? Anyway my locker was locked, and nobody but me knew the combination.

As if speaking my thoughts, Hal said, "How could Amanda even have gotten inside our lockers?"

For the first time since we'd entered his office, Mr. Thornhill smiled. "An excellent question, Hal," and he slipped his hands behind his head and leaned back in his chair. "Why don't *you* tell *me*?"

* * *

17

"I just like having them, knowing somewhere there's a lock and I could open it if I wanted to."

Outside it was pouring, a freezing February rain that seemed as if it might continue forever. The rain only made my room, which I generally love anyway, feel even cozier, like a tiny haven that the wet and cold could never penetrate. Even the fact that the silence from my dad's workshop meant he was probably drinking and not working didn't bother me when Amanda started talking about something cool, like why she collected keys.

"They're not worth anything," I pointed out. As usual, my mind was quick to turn to money. It's funny how when you don't have any, suddenly all paths seem to lead to it.

"True," said Amanda, fingering the tiny, ancient-looking key she always wore on a ribbon around her neck. "But I like their symbolic value."

We were sitting on the floor, Amanda resting her back against the big armchair and me facing her, my back against the bed. We were both wearing a pair of slippers from the basket by the front door, and I had my comforter wrapped around my legs. The day before, Amanda had cut her hair short and blunt, but today she was wearing a long, platinum wig. I'd asked her if it was because she didn't like the cut, but she'd said, "No, I like it. Why do you ask?" in this way that made it seem like wearing a wig the day after you get your hair cut was just something anybody would do.

"But where do you get used keys?" I asked.

"Oh, the Salvation Army or antique stores. Or if someone's

got a really big ring of keys it usually means there's at least one they don't use anymore." She swung the key chain back and forth, admiring her collection.

"It's like something a custodian would carry," I said. Once I watched a custodian get something out of a supply closet at Endeavor. Even though his key ring must have had a hundred keys, he found the one he needed in less than a second. "I could never find the right key if I had as many as they do."

Amanda looked at me. "You don't carry a house key." It was a statement, but there was a little question mark at the end of it, like I should explain if I wanted but I didn't have to.

My family never locked the front door. Not that there would have been any point to locking it. Farmhouses built at the turn of the last century might have a lot of charm, but they weren't usually designed with airtight security in mind. Even if we did bother to lock the doors, anyone who really wanted to break in would have needed about ten seconds to do so.

"I don't *have* a key," I said. "My mom lived in New York City for a while, and when she and my dad bought this house she said her favorite thing about living in the country was not having to lock her door." As soon as the words were out of my mouth I realized my mom might never again open our front door with or without a key. The thought made my eyes burn.

Amanda didn't say anything, just looked away from me and studied her key chain. I knew she wasn't avoiding the subject, she was giving me a minute of privacy. I took a deep breath.

"Here," she said suddenly, and she flipped the keys fast around the circle before slipping one off. "Take it."

I took the key from her hand and studied it. It was just a regular key, but it had a five-digit number and the words DO NOT DUPLICATE stamped on the top.

"What does it open?" I asked.

Amanda shrugged. Then she smiled, her bright eyes sparkling with the joke. "Well, whatever it opens, I sure hope they duplicated it before they lost it."

I laughed and slipped the key into my pocket. "Thanks."

"Unscrew the locks from the doors! / Unscrew the doors themselves from their jambs!" she said.

"Totally." Seeing she was ignoring my confused expression, I stood up. "Now let's eat. I'm starving."

CHAPTER FOUR

Vice Principal Thornhill marched us to our lockers so we could show him anything Amanda might have stashed inside. While we were in his office, first period had ended and second had started, so the halls were empty again. This time I was glad rather than creeped out by the stillness; the last thing I wanted was the population of Endeavor staring and pointing at the three of us as our lockers were inspected like we were criminals or something. I distracted myself by reading the flyers for chess club, band rehearsal, call-outs for newspaper contributions, and the formation of some new after-school jazz quartet. None of these were I-Girl activities.

Nia's locker was in the humanities corridor, just a few feet from Mr. Randolph's room, and I realized I'd passed it on my way to class this morning and definitely hadn't noticed anything weird (not that I would have even known it was hers if I had). As we stood in front of it now, though, I saw that in the bottom right-hand corner was a small stencil of an animal, a bird of some sort, painted a metallic gray slightly paler than the gray of the metal locker. Nia's expression definitely changed when she looked at it—as we'd walked from Mr. Thornhill's room, she'd been scowling as usual, but suddenly her face was the picture of amazement. The look was gone almost as soon as it appeared, and I didn't know if Mr. Thornhill had seen it or not.

"Anyone could have done this, Mr. Thornhill," she said. "What makes you think it was Amanda?" Her hand fluttered up, and it looked like she was about to touch the picture, but then she seemed to think better of it and jerked her hand back, pulling the sleeves of her pale blue sweater almost to her fingertips as she crossed her arms tightly across her chest.

Mr. Thornhill gave her a long look but all he said was, "Open it, please." She hesitated for a second, like maybe she really did have something to hide, but then expertly turned the combination lock and jerked the door open.

I couldn't help being curious to know what someone like Nia would have in her locker. She was so serious—it wouldn't have surprised me if there'd been a bound set of Supreme Court cases or a collection of Save the Whales bumper stickers in different languages. While Mr. Thornhill rifled through the unexpected amount of junk piled high inside—books and notebooks, two pairs of broken sunglasses, a bunch of empty candy wrappers, a bag of marbles, some Mardi Gras beads—I

snuck glances at the postcard of the poster for a movie called *The Thin Man* taped next to a picture of a Mayan or Aztec warrior-looking guy on the inside of the door under a magnet in the shape of a fish with the word *DARWIN* written inside it. Pretty surprising stuff compared with what I'd imagined.

Mr. Thornhill didn't find anything that would have definitively proven Nia's guilt, and it obviously pissed him off. He slammed her locker shut and started walking. Hal and I followed a few paces behind. When I looked around to see what had happened to Nia, she was standing, staring at the closed door of her locker. A minute later, she turned and ran to catch up with us.

As soon as she was walking alongside me and Hal she said, "I—"

"Not now," said Hal. His voice was somewhere between a whisper and a hiss.

"But—"

"Not now," he said again.

Hal's face remained completely blank as we stood in front of his locker, where there was a stencil of another animal— some kind of cat or maybe a lion—also in pale gray, also in the lower right-hand corner. He was wearing a long-sleeved white T-shirt, and he looked almost bored as he leaned his hip into the wall of lockers next to his own, toying with one of the cuffs while Mr. Thornhill rifled through his stuff. Hal's locker was really organized for a boy's—there were books and notebooks neatly lined up, and hanging on the inside of the door was a small pouch with a bunch of colored pens in it. At one point,

Mr. Thornhill took what looked like a sketchbook off the shelf and held it, closed, for a minute, looking at Hal as if to see if he'd flinch.

I flinched for him. I mean, Hal's a great artist and I can barely draw a stick figure, but my artistic talents (or lack thereof) aren't the reason that if Mr. Thornhill ever looked through my Scribble Book, I'd die of shame. The whole thing is just so . . . personal. It's the closest thing I have to a diary, and the only person I'd ever let see it was Amanda. I realized that if I hadn't left it at home today, Mr. Thornhill, Hal, and Nia might have had the opportunity to look at my most private thoughts, and I wondered if that was the kind of thing Hal sketched. If so, he must have been crying inside.

But Hal's face remained blank as Mr. Thornhill raised the book slightly, then lowered it, as if he were weighing the decision to open it, literally and metaphorically. After a minute, he slipped the book back where it had been and slammed Hal's locker shut, too. Hal stayed behind to lock it after Thornhill had walked away, and when I turned back to check if he was following us, I saw him standing with his head leaning against the cool metal.

I could feel my heart beating in my throat as we turned the corner into the science wing, where my locker was. I never go to my locker until after first period since all of my first period classes were about as far from the science wing as you can get without actually leaving the town of Orion. The last time I'd been here was yesterday, right before math, my last class. I'd actually been standing right here when I got Amanda's text—

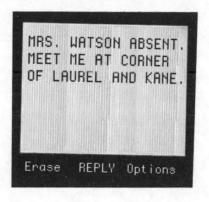

MRS. WATSON ABSENT.
MEET ME AT CORNER
OF LAUREL AND KANE.

Erase   REPLY Options

My locker is halfway down the hall, and it seemed to me that the trip was definitely proving Zeno's Paradox—you can't travel from point A to point B because the distance must be divided by half each time, and you can divide distances in half indefinitely until you've proven you can't move forward at all. I watched the numbers climb from 100 to 110 to 120 and then, finally, 128. My locker.

I scanned the scuffed, metal surface, but I didn't see anything in the corner where Hal's cat and Nia's bird had been. I had time to feel an instant of confusion and disappointment when suddenly my eyes caught a shape, the same gray color as theirs had been, up on the top right-hand corner.

It was a little bear. And in spite of myself, I let out a tiny gasp of amazement.

chapter 5

"**Y**ou're getting the bear."

It was weird to be out of school so early, but since math class was canceled, Amanda convinced me to go with her to Lakshmi's Henna Tattoos. She'd said it was because she was thinking about getting one, but almost as soon as we walked in the door, the focus changed from which tattoo she might get to which one I would.

"Amanda, I'm not getting anything. I don't even have any money on me." I added the "on me" quickly, though the sentence would have been equally true without it.

"It's my treat." She walked over to the wall where the tattoo designs were displayed. There were hearts, anchors, letters, and words. Some of the designs were enormous, like a skyline of New York City with the Empire State Building in the middle, some were tiny, like the peace signs and doves I associate with hippies.

Amanda focused on a spot on the wall. "I think this is the one."

"You're crazy," I said, but I went over to see what she was looking at.

"Remember, the bear *is* your totem."

Amanda had already taught me about totems. Apparently we have animals that can protect and guide us. Usually it takes a while to figure out which animal spirit we're associated with, but because of my name, Amanda had immediately known my totem was the bear.

Most people are named for normal things like family members and important historical figures. Not me. I'm named for a constellation. No, really. Callista is for Callisto, also known as Ursa Major (the Great Bear). I know, you've never heard of it. No one has, unless your mom, like mine, happens to be a world-famous astronomer. If you've ever heard of anything even remotely connected with Callisto, it's the Big Dipper (which, sorry to burst your bubble, isn't actually a constellation, it's an asterism), which is part of Callisto. My mom is named Ursula, for Ursa Minor, the Little Bear (of which, yes, you guessed it, the Little Dipper is the most famous part). Technically, I'm named for *both* Callisto and Ursula, since I'm Callista Ursula Leary.

I looked at the bear on the wall. It was a small brown bear standing on its hind legs, its right front paw reaching up as if it

were about to grab some honey or whatever it is bears reach for. The bear was cute, the way bears are, but there was also something brave about it. It looked strong and steady, like nothing could knock it over. Without realizing what I was doing, I reached my hand up and touched the plastic display.

I hadn't noticed Amanda watching me, but when I turned my head, her eyes looked deep into mine.

"You were destined to have this tattoo."

I laughed. "You can't be destined to have something that's going to disappear in a few days. Destiny's about bigger stuff. You know, things that last. Things that are permanent."

"But nothing is permanent," said Amanda. "The only permanent thing is change."

Everything seemed to stop for a second, to freeze, as if all the energy of the universe was focused on me, on my face and my arm and my locker right in front of me. I couldn't quite catch my breath, and I felt my hand lift slightly as if the bear on my locker were calling to the one on my forearm.

"You recognize this. It means something to you." Mr. Thornhill wasn't asking a question at all, he was making an observation.

His tone was gentler than it had been all morning, and for a second I was tempted to tell him the truth. *Yes, I recognize this. Yes, it's a message from Amanda. Where is she? I need to talk to her.*

"I'm named for Ursa Major," I said, surprised that my voice didn't shake.

"The Great Bear," he seemed to think aloud. "Who would know that?"

I forced myself to shrug. "Anyone who knows the legend of Callisto, I guess. Or who knows about astronomy. It's not like it's privileged information." Remembering how casually Hal had leaned against his locker while Mr. Thornhill stared at him, I forced myself to meet the vice principal's gaze.

"Does Amanda know?"

I made myself shrug. "I really don't know what she knows about astronomy."

"She's a brilliant math student."

She's a brilliant everything. "There's more to astronomy than math," I said.

Mr. Thornhill gave me a look that made it clear just how furious he was, then he gestured for me to open my locker. Once I had, I moved to the side, and while he went through my books and notebooks, I made myself stare at the pictures of me, Heidi, Traci, and Kelli that lined the inside of the door. In every single one of them we were all smiling, like nothing bad had ever happened to us. Like nothing bad *could* ever happen to us.

Mr. Thornhill didn't take anything out of my locker, just poked at what was inside it and stepped away, as if there were nothing even remotely interesting there. If I hadn't been so relieved, I might have been offended.

I shut the door and slipped the lock through the hole of the handle as Mr. Thornhill started walking back down the corridor toward the main office. I wondered if we were supposed to go with him or if he was finished with us now that he'd seen we weren't hiding anything, but he'd only gone a short distance before he snapped, "Follow me." He set a fast pace, and I had to jog a little in order to keep a few steps behind him.

Just as Mr. Thornhill turned the corner to the main lobby, I felt a hand on my arm. I looked down and saw that Hal was gripping me just below the elbow. Nia was on his other side, and he was holding her the same way.

When he saw we were both looking down, he let go of us and eased the sleeve of his shirt up about six inches. There, in the exact same spot as mine, was a brick-colored tattoo of the same cat that had been on his locker. As soon as she saw it, Nia looked up at Mr. Thornhill's back, then reached over to her left arm with her right hand and slid her sweater up just enough to reveal the image I'd seen earlier on her locker. A second later, she slid it back down again.

"Let's go, kids," said the vice principal. He was already at the door to the main office, holding it open with his back. We were no more than twenty feet away from him.

Fifteen feet. Ten feet. I raised my right arm in front of my face and reached behind the back of my arm with my left hand, like I had an itch on my shoulder I needed to scratch.

Seven feet. Five feet.

Pressing my hand against my bicep, I slid the fabric of my shirt up just enough to reveal the bear's reaching paw.

"Oh my god," whispered Nia, and we crossed the threshold from the lobby into the office.

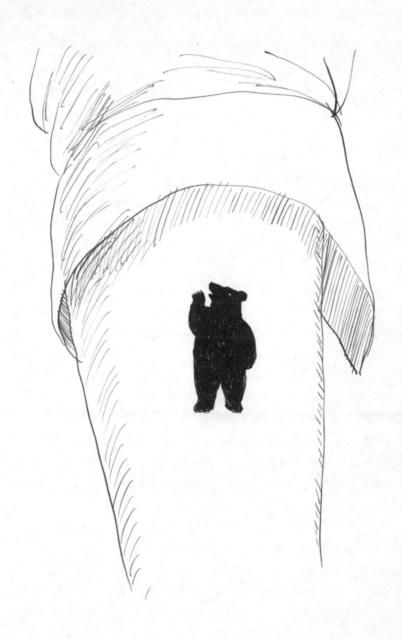

CHAPTER SIX

"Have a seat," said the vice principal, gesturing to three empty chairs outside of his office. "I have a meeting, so, Mrs. Leong, I'm going to ask you to keep an eye on these three. I want them sitting here silently until I come back."

"Yes, Mr. Thornhill," said Mrs. Leong.

"Now." He turned back to the three of us. "While it is true that, historically, Amanda has felt that her attendance at Endeavor was . . . optional, this is different. Today as part of her absenting herself, she chose to send me directly to three people to ask about her whereabouts."

"If you want to know where she is so badly," snapped Nia, "why don't you just call her house?"

Mr. Thornhill's eyes flashed with irritation. "I'll thank you not to tell me my job, Nia. You can rest assured that I'm handling things on that front. Meanwhile, I want the three of you to think very, very carefully about everything you've just seen."

My heart was beating hard enough that I could barely hear him, so it was a relief when Hal took it upon himself to answer for all of us. "We certainly will, sir. We certainly will."

Despite Mr. Thornhill's instruction of silence, I thought for sure we'd have a chance to talk about our tattoos, but the one time Hal started to whisper something, Mrs. Leong jerked her head up and stared at us so fiercely I was actually afraid. Two periods passed while I tried and failed to make sense of what was going on, and by the time Mr. Thornhill walked back into the office and asked if we were ready to talk, I was so tangled up it was all I could do not to tell him everything I knew about Amanda just so he'd help me make sense of it.

But after Hal had answered, "I'm just as confused as you are," and Nia had said, "Has it not occurred to you, Mr. Thornhill, that we, too, are simply victims of a troublesome student's practical joke?" I couldn't start spilling my guts. When he looked at me for an answer, I just shook my head.

"Well, I'm sorry to hear that. Very, very sorry to hear that. Perhaps you'll feel differently after you wash my car this afternoon after school—"

"But—" began Nia.

"And, if not, I'm sure a month of Saturday detention will change your mind."

"That's—" said Hal.

"That's final," finished Mr. Thornhill. "Unless you can convince your friend Amanda Valentino to come by my office and explain everything herself." The bell rang right then, as though Mr. Thornhill had planned it. "You may go to lunch."

I'd expected Nia, Hal, and me to start dishing everything we knew as soon as we stepped into the corridor, but once the office door closed behind us, Nia clutched Hal's arm and pulled him into the sea of humanity that fills the hallways during period changes. It was like I hadn't been with them in Thornhill's office, hadn't shown them my tattoo. I didn't know what to do—was I supposed to trot after them like some kind of desperate puppy? *Take me with you! I want to talk about Amanda, too!*

Um, no. If they thought they were too good to include me in their little powwow, let them think that way. I'd go straight to the source.

Cell phones are totally forbidden in school, so I had to slip into one of the stalls in the bathroom to dial Amanda's number.

"Life is too short to wait. Except for the beep."

Beep. "Okay, wherever you are, you have *got* to get back to school. *What* is the deal with Thornhill's car and the lockers and everything? Call me as soon as you get this. Okay, bye." When I hung up I wished I'd said something about her knowing Hal and Nia. But what? *I happen to know for a fact that you're good friends with two other people at Endeavor besides me.* It wasn't exactly like I didn't have friends other than Amanda. I mean, a table full of people was waiting for me right now in the cafeteria. So Amanda had other friends, too. What was the big deal?

But as I made my way to the lunchroom, I couldn't deny that it *did* feel like a big deal. After Amanda had chosen me, I'd just assumed that I was her only real friend. Now it turned out that I was one of three people she assigned totems to. Three people she'd gotten involved in her prank (whatever it was). I mean, *she* knew about the I-Girls. So why didn't *I* know about Hal and Nia?

The cafeteria was packed, but I spotted Heidi, Traci, and Kelli at our usual table. They'd clearly been looking for me because the second I walked into the room, Kelli's hand shot up in the air and she said something to Heidi who turned around to wave. As I made my way toward them, I passed Hal and Nia sitting together at one of the small tables by the windows that someone must have thought would make the place feel more like a café. They were leaning toward each other and Nia was talking and gesturing.

Even as every atom in my being longed to know what she was saying, I couldn't not be conscious of the nearby table of upperclassmen, some of whom I recognized, who were looking at me. I realized everyone must have heard about the VP's car by now. And if they'd heard about the car, they'd probably heard about the three people who'd been called into the office: Nia, Hal, and me.

Would they think the three of us were friends now?

At our school, there are a lot of what I think of as social neutrals in the ninth grade. You know, they're not popular, but they're not unpopular. Nia Rivera was so totally not one of those people. The irony of it is, she'd had to *work* to be the outcast she'd become. I mean, even with her baggy sweatpants and lumpy ponytails and geeky glasses and angry, confrontational attitude, I *still* think that, if for no other reason than her brother, she could easily have spent her life as a social neutral.

Could have, that is, if she hadn't turned Heidi and Traci in for cheating on a math test two years ago.

Remembering the poisonous song Heidi had made up about Nia after the cheating incident (the song she'd then taught to the entire grade) made it easy for me to turn my feet in the direction of my usual table. I may have wanted to know what Nia was saying, but this was a perfect example of curiosity having the potential to murder the cat.

Or at least the cat's social life.

"OH MY GOD!" Heidi yanked me into the seat next to her. "I heard everything!"

"This is the most insane thing *ever*!" said Kelli.

"Everyone's talking about it," said Traci.

"We were, like, freaking out," said Kelli.

Kelli and Heidi both have long blond hair, and when we're all out together, people think they're sisters, which they sometimes pretend that they are. Traci gets her straight black hair from her mom, who's Chinese, and her blue eyes from her dad. All three of them look like they could be models, which, as you can imagine, does wonders for my self-image. I mean, I'm not a dog or anything, but my legs are kind of on the short side, and my hair's more frizzy than curly, and even on my best, best day, I could never be taken for someone whose only job is to look good. Which is probably about reason number one

hundred and fifty why it's so incredible that I'm one of the I-Girls and that a popular and great-looking guy like Lee would choose me for his girlfriend. Or kind-of girlfriend. Or whatever we are.

"So first of all, *what* did he want *you* for? You don't even *know* that girl."

Heidi always called Amanda "that girl," refusing to dignify her with a name. Heidi's mom is kind of a celebrity in Orion because she's a TV reporter, and her dad is the police chief, so everyone knows her and her family. Even if she weren't beautiful and rich and popular, Heidi would definitely be *somebody* because of who her parents are, and everyone at Endeavor is a little intimidated by her. Even the senior girls (even the *popular* senior girls) always say hi to her in the halls. The four of us were almost always the only freshmen at parties, and no one ever gave us a hard time because we were with Heidi.

But Amanda never acted like Heidi was anything special. Her first article in *The Spirit* (the Endeavor paper) was called "Do You See What I See? A Newcomer's Take on Orion," and she included something about watching the local news and referred to Heidi's mom as a "small-town TV reporter." Heidi was furious, but not nearly as furious as she was after she confronted Amanda and Amanda said simply, "Well, that's what she is, isn't she? I didn't mean it as an insult or anything. But Orion's a small town, and she's a TV reporter here." After that, Heidi was happy to take any excuse to say something bad about Amanda, and Amanda provided her with plenty of excuses, like the time she beat Heidi out for a part in *As You Like It* and then didn't even *take it* because she said she was too busy.

For her second article in *The Spirit*, Amanda exposed a secretary who'd been giving kids late passes in exchange for money. The secretary was transferred, so the whole situation stopped, and Heidi informed us that Amanda was the devil because Mrs. Rifkin had just been providing a service and sometimes you really, really need a late pass but then Amanda went and ruined everything.

Amanda's third article was all about how teachers are afraid of popular students. It said that if a student had a lot of friends or if the student's parents had money, he (or she, of course) is less likely to be yelled at in class, get detention, receive bad grades, or be asked to provide an excuse if he (or she) didn't have the homework or couldn't meet a deadline. The article, which came out right after February vacation, caused a *huge* scandal, which I thought was kind of weird since it seemed like Amanda was just stating the obvious. I mean, *everyone* knows that who gets in trouble and who doesn't is totally unfair and teachers have favorites and some kids can basically do whatever they want in certain classes.

But I guess even something everybody already knows can cause a scandal, especially since Amanda backed up her argument with tons of statistical evidence. Like Mr. Thornhill said, she's a math genius, and she'd managed to get all this data she was definitely *not* supposed to have access to (like who had served detention when and for what). It was this huge deal, and some students (okay, Heidi) who had enjoyed a certain . . . privileged status—and who, as far as I knew, had never been held to a deadline, or asked to show their work on a math problem (even after said students had been caught cheating, if you can believe it), or told to stop chatting with a friend—found that once Vice Principal Thornhill had finished lecturing the faculty of Endeavor on fairness, their classroom experience was suddenly quite different from what it had been before.

"Is it true? Was she expelled?" Kelli's face was pink with excitement.

"Expelled? Actually, I—"

"God, I *hate* that girl," said Heidi, and she stabbed viciously at a piece of sushi.

Part of me wanted to say something in Amanda's defense, but when Heidi really hates something or someone, it's scary to try and defend it. Plus, after the morning I'd had and the disappearing act she'd pulled, I wasn't exactly in the mood to defend Amanda.

Traci, who rarely eats, snapped her gum thoughtfully. "I still don't get why they even called you into the office with those weirdos. You don't even *know* them."

"I don't know," said Kelli. "Nia's a weirdo, but Hal's kind of a hottie."

Was it my imagination or did Heidi look uncomfortable for a minute as she drew her chopstick through a small pool of soy sauce on her Styrofoam plate?

Traci was too busy brushing some invisible lint off her bright red T-shirt to notice Heidi's behavior, and she didn't acknowledge Kelli's comment. "Was it just some kind of

monster mistake or something?" As she pressed her chin into her neck, it was impossible to know if she was checking her shirt for cleanliness or admiring her chest, which she tends to stick out as much as possible. "How'd Thornhill get the idea that you would ever have done anything with Amanda Valentino?"

The thing was, I'd never intended to keep my friendship with Amanda secret from the I-Girls, it had just kind of . . . worked out that way. In the brief time between my meeting Amanda and our becoming friends, Heidi had started hating her intensely, and like I said, you *really* don't want to try and point out the good side of someone Heidi's decided to hate. Amanda made it easy, always at newspaper or some other activity at lunch, so hard to pin down during the school day that she was practically the invisible friend. Keeping our friendship very low profile was no problem. But what was I supposed to say *now? Um, listen guys, the thing is that I actually am friends with Amanda. Really good friends. I hope that's not weird or anything.*

Great idea, Callie. And why don't you bring Nia Rivera to that party on Saturday.

The three of them were staring at me, and I thought about Nia and Hal talking at their table. Maybe they *did* know Amanda better than I did. Maybe despite what she'd said about my being special and her guide and everything, she and I *hadn't* ever really been friends.

"Yeah," I said slowly. "It was just a total mistake."

Kelli put her arm around me. "You poor thing. I can't believe you had to spend the whole morning trapped in a room with the biggest freaks in the school." She squeezed me to her.

"Even if one of those freaks *is* a hottie freak."

From my other side, Traci put *her* arm around me. "Do you need a cootie shot? Like the old days?" She laughed and then reached for my arm, starting to say the words even before she touched me. "Circle, circle, dot, dot—"

As her fingers reached for my wrist, I realized what was about to happen.

"Don't." My voice was sharp, and I yanked my arm away from her as if her hand were a flame.

Traci looked up, a hurt expression on her face. "God, Callie, what's your deal?"

"I just . . . I burned myself last night. Making pasta. And my arm's kind of . . . it's still sore."

"Oh," she said, suddenly contrite. "I'm really sorry. Are you okay?"

"Yeah." I was relieved to see that my sleeve actually covered half my palm. "I'm fine."

"Cool," said Kelli, ready to move on. "Okay, can I show you guys the *cutest* lip gloss my mom picked up at the mall yesterday?"

"Sure," I said, and when Kelli went to put it on me, I puckered my lips and let it roll.

Is it possible for forty-five minutes to last a millennium? I must have looked at the clock over Heidi's head fifty times between when I sat down and when the bell finally rang to end lunch period.

"Oh my god, is lunch over already?" asked Traci, her face

crumpling. "I have double bio now. Kill me."

"Do you guys want to come over and hang at my place after school? Maybe the guys would come, too," said Heidi. She'd also sampled Kelli's lip gloss, and the shiny, bright pink—the perfect color for her—made her supermodel smile even more sparkly.

"Sure," said Traci.

"Yeah," said Kelli.

"I can't," I said, and my mild irritation with Amanda grew into actual anger in the face of their matching, glossy smiles. My friends and my kind-of boyfriend were going to have a great afternoon together while I spent the hours after school scrubbing spray paint off a car with two social outcasts who had the nerve to ignore me. Great.

"And why not?" asked Heidi.

"I've got to clean the vice principal's car."

"What? But you said it was just a big mistake that he even made you come into his office." Traci had been checking her nails for chips, but now she looked at me, completely confused.

"Yeah, why didn't you just tell him you had nothing to do with that stupid psycho painting on his car?" demanded Heidi. She did not like it when her vision of an afternoon was thwarted.

"I did," I said. And I comforted myself with the fact that I wasn't lying. That *was* what I had told Thornhill.

Kelli pulled a pack of Orbit gum out of her bright green Coach bag. "Can't you have your parents call and complain or something? That is *completely* unfair."

I thought about my dad, who was probably about halfway through his second bottle of wine by now, and tried to imagine his making a coherent case to Mr. Thornhill about my innocence. Not exactly a pretty picture. And it wasn't like my mom was reachable by phone.

"I think it's easier to just get it over with," I said, accepting the piece of gum she held out in my direction. "Trust me."

After we'd hugged good-bye, I slung my bag over my shoulder and turned to head to English. As I left the cafeteria, I almost walked right into Beatrice Rossiter, a ninth grader who was hit by a car over winter break. The whole left side of her body including her face was totally disfigured—she's got all of these scars and she wears a patch over her left eye and she always walks really close to the wall, like maybe nobody can see her when she does it. Once when we walked past her, Traci whispered to me, "Every time I see her, I'm thankful I'm me."

I didn't say anything to Traci at the time, but what I was thinking was, *If you were me, Traci, and if you knew what I know, then every time you saw Bea, you'd wish you were just about anyone but me.*

I snuck my phone out of my backpack and turned it on, but there were no new messages.

CHAPTER 7

Bio and English were a total blur except for when Ms. Burger pointed out that today was March fifteenth and warned us to "beware the Ides of March." Her words created a flicker of anxiety in the pit of my stomach. Could there be some connection between the date and Amanda's prank? But what? I couldn't even remember *why* we were supposed to beware the Ides of March, and by the time Ms. Burger told us to open our books to Shakespeare's Sonnet 138, I'd gone back to ignoring what was going on around me, just focusing on the clock as I counted the seconds until last period.

I was totally sure Amanda was going to be in math class, so sure that I actually jogged the last fifty yards to the room. Even though I was pretty confused and starting to get more than a little annoyed about everything that had gone down over the course of the morning, it would be such a relief to see her. Was she really friends with Hal and Nia? Why had she spray-painted Thornhill's car and our lockers? I'd run over in my head what I was going to say to her so many times I practically had it memorized.

It didn't mean anything that she wasn't there when I pushed open the door of room S-51 (when was Amanda ever on time for *anything*?). It didn't even mean anything that she hadn't shown up by the time the late bell rang. But as the minutes ticked by and Mrs. Watson took us through the homework problems (problems Amanda and I had just done *together* the night before), the excitement I'd felt started to morph into frustration. Where *was* she? It was one thing to cut school; god knows Amanda did that fairly regularly. It was another thing to cut school on a day when you'd pulled a prank that got several other people in mad trouble. Of course, knowing Amanda, she would just respond with a raised eyebrow or a quotation of unknown origins to direct questions she didn't care to answer.

That was so not going to fly this time.

It's not exactly a major problem when I can't concentrate in math class. When I don't pay attention in history, I know I'm a goner on the next test. But math is totally different. Math is like . . . okay, you know when you're shopping for jeans and you try on ten million pairs and each one is just a little too tight, or a little too loose, or it's got some freaky acid washed thing going on, and then all of a sudden, right when you're like, *Oh, forget it, I'm just going to live without a new pair of jeans*, you try on one last pair and as they slide up your legs it's . . . it's

45

like you were born to wear them. That's what math is like for me, like a language I was somehow born knowing.

Actually, I probably *was* born knowing it. My mom is one of the best mathematicians in the world. I mean, I might be good at math, but she's *brilliant*. Like, if you ask me to multiply two three-digit numbers, I can do it in my head pretty fast, but that's nothing compared to my mom. If we're at the grocery store and she's trying to estimate what everything's going to cost, she can glance at the cart and figure out to the penny what the total's going to be. And if you ask her in July how many days until Christmas, she can tell you the answer in less than a second.

For me, it's more . . . well, when Mrs. Watson puts a new concept up on the board, like when we learned sine and cosine this fall, it feels like the whole time she's talking and writing stuff down, I'm just thinking, *Right. Right. Of course. That makes total sense*. I can't really explain how I understand something when it comes to math—I just understand it.

That was why I was so totally bummed back when Mrs. Watson asked me to catch up the new girl in our class, Amanda Valentino, on one of her first days in school, maybe Halloween or the day after. First of all, I was already half out of my mind because of everything that was going on with my mom, but even when I'm functioning normally, I'm lousy at relaying math concepts to other people. Traci used to ask me to help her with her math homework when we first became friends; after I tried to teach her a few times, she got so irritated by my inability to show her how I was getting my answers that

46

she just told me to forget it. So I knew assigning me to teach Amanda Valentino two months' worth of math was destined to end in failure, but I mean, what can you say? *I'm sorry, Mrs. Watson, I swear I wasn't cheating, but there's no way I can explain my work to another human being.*

Instead I just said what you always say when a teacher asks you to do something. "Sure."

"How long have you lived in Orion?"

"My whole life." My answer was more terse than polite because Amanda struck me as kind of weird. First of all, she was wearing bright, bright red lipstick, which looked even brighter because her face was super pale, like she'd powdered an already über-white complexion. She wasn't ugly or anything. Actually, she was pretty; not like Heidi and Traci and Kelli are pretty, not the kind of pretty you'd find in a catalog, but there was something about her that would definitely make you look at her twice if you saw her in a crowd. It might have had something to do with what she was wearing—her black hair was pulled back in a tight, high bun held up by two crisscrossed chopsticks, and she was wearing a gray dress that was really plain but somehow chic, like something you might see on a *Vogue* model. Around her neck was a thin blue ribbon necklace that disappeared under the front of the dress. It was nothing that anyone at Endeavor would ever wear.

"That must be wonderful, living in one place." She sounded wistful, which was surprising considering I'd heard she grew up all over the world. I mean, why would someone with a childhood like that envy someone who'd spent her life in Orion, Maryland, capital of nothing?

"I guess," I said. Then I felt bad for being so rude. "Um, do you have a favorite country?"

"Country?" she asked.

"Yeah," I said, realizing too late that it might freak her out to know the Endeavor population was already gossiping about her. "I heard you grew up all over the world."

Amanda laughed this totally unself-conscious laugh that I wouldn't have expected to come from someone looking so tailored. "Fascinating. Who told you that?"

I'd heard it from the note Heidi passed me in history.

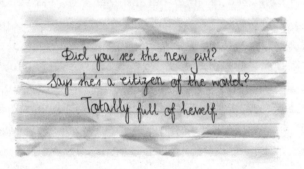

Did you see the new girl?
Says she's a citizen of the world?
Totally full of herself.

I shrugged. It wasn't like the name Heidi Bragg would mean anything to Amanda. "A friend."

Amanda nodded. "And what else did she say about me?"

Okay, the rest of the note so did not need to be repeated. "That was all," I said. Amanda gave me a look that said she knew I was lying. It was a look I'd get to know very well over the next few months. "Did you *not* grow up all over the world?" I asked, not one hundred percent sure what "citizen of the world" actually meant.

"Not a bit," said Amanda. "I grew up in this country."

I thought it was strange how she didn't name a city or even a state. "Where?"

"Here, there, and everywhere." Her smile was impossible to read.

"Oh," I said. I mean, what are you supposed to say to something like that? (It wasn't until much later that I would learn about her penchant for quoting others.) "Well, welcome to Orion."

"Thanks." She nodded, looking around the corridor where we were sitting. "I really feel I'm going to like it here."

"Don't count on it," I said. "Not much here." Okay, I realize I wasn't exactly being the Orion Township Welcoming Committee, but I wasn't feeling all sunshine and light right about then. My mom had been gone for two weeks, and my dad was already starting to lose it.

Amanda didn't seem to mind my negativity, and she didn't ask why I was so down on my hometown. Instead, she continued to nod, like I'd just given her a really helpful, insightful piece of information. "I'll keep that in mind."

I wasn't in the mood to keep talking. I wasn't in the mood to do much of anything besides stare out the window and figure out when my family was going to get back to normal. I knew attempting (and failing) to teach someone math wasn't exactly going to improve my mood, but anything was better than chatting.

"So," I said. "Sine and cosine." I flipped open my book to the page we were on, then started to work backward to the beginning of the chapter.

"Right," said Amanda. "About that." Suddenly she sounded embarrassed. I was kind of surprised given that she'd been so cool and collected when Mrs. Watson had introduced her while making her stand at the front of the class like livestock to be judged at a county fair.

I held my book open at page 217 and looked up at her. On her index finger was an enormous silver ring shaped like a bunch of grapes, and she was twirling it around distractedly.

"What *about that*?"

"I actually know about sines. And cosines. My father taught them to me. I'm sure that sounds completely strange to you," she added quickly.

"No it doesn't," I said honestly. "My mom knows tons of math. She's always teaching me stuff." I was kind of psyched. All my friends thought it was really bizarre that my mom and I talked about math so much. Back when we were first hanging out, Heidi asked me one day what I'd done the night before, and I said my mom and I had used her telescope to find M31 in the Andromeda Galaxy, only we'd purposely used an out-of-date star planner so we'd have to do the computations to figure out where to look in the night sky. When I finished, Heidi looked at me like I'd just confessed to being a victim of domestic violence.

"Oh, this is such a relief," said Amanda. "I was debating between pretending not to understand what you were talking about or saying I learned it at school. I didn't want you to think I was odd."

Now I was the one who laughed a real laugh. "Wow, I'm so the last person to think that you're a freak for learning about math with one of your parents. And you would have been really sorry if you'd pretended not to know what sine and cosine are. I'm the worst teacher."

"Me too!" Amanda's voice was a shout, and she put her hand over her mouth. "Me too," she repeated, whispering this time. "I can never explain how I got my answers on tests. I just . . . I see them. Teachers are always accusing me of cheating." She practically glowed with pleasure.

"That used to happen to me!" I said, almost as loudly as she'd spoken before. And then we were both laughing, like being accused of cheating on a math test was the funniest thing that could ever happen.

Amanda stopped laughing first and gave me a look that lasted so long I started to get weirded out. "What?" I asked, rubbing under my nose self-consciously. Did I have a horrible embarrassing something?

"Do you ever get a feeling about the future?" she asked. Her eyes were enormous—a deep, storm-cloud gray that I would later learn changed color with the light.

"What, you mean, like, ESP?" My nose felt clean, and I put my hand down.

"Not exactly," she said, gently tapping the tip of her pen against her top lip. "More like the sense that something is destined."

"Um . . ." Okay, this was getting a little intense. A second ago we'd been joking about math tests and now we were suddenly onto destiny?

Amanda didn't seem to mind that I wasn't answering her. She leaned forward and touched me lightly on the shoulder with her pen. "It's you," she said.

"What?" I said, not sure how to communicate to her that she was starting to freak me out.

Oblivious to my monosyllabic, unenthusiastic response, and with a sure smile on her face, she exhaled, leaned back against the wall, and closed her eyes. "You're going to be my guide." Her voice was quiet.

Even though I had no idea what Amanda was talking about, I felt my heart pounding in my chest. "Your guide?" I asked, and my voice was as low as hers had been.

Amanda opened her eyes and stared straight at me. "I knew I'd find you," she said.

And since I didn't know what to say back, I didn't say anything at all.

Occasionally a geological occurrence takes place that is so dramatic, it actually shifts the earth on its axis. A tsunami. An earthquake. If you could go into outer space and film the planet at the exact moment the event occurs, you would literally witness the world move.

I didn't realize it at the time, but that is what meeting Amanda Valentino would be for me.

chapter 8

Nia snickered when Mr. Thornhill offered us a chance to "come clean" right after we'd each picked up a bucket filled with rags, rolls of paper towels, and cleaning products piled by the door. It took me a minute to get the joke about cleaning, but I'm not sure if that was because Nia's smarter than I am or if it's because I was so confused by all the thoughts whirling through my head that I didn't have room in my brain for a pun.

When nobody said anything, he just gestured toward the door and we trooped out in a line: Hal first, then Nia, then me.

"It's not like we're going to be able to get the stuff off his car with this," I pointed out, rattling the bucket toward their backs. "Spray paint doesn't exactly wash off."

Neither of them said anything, as if during lunch they'd made a pact to ignore me. Well, two could play at that game, and I didn't say anything more. A crowd was gathered by the gate to the faculty parking lot to gape at Mr. Thornhill's car (some people had out their phones and were taking pictures); at first the security guard, who was holding them back, wouldn't let us through. Hal had to explain for about fifty years that we *had* to go to the car, and even then the guy was reluctant to let us pass. As we walked past him, I spotted Lee's curly dark hair towering above the crowd and then I saw Traci, Heidi, and Jake, who were all standing with him. Lee saw me before they did, maybe because he's so tall, and he put his fists up over his head and shouted, "Go, Callie!" as Traci and Heidi clapped and Jake whistled. I hoped Hal and Nia heard them. I hoped they realized who they were ignoring.

The VP's ancient Honda Civic was parked far enough away from the crowd that the noise of the onlookers was muffled, or maybe it was just that the sensory overload of looking at something so vivid made it difficult to register anything else. The clouds had rolled in since we'd first looked out Thornhill's office window, but even in the watery sunlight of a March afternoon, the car pulsed with color and energy.

"Wow," said Hal.

I had to agree. From a distance, we'd only been able to see the biggest shapes, but up close you could make out the detail work—tiny birds carrying intricate olive branches, long daisy chains intertwining with meticulously drawn rainbows. It wasn't just bright and colorful, it was really, really good art.

Suddenly, I thought of something. Despite my private vow not to talk to either Hal or Nia, I turned to Hal, who was standing next to me admiring the lunar landscape that covered the driver's side of the windshield. "Did you draw this?"

Either Hal was *seriously* ignoring me or he hadn't heard what I said. He reached out with his index finger and traced the edge of the moon. "Hey, it's—" he started to say, but before he could finish, I grabbed his arm.

"Did you do this?"

"What?" He turned to face me but I could tell he was still absorbed in admiring the masterpiece that was Thornhill's car. I noticed that after he'd touched the moon, his finger had a light coating of bluish-white.

"I said, did you draw this?" Hal was the best artist at Endeavor, and there was no doubt someone with real talent had decorated this car.

"I wish," he said. He turned back to admire the car. "Maybe I could have done this, but only *with* her, you know?" I wasn't sure what he meant, but I couldn't deny that Hal's tone was friendly enough. I wondered if I'd been paranoid to think he and Nia were ignoring me.

"How did you even *know* her?" I hadn't meant to sound so accusatory, but my question came out like an attack.

Hal didn't say anything, but Nia did. "Oh, what, now you're the holder of the social registry for the entire grade?"

None of the other I-Girls would have tolerated Nia's being so rude, but the three of them are way better at confrontations than I am. For a second I tried to think up a snappy comeback,

55

but when nothing came to me, I just ended up with, "I didn't realize you guys were friends, that's all." Then I shrugged, like there hadn't been any judgment in my assumption.

I'd expected Nia to back off, but instead she kept going. "Oh, right," she said. "You and your friends just—"

"Look!" said Hal. He'd been circling the car, and now he was pointing at the trunk.

Glad to have an excuse not to fight with Nia without having to feel like a wimp, I went over to where he was standing and followed his finger. Scattered across the trunk were half a dozen bears, birds, and cats that were the same as the ones on our lockers. There was another animal, too—a lizard of some sort. Then there were stars and moons and a bunch of peace signs.

"That's a lizard," I said, half to myself and half out loud. "And that's a cat—"

"It's a cougar," said Hal, rubbing his wrist unconsciously for a second.

I hadn't noticed that Nia had come up behind me until she spat out, "You thought it was a cat? It doesn't look anything *like* a cat."

This time my comeback was out of my mouth before I even realized I'd formulated it. "Gee, I didn't realize you were such a friggin' nature girl, Nia," I snapped. "When you're on the Discovery Channel talking about the indigenous wildlife of Orion, I'll be sure to watch."

"Like I'd even *care*."

"Um, could you two—" said Hal quietly.

But Nia was on a roll. "And where do *you* come off questioning *our* friendships with Amanda anyway? What about *yours*? I mean, I never saw her hanging out with you and your stupid I-Girls. You probably tried to get her to be friends with you, only she wouldn't let you call her *Mandi* so you dropped the whole idea!"

I could feel my face getting red, and I was so mad I forgot I was still holding the bucket as I reached out my arm to point at her. "Nia, you're so jealous it's pathetic. Like Amanda would ever, *ever* in a million years have hung out with someone as—" The bucket swung wildly in my hand, and one of the bottles of cleaner fell to the pavement.

"Hey!" Hal's voice was a shout this time. I'd never heard him yell before, and it shut me up.

"Listen," he continued in his normal voice. "I don't pretend to understand Amanda or what motivated her or anything. But one thing I do know is that she didn't do anything randomly. And I have a really strong feeling right now. This"—he pointed at the car and looked from me to Nia—"is a message."

I'm basically the least superstitious person in the world, but as soon as Hal said that, I shivered. Was it possible? Was Amanda trying to tell us something?

Hal continued. "Now, here's what I can tell you about what she's drawn. My totem is the cougar. Strong but solitary." I felt myself blush again when he described himself that way, but he didn't seem at all embarrassed.

Hal's words had some kind of magical softening effect on Nia, who pointed at the bird. "That's me," she breathed, her voice quiet and almost dreamy. "Night owl. Wise. Independent."

I managed not to laugh when she said "independent." Was that what we were now calling people who were incapable of functioning in a social setting?

Hal jostled me gently in the shoulder, and I realized it was my turn. "Bears are strong," I said slowly. I didn't add the other important bear fact Amanda had reminded me of: Bears hibernate.

Nia had leaned against the car while Hal and I were talking, and when she stood up, she instinctively brushed some dust off her hip. I remembered Hal's finger.

"It's chalk," I almost shouted.

Hal smacked his forehead. "Yes! That's what I was going to tell you before. It's not paint at all."

"What?" Nia looked from me to Hal.

"The drawing. It's chalk. Look." I touched my finger to a bright red apple and dragged it against the metal surface of the car. When I pulled my hand away, there was a red streak along my skin.

Hal leaned down until his face was less than an inch from the car's surface. "You know, now that I'm looking more closely, I think it's chalk *and* pastels," he said. "This should come off the car really easily."

"I hate the idea of erasing it," said Nia.

I knew exactly what she meant. Even if this wasn't some kind of *message* from Amanda, it was *from* her. And it was *so cool*. I couldn't wait to ask Amanda about it.

Wishing I could talk to Amanda made me think of something. "Hey, have you guys heard from her? I tried texting her and calling, but she didn't answer."

Both Hal and Nia shook their heads. "Nothing," said Nia, and the way she said it made me know they'd spent the day calling her, too.

"I'm going to take pictures." Hal took out his phone even as he said it. "Will you guys help me?"

Neither of us answered him, we just grabbed our phones and began circling the car with them.

"Look!" Nia was sitting on the pavement by the driver's side door, pointing at the very edge of the car's side panel, just behind the tire.

Unlike the cougar, this animal was immediately recognizable to me.

"The coyote," said Hal.

"Amanda's totem," announced Nia.

"**M**e? I'm the coyote. The trickster." She made a fist with her hand, then opened it and showed me her empty palm. "Now you see me, now you don't."

Supposedly I was catching Amanda up on quadratic equations, but really she was teaching me about totems, specifically hers and mine. When I pointed out that totems and superstition and ancient belief systems were about as far from trigonometry as you could get, Amanda gestured at me with her quill pen.

"Au contraire," she said. "Belief systems are belief systems."

"Oh, come on!" I said. "Math isn't a belief system, it's an explanation for how things work."

"Right," said Amanda. "In other words, it's a belief system."

She was wearing something in her hair that made it look as if she'd grown a waist-length ponytail overnight, and her dress, with its puffy sleeves and lace edging, definitely looked like it was something out of another century. I'd meant to ask her about the outfit—the hair and the pen and the dress, but as usual, I'd gotten sidetracked. That was the thing about talking to Amanda: I could never figure out how we'd gotten on the subject we were discussing or how we'd gotten off the subject I'd thought we were on.

"Wait, are you telling me you don't believe in math?" Over the course of the past two weeks, I'd discovered that Amanda was probably the best mathematician I knew outside of my mom. She was truly a genius with numbers. How could she question their fundamental truth?

"I believe in math," she said. "It's not like the tooth fairy or Santa. I believe it exists. I just don't think it explains things any better than a lot of other belief systems just because it happens to be in fashion in this particular place at this particular moment in history."

"So, what, are you talking about, like . . . God?" This was definitely the weirdest conversation I'd ever had with someone. I tried to imagine talking about God with Heidi or Traci or Kelli.

"Religion is another belief system," she said. "It happens not to be mine."

"So, like, what's yours?" I didn't mean to sound defensive, but sometimes talking to Amanda made me feel like I was always one crucial step behind her.

"What's my belief system . . ." She leaned her head against the wall and closed her eyes for a minute. Then, without opening them, she said, "There are more things in heaven and earth, Horatio, than are dreamt of in your philosophy."

I shook my head. "There may be a lot of things in heaven and earth, but the point is, you can still count them."

She opened her eyes and locked them with mine. "That's what I'm telling you, Callie," she said. "You can't."

Nia's camera clicked, and without really looking at what I was photographing I pointed my phone in the general direction of the coyote and took a picture. None of us said anything for a minute.

"Okay," said Hal finally. "Amanda needs us to do something for her."

A car pulling out of the circular driveway at the front of the school honked its horn, and when I looked up, I saw Heidi's mom's BMW SUV pulling away. Heidi was in the passenger seat and Traci was sitting in the back. She shouted out something that sounded like, *Call me!* as the car turned onto Ridgeway Drive.

It was so weird that I could be having these two interactions at once: one, the most mundane and transparent, the other unique and mysterious. It was like existing in two parallel universes simultaneously.

But I couldn't ignore the gravitational pull of what Hal had just said. Turning back to him, I said, "But *what* does she want from us? And why couldn't she just *ask* us for it?"

"He's not a *mind reader*," said Nia. Any softness that had been in her voice earlier was definitely gone.

Okay, I'd had just about enough of this. "Do you have some kind of *problem* with me or something?" I asked. "I mean, how, exactly, did I manage to offend you in the past five minutes?"

"Let's see," said Nia, tilting her head to the side and pressing her index finger to her temple in imitation of someone thinking hard. Then she straightened her head and sneered at me. "No, I'd have to say you *have* managed not to do anything offensive in the past five minutes."

"Are you two going to keep—" Hal interrupted, but this time I didn't care what he had to say.

"Nia, I have never, *never* done anything to you and now you're acting like—"

"You've never done anything to me?" Nia stood up and took a step toward me, lowering her voice until she was practically hissing. "You've never done anything to me? Oh, that's a good one, Callie. Um, do the words *Keith Harmon* mean anything to you?"

I took a step back, but it wasn't just to get away from Nia's scary voice. The words *Keith Harmon* did mean something to me.

"That wasn't me."

"Yeah, right," said Nia, turning her back on me.

I reached out and grabbed for her arm. "Seriously, Nia, that *wasn't* me."

She snatched her arm away from me, like there was something revolting about my touch, and I was reminded of Traci's aborted cootie shot earlier. "Well, like my mom says, 'Lie down with dogs, get up with fleas.'"

At first I didn't realize what she was saying, and then I did. "My friends are not *dogs*!"

"Maybe not on the outside," said Nia, and she went back to snapping pictures of the car.

My heart was pounding. If I was all about avoiding confrontations, Nia was all about *having* them. No wonder she didn't have any friends.

But even as I thought that, I couldn't help cringing a little at the memory of what Heidi had done to Nia in seventh grade.

Nia and Heidi weren't just in the same math class that year, they also had English together. One day, maybe a week after she'd turned Heidi and Traci in for cheating, Nia left her English notebook behind in class. Heidi picked it up because, as she told us at lunch, she wanted to be a good citizen, and then she dropped it; it happened to flip open, and what did it happen to open *to* but a page with a few notes on direct objects and predicate adjectives and a small heart in the margin with the initials NR and KH inside of it.

The truth is, I really *don't* know exactly what happened or whose idea it was because my dad and I went to Washington, D.C. that weekend to meet my mom at a NASA conference she'd spent the week attending. But apparently, Heidi or Traci or Kelli or maybe all three of them created keith.harmon95@ yahoo.com or some address like that, and they emailed Nia and then Nia emailed "Keith" back and then "Keith" emailed Nia and so on. By Monday morning, Heidi had a whole string of emails to show me *and* the rest of the seventh grade, emails in which Nia admitted she'd always thought Keith was cute and agreed to go out with him sometime. At that point, Nia was just a little geeky with her goofy braids and glasses, but she wasn't a leper. And even then Cisco Rivera was Cisco Rivera, so maybe if she'd never pissed Heidi off, she could have survived middle school as a neutral. But no.

The whole thing was really, really bad. For a long time, Nia couldn't walk by anyone without hearing something like, *Going to meet your boyfriend, Nia?* Or, *Oooh, Nia, I think I just saw Keith, were you looking for him?* Every time I passed Nia's locker, I'd see something stuck on it—a piece of paper with NR and KH on it or a dead flower or, once, simply the words *AS IF!!!!!!* As far as I was concerned, she'd brought the whole thing on herself (what had she been *thinking*, that Heidi and Traci would allow her to live in peace after she turned them in?), but even I felt kind of bad for her by the end.

Part of me *knew* I should say something to them, but it wasn't like I was *that* good of friends with Heidi and Kelli and Traci. I still felt a little as if . . . I don't know, as if I were on probation or something. I mean, now if they did something like that, I would *definitely* tell them to stop. And anyway, they wouldn't do anything like that anymore. People do a lot of stuff in middle school that they wouldn't do in high school. You can't judge someone forever based on one mistake.

Right at that moment, as if she'd been *sent* or something, Bea Rossiter limped out the front door. I watched her get into her mom's waiting car and drive away.

I closed my eyes. What had happened with Bea was different.

But a little voice in my head said, *Was it really?*

CHAPTER NINE

I was glad when Hal's voice interrupted my thoughts. "We can't help Amanda if we don't work together."

Nia whipped around to face him. "You know what, Hal? Just shut up already. You don't know that she wants our help. You don't know why she did this. So why don't you stop with your whole I-can-read-the-tea-leaves-guru thing, okay? Because it's starting to get on my nerves."

I gave Hal a look like, *What can you do with a lunatic like that?* but he was looking intently at Nia, which kind of annoyed me.

"Hey," he said quietly. When she didn't meet his eyes, he said it again. "Hey." I couldn't help being jealous of his gentle tone. It was like even though she'd just yelled at him, he really cared about her.

She covered her face with her hands for a second and breathed in deeply. "I just don't understand. Nothing makes sense. I thought I was . . . never mind. I am so freaking out."

Hal took a step toward her and put his hand on her shoulder. "You thought you were what?"

"Nothing," said Nia, and she shook her head, like it was a door closing. "Anyway, why won't she call us back?"

"I don't know," said Hal. He briefly touched his pocket, where I could see the outline of his phone through his jeans.

"It's not like her," said Nia, her statement a question, like things had gotten so topsy-turvy that she needed Hal to confirm something she already knew.

"It's not like her at all," agreed Hal.

It was weird to be standing there with no one to talk to while the two of them had their little moment. I couldn't remember the last time I'd felt like such an outsider. That's the thing about being an I-Girl: you're *never* on the outside. Of anything. I went back to taking pictures of the car, but I couldn't focus, and I knew none of my shots were going to be any help if we were trying to decipher a message. When my phone's memory was full, I just stood there. Nia and Hal were talking quietly on the other side of the car. For something to do, I went up close to one of the windows, but I'd looked at the design on it (a rainbow with a huge, puffy cloud at either end) so many times that I didn't really know what the point was of looking at it again.

What was Mr. Thornhill's car like inside? I was sure he was a total neat freak, and I pushed my nose against the window to see if I was right, but it was impossible to see past the stripes of the rainbow.

"Okay, we should probably start cleaning," said Hal, standing up and addressing me over the roof of the car.

I couldn't help being annoyed. What, now that they'd had their little chat we could get on with our work? Did they get to decide everything?

Without saying anything, I went over to my bucket, got the spray bottle, and started shooting cleaning fluid at the car. Almost the second the stuff hit the drawing, the chalk began to dissolve. I barely had to rub at the surface to get it to disappear. For a minute, I found myself thinking that it was nice of Amanda not to make us work too hard, but then I was irritated with myself. Whatever Amanda's purpose, she so clearly was not trying to show how deeply she cared about me, Hal, or Nia. Maybe she thought it was hilarious to play a trick on us or maybe she just wanted us to know that each one of us was an idiot. But the idea that she'd wanted to do us a favor of any kind was nothing short of hilarious.

None of us spoke as we wiped away the brightly colored surface of the car, revealing the dark blue paint beneath. When I could finally see inside the car, I was surprised to discover how messy it was. Empty takeout cups were lying in the back on a bunch of folders and a pile of newspapers on the passenger seat. At least a dozen CDs were scattered on the floor of the passenger seat; I put my nose up against the car, trying to read the titles. On one I could make out the word *Mozart*, but the others were either upside down or had the writing covered up.

I tried the car door because, hey, you never know, but it was locked. Whatever. It wasn't exactly like I needed to know what music Thornhill listened to.

It felt like we'd been cleaning for years by the time we wiped the last streak of color off the car, but when I looked, it was only a little after five. Without speaking, we all stepped away from the car and surveyed our handiwork.

Suddenly a phone rang. *Amanda. It had to be Amanda.* We all jumped, fumbling for our respective cells.

It was Nia's. "Hi, Mom," said Nia, and she gave us both an apologetic look, like it was her fault we'd gotten our hopes up briefly. "Nothing."

I looked back to the car, surprised at how dull and normal it appeared now that all of the artwork had been cleaned. Suddenly I had this really bad feeling about my life, like I was the car and Amanda was the artwork and now she was gone . . . but I pushed the thought away. Thornhill was being a total drama queen. Everyone knew Amanda cut school all the time. She'd be back tomorrow and all of this would be explained.

Nia was still talking to her mom. "Model Congress," she said, then added quickly, "It was a last-minute meeting."

There was a streak of purple left on the driver's side window, and I headed back to the car to wipe it off, but when I got up close, I realized it wasn't on the driver's side, it was on the passenger side. I went around the car; now that we'd spent all this time cleaning it, I wanted it to be perfect.

"Hey, Mom, it's me." Hal's voice this time. Now I was the only one not talking to her mother. Well, no surprise there. I went up to the passenger-side window, but there wasn't any purple that I could see. Still, I was sure I'd seen some color here a minute ago. It was getting dark, and it was harder to see into the inside of the car.

Hal was still talking. "No, I just decided to stay for a while, hang out." So they weren't telling their parents about what had happened. Would I? I couldn't exactly imagine my dad being in any state to care by the time I got home. You didn't have to be in an advanced math class to know that one bottle of wine per hour times three or four hours equaled someone who wasn't able to keep tabs on his daughter's whereabouts.

"Well, the building's unlocked if she wants me to get it for her," said Hal, and I remembered his little sister, Cornelia, who must have been in the sixth or seventh grade by now. Even though the middle school and high school are in the same building at Endeavor, their classes are in separate wings from ours, so we almost never see the younger kids. The last time I'd seen Cornelia, she'd been about nine; I wondered what she looked like now.

I pressed my nose up to the glass again, not really looking for anything.

Which is exactly when I saw it.

In the middle of the pile of newspapers was a piece of purple paper. Or was it an envelope? In the fading light, I couldn't tell. But one thing I could tell was that in the corner of the mysterious purple object was the outline of an animal.

And the animal was almost definitely a coyote.

CHAPTER 10

My heart pounding, I yanked at the handle of the door, but of course it wouldn't open.

Suddenly Hal's voice was at my shoulder. "What?" he asked. "What is it?"

"Nothing," I said quickly. I turned my back to the car and leaned against it, smiling up at him in what I hoped was a normal way. "It's nothing. I . . . wanted to see what music Thornhill listens to. But it's just classical stuff."

I hoped Hal wouldn't have a passion for classical music, one that would make him desperate to know the titles of the VP's favorites. He took a step closer to the car, and for a minute I feared he was going to try to see the CDs for himself, but then he stood next to me and leaned his back against the window.

My heart was still racing. Could what I had seen been a note from Amanda? But why would she have written him? She *hated* Thornhill. How many times had he dressed her down for an article she had written or was writing, or an interview she'd tried to schedule with someone he didn't want her "bothering," or a document she'd demanded to see? The argument I'd overheard them having that day in the office was only one of at least half a dozen they'd had.

"So, what do you think it means?" asked Hal.

For a minute I wondered how he knew what I was thinking, but then I realized he was just talking about the car in general.

"I don't know," I said. And the truth was, I *didn't* know. Not why Amanda had done this *or* why I didn't want to tell Hal and Nia about possibly seeing the piece of paper with Amanda's totem inside the car. It was like there were so many things I was suddenly being forced to share with the two of them, but the note from Amanda (if that's even what it was) was just mine.

Well, mine and Vice Principal Thornhill's.

"I feel like she wants something from us," said Hal. "Like she's . . . talking to us. All those peace symbols. The totems . . ."

Nia was still on the phone with her mom. She sounded frustrated, and I couldn't help being jealous. I remembered that feeling of frustration when I wanted to get off the phone and my mother kept talking to (well, at) me.

Was I ever going to have that feeling again?

When I didn't say anything, Hal continued. "You know, Amanda had a lot of personas. She could have done the car in goth or punk or ante bellum. But she picked this whole sixties hippie thing."

I wasn't sure what ante bellum was, but I knew what he meant. It wasn't like Amanda was a hippie. Or like she was a hippie *more* than she was anything else. Or *wasn't* anything else.

"This car," said Hal definitively, "is a happy message. I'm sure of it."

I turned to look at him. Under his chiseled jaw and tousled hair, I could just make out the soft cheeks and bowl-cut that belonged to the geeky kid he'd been back when we hung out. Back when we'd been friends.

Which may explain why I suddenly blurted out, "I feel like everyone is disappearing." As soon as the words were out of my mouth, I was afraid I might start crying or something. And what a stupid thing to say to Hal who didn't even know anything about my mom. Now he'd think I was some kind of hysteric.

I rubbed at my eye, hoping it would seem as if there was an eyelash lodged in it.

"She hasn't disappeared," said Hal, looking over my shoulder. "She's here."

The combination of his saying "she's here" and looking behind me made me spin around, expecting to see Amanda walking toward us. But all I saw was Nia, slapping her phone shut.

73

"Well, *that* was annoying." She slipped her phone into her bulging army knapsack and came toward us. "So," she said, looking at Hal in a way that made it hard not to think she was ignoring me.

"So," he said. "What's our next step?"

"You think this car thing is more than just a prank," said Nia.

Hal nodded. "I think this car thing is more than just a prank," he echoed.

Nia cocked her head to the side and for the first time I noticed her glasses. They had thick black rims that were so retro they were almost . . . cool. And her jacket, which I hadn't paid any attention to, was pale blue wool, cut short, that looked almost vintage. How long had she had this new look? Had Amanda taken her shopping for her clothes and glasses?

Thinking about Amanda and Nia shopping at a vintage store together made me feel jealous and humiliated, almost like I'd discovered Lee had another girlfriend or something. Which might explain why the next words out of my mouth were so incredibly snotty. "So, what, you think there's some kind of secret code here? Each animal equals a letter? Find the hidden message inside the picture?"

"I'm not saying it's something all that complicated," answered Hal, unfazed by my tone. "I mean, if it's a message, maybe it's just, I don't know, *You're all really special to me.*"

If we were so special, why had she been hanging out with Nia and Hal behind my back? I laughed, but not because I thought what Hal had said was especially funny. "Why couldn't the message be *None of you is really special to me*? I mean, the result of her whole 'message'"—I put air quotes around the word—"is that we're all stuck in detention for the next month."

"Oh, give me a break, Callie," scoffed Nia. "She's not going to be gone for a month. We're probably not even going to have to go to detention once."

I hated the way Nia sounded so confident, like she was the one who really knew Amanda while I was some kind of . . . stranger to her. "So, what, now you're predicting the future?"

Hal shook his head. "Guys, I wish you'd cut it out. This prank was meant to bring us together, okay?"

I was actually glad when Nia snorted, since it was exactly what I felt like doing. "I don't get it," she said. "Amanda's so smart . . ." she trailed off, but the end of her sentence was as clear as if it were written on the car in front of us. *She's so smart. How could she have thought we would want to do anything together?*

"That's right," said Hal, and now he, too, sounded annoyed. "She *is* so smart. So maybe the two of you could stop fighting for one minute so we can figure out what she's trying to tell us."

And with that, he stormed off. It was dark enough now that before he'd gotten to the edge of the parking lot, he was no more than a shadow.

"Well, he sure is pissed."

I don't know what I expected Nia to say, even a simple "yeah" would have sufficed. Instead, she just gave me a look.

"What?" I said. Even nonconfrontational me had had

enough. As far as I was concerned, if she wanted to get into it with me, she could bring it on.

Nia gave a little laugh, more like a sharp exhale of breath, then shook her head. "Nothing," she said, and she, too, walked toward the school exit.

I watched her leave, then turned back to the car and pressed my nose up against the window so hard it hurt. Teachers had been walking past us for a while, getting into their cars and driving off, and I realized that the vice principal would be coming out soon. Should I ask him about the letter? Would I get in trouble for spying into his front seat?

While I was trying to decide what to do, I realized all three buckets with their dirty rags and used paper towels were still sitting on the pavement next to the car and that I'd have to bring them back inside the school.

"Thanks a lot for sticking me with returning the garbage!" I shouted.

But no one heard me, and I just gathered up the buckets and carried them toward Endeavor.

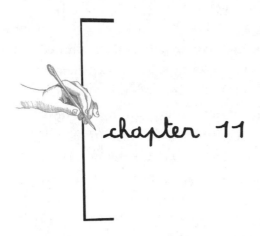

chapter 11

Lately, whenever I came up the driveway to our house, I played a little game with myself. It's called: Name the point when a stranger would realize something is very, very wrong with this place. For a while after my mom left but before my dad lost his job, you could get all the way to the refrigerator before noticing a problem, and then you would have actually had to open the door and see there was nothing inside but some condiments, at which point you might wonder what, exactly, the inhabitants of 90 Crab Apple Road were eating.

More recently, though, you couldn't make it up the driveway without knowing something was up. Back in December, my dad had stopped paying the guy who used to mow our lawn, and now it came almost up to my knees in some places.

The light over the front door had burned out months ago, but no one had bothered to replace it, and there was a whole mess of leaves and twigs and dirt that had blown up onto the front porch during the storms we'd had over the winter.

Inside was where the real fun began, though. After my dad got fired, he came up with this whole plan to make furniture for a living. Now, this wasn't actually as crazy as it might sound—my dad makes beautiful furniture. We have this amazing dining room table that he built my mom for their anniversary last summer. It's created entirely of wood (even the pegs that hold the legs on are wood—there aren't any metal nails or anything) that he took from an old barn someone was tearing down to clear the way for one of the new developments that keep springing up in Orion. Right after he gave it to my mom, her boss came over for dinner, and his wife couldn't stop admiring it. She kept going, "Tell me what you want for it." And my dad kept going, "Oh, it's not for sale." And then she'd go, "I'll give you a thousand dollars." And my dad would say, "I'm sorry, Sheila, it's just not for sale." I swear, she got up to five thousand dollars before her husband finally told her to stop. (I'd wanted to tell her to stop the second she opened her mouth.)

You could tell my mom was irritated by the whole thing, and after they left she went on one of her usual rants about people who think they can just buy up whatever they want and who are totally convinced everything has a price tag and what right do they have and how dare they and blah, blah, blah, blah, blah. Finally my dad managed to tease her out of it by going, "Okay, honey, just tell me what you want for doing all the dishes? I'll give you a thousand dollars. Two thousand dollars. Three thousand dollars if you throw in taking out the garbage." Finally she stopped being mad and started laughing and then they started kissing, and I was like, *Give me a break, I'm going to bed!* since I was already mad about having had to miss a night with my friends to have dinner with my mom's boring boss and his wife—the most annoying woman in the universe.

Sometimes, like when I think back on nights like that one, I'm convinced that what pushed my dad over the edge was that everyone kept assuming they'd been unhappy together. By Christmas, even his friends were saying things like, *You know, Dan, she did pack a bag and take her computer and all of her files. She clearly left of her own volition. Maybe things with the two of you weren't actually as good as you thought they were.* That just killed him. So to prove them wrong, he took all of this high-level security clearance from back when he was running security for my mom's NAVSTAR-GPS team (this was in Colorado, where they met), and he started using it to look into my mom's disappearance, logging into databases he wasn't supposed to use. That's when they fired him.

But sometimes I think if anyone, *anyone*, had believed that she hadn't wanted to leave (even though technically she got in her car and drove away), that instead she'd gone because she was somehow chased or frightened into leaving by something (or someone), maybe he would have been able to make a life while he waited for her to come back. Maybe he could have gotten out of bed every morning in order to do something other than drink his way through the wine cellar they spent years creating with their favorite vintages.

By the time I pushed open the front door, I didn't have the heart to play my game anymore. Because inside, our house doesn't look like *something is very wrong*, it looks like *someone has gone completely insane*.

There were about a million pieces of old wood stacked everywhere—everything from huge planks my dad had ripped off collapsing old structures in and around Orion, to strange (usually enormous) branches that caught his eye because of their shape or their color. In the front hall alone is enough wood to build an entire house, and you literally have to step over a pile just to get to the coat closet.

"Hello?" The house was cold, and I wondered if my dad hadn't paid the heating bill or if the furnace, which he was always saying was about to quit, had finally given up. "Hello?" I called again. There was a flicker of fear in my voice, an echo of the fear I felt every time I came home now. Because to anyone who looked around, it was very, very clear that the owner of this house didn't feel like he had much to keep living for. And once you start thinking about it, you realize there's really no way to know when having *little* to live for becomes having *nothing* to live for.

A light was on in the dining room, and as soon as I crossed the threshold, I saw my dad, snoring, his head on the table, his hand inches from the base of an empty wineglass. It was a sign of just how bad things had gotten that all I could think was

Dead people don't snore. I considered waking him up, but then I was like, *Why?* Maybe after I'd boiled some water for pasta or something. Usually once he'd gotten some food into him he was a little more coherent.

As I opened the cabinet to get a pot, my eyes passed over the Post-it that had been stuck on the fridge for months now.

Callie: Your parka's in the dryer.

Not like I hadn't seen that note, the last one my mom ever wrote me, a million times before, but after the day I'd had, seeing her handwriting and her lab's familiar logo—the spinning red galaxy—was more than I could handle. I closed the cabinet without taking anything out and headed from the kitchen. My dad could make his own dinner; I'd just lost my appetite.

I flicked the switch at the bottom of the stairs, but the upstairs hall remained dark. I made a mental note to pick up some lightbulbs at the store this weekend.

At least we could still afford lightbulbs.

My room is a corner room at the end of the hall, and I've always loved it. From the back window, you can see Crab Apple Hill, where my mom and I used to go and look at the stars with this super high-resolution telescope she has. Though technically I suppose *I* have it now. Not that I ever use it anymore.

The switch just inside the door of my room clicked, but nothing happened. "Oh, come on," I groaned out loud. I flicked it again, and again nothing. Had the electricity been turned off? But then I remembered the light in the dining room. So

81

clearly there was *some* electricity in the house. I made my way over to the bed and the small lamp on my night table.

I pulled the chain on the old-fashioned lamp and the room was awash in soft, rosy light. That's what my room is like—soft but not in a cheesy girlish way. The walls are covered in wallpaper with tiny yellow roses, there's a big fluffy white down comforter on the bed, and the furniture is all old wood that's so smooth to the touch it feels like satin. I used to lie in my bed at night and think about all the families that had lived here over the two hundred years the house has stood—the happy families, the unhappy families, the weird families, the normal families. Lately I mostly try getting into bed and going right to sleep, not thinking about anything if I can help it.

I lay down, pulling a pillow over my face. My back was sore from all the hunching over I'd done as I made my way around Thornhill's car, and I reached my arms up over my head to try to stretch out. As I did, my hand brushed against the edge of what felt like a piece of paper.

Still lying down, I folded my hand around the paper, remembering how I'd fallen asleep two nights ago studying for a bio test. I could tell now that what I was holding wasn't a piece of paper, it was a card, and I figured one of my flash cards must have gotten left behind when I made my bed. You'd think I would have seen it yesterday or today, but maybe when you live in a house piled high with crap, you stop noticing even when there's stuff right in your own bed. I slid the card out from under my pillow and pulled my arm in front of my face, wondering if it was going to have on it a fact I knew or one I'd totally forgotten to memorize.

And then I was looking at the card, and I wasn't wondering about biology at all. Because the index card I was holding wasn't an index card. It was a purple envelope, the exact same shade as the one I'd seen in Mr. Thornhill's car. And in the top left-hand corner, where you'd normally find a return address, was an imprint of a coyote.

Hands shaking, I tore open the envelope. Inside was two thousand five hundred dollars in crisp, fifty-dollar bills.

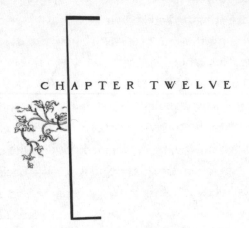

CHAPTER TWELVE

"Don't tell me that, George. Do not tell me that."

I was on the stairs, and my dad was in the living room, but still his voice boomed. My Scribble Book was under my arm, and I almost dropped it as I rushed to the kitchen, where Amanda was sitting.

"Let's go upstairs," I said.

"George, you've been my lawyer since Ursula and I got married. You know what this house means to us."

Amanda looked up at me. "Callie, it's okay." The cups of cocoa we'd been drinking were half-full, and I grabbed both of them, like they were the things that would lure Amanda away from my screaming father.

"Will you just . . . will you please come upstairs with me?" Why had I left her downstairs when I went to get the book? I knew my dad was on the phone. I knew how quickly things with him could get out of hand.

My eyes were stinging and I blinked hard.

"I am not losing this house, George. Not for twenty-five hundred dollars. This is our home."

Amanda slid her chair back from the table and walked around to where I was standing. She didn't say anything, just took my wrist and gently touched the tattoo I'd gotten earlier in the day. Then she followed me as I headed back up the stairs.

"No, that's where you're wrong. She is coming back. She is coming back, and when she does she's not going to find out that I've defaulted on our mortgage. I'll get the money. You have to tell them that . . ." We were halfway up the stairs now. If he would just stop shouting, we'd be out of earshot.

But what came next was even worse than the shouting had been. "Please, George. I'm begging you. I can't lose this house." As I pushed shut the door to my room with my foot, I could hear his voice breaking.

"I'm really sorry," I said. My voice was shaky and so were my legs. I slid down the wall to the floor, placing the mugs next to me. Just the thought of drinking the thick, sweet liquid turned my stomach.

"You don't have to be sorry," said Amanda. She was sitting on the edge of my bed, and her big eyes, heavily outlined in black to match the rest of her Patti Smith punk-rocker look, bore into mine.

"I'm just . . . I'm so embarrassed. He's not usually like this." But even as I said the words, I knew they were a lie. Sure, once

upon a time he hadn't been like this. Once upon a time he'd been Funny Dad. Nice Dad. Even Handsome Dad. The first time Kelli met him, she'd said, "Your dad is soooo cute. He totally looks like George Clooney." Now, with his pale, unshaven face, sunken eyes, and thickening belly, he was almost scary looking.

"Really, Callie," said Amanda. "It's going to pass. He'll be okay."

In spite of my attempts to stop them, two tears rolled down my face. I swiped at them angrily. "You don't know that," I said, and my voice was sharp. "He's never going to get better. He's never going to change." I'd been so excited when Amanda offered to come over after we'd gone to town. She was usually too busy to hang out for an entire afternoon, and she was literally the only person I didn't mind having at my house. And now she'd seen this.

"*Plus c'est la même chose, plus ça change*," said Amanda.

In spite of myself, I laughed. "I hope what you just said translates to 'Your distant relative is going to die tomorrow and leave you twenty-five hundred dollars.'"

She came over and kissed me lightly on the cheek.

"It does," she said. Then she stood up and put her hand on the doorknob.

"I don't blame you for going," I said. If I'd been her, I would have left while we were still downstairs.

Amanda knelt down next to where I was sitting. "Don't, okay?" she said. "Seriously. Do not blame me for going." Her voice was more intense than I'd ever heard it. For a second, I looked at her.

"I so didn't plan on something like this happening when I invited you over."

She stood up. "Life is what happens when you're busy making other plans."

I gave a little half laugh. "Sure," I said. I leaned my head back against the wall and closed my eyes. "See you tomorrow."

"Good-bye, Callie." There was the slight click of the door closing, and she was gone.

My hands were shaking so much it was almost impossible to get the money back in the envelope. Where had Amanda gotten over two thousand dollars? She definitely wasn't someone who threw money around like Heidi or Traci. Sometimes she paid for stuff, like the tattoo I'd just gotten yesterday, but that cost twelve dollars. Twelve was . . . I thought for half a second. Twelve was .0048 percent of twenty-five hundred.

Doing the math made me feel calmer. There had to be some kind of explanation. Maybe she *had* been saving the money for something. Maybe she'd been saving it and she'd been so worried about me and my dad that she just . . .

Just what, exactly? She just thought, *Hey, what the hell, I'll give them the money and then, once I've helped her out, I'll get Callie in trouble with Thornhill and laugh and laugh while she tries to make sense of it all.*

Okay, that scenario was a bit too ridiculous. So could Amanda have *stolen* the money? Could she have stolen it and then needed to leave in order to escape detection? That was definitely a whole new reason for her to have cut school today.

But then why the elaborate prank with the car and the lockers? If she were on the run from the law, wouldn't she have wanted to get as far as she could as fast as she could?

It didn't make any sense. Was it just a coincidence that the car and the money had happened right at the same time? Or were the two events connected somehow?

Trying to keep everything straight was making my head swirl. I couldn't do this by myself, I just couldn't. But who was I going to tell, Heidi? Traci? Yeah, right. Lee? Technically he was my boyfriend, but so far that was more about, like, exchanging Valentine's Day cards and holding hands when we were all at the Orion diner together, not something like this. For a minute I thought about calling Hal or Nia, but that would mean telling them more than I wanted them to know. Did I really want Nia Rivera knowing my family was broke?

There was only one person who could help me.

I stopped trying to straighten out the bills and just jammed the money in a wad into the envelope. Then, carrying the envelope in front of me like it was a precious object, I made my way along the hall and down the stairs.

My dad was still where I'd left him, his snoring replaced by more rhythmic, gentle breathing. For a minute, I questioned the wisdom of what I was about to do. Here was a man who spent his mornings collecting old, abandoned wood and his afternoons drinking himself into unconsciousness. Was he really the person I was going to turn to for help?

To stop myself from answering, I called, "Dad?"

He didn't respond.

"Dad?" I called again, and this time I reached down and shook him by the shoulder. Like a cartoon character, he jerked his head up and looked around, as if nothing could be more disorienting than being awakened in your own dining room by your own daughter.

"What? What? I . . ." He looked up and saw me standing there. "Oh, Callie," he said. He rubbed his eyes with the palms of his hands, then pressed his palms into his forehead as if he had a headache. "I must have fallen asleep. What time is it?"

I didn't answer him. Instead, I pulled out the chair next to his and sat down. "Dad," I said. "I need to talk to you."

"Sure, honey," he said. His gaze was unsteady, but at least he was looking at me. "What's on your mind?" He reached out toward his glass of wine and went to pull it closer to himself, but I put my hand on his arm.

"Dad," I said. "You have to help me."

"Of course," he said. He looked at his glass with what I can only describe as longing, but he didn't reach for it again.

Without saying anything, I held the envelope out toward him. The flap was down, so you couldn't tell what was inside of it.

"What are we going to do with this?" I asked.

He looked at my face as if he were seeing it for the first time in a long time. Then, without speaking, he reached for the envelope.

CHAPTER 13

"I am telling you, that girl was an F-R-E-A-K, freak!" said Traci, dipping a carrot into Kelli's container of ranch dressing. "She was in my history class, and she was always going, like, *How do we know for sure? How do we know for sure?* It was soooo annoying. I thought Mrs. Balducci was going to smack her."

"God, can you imagine the article she would have written? 'Schools Return to Capital Punishment.'" Kelli framed an imaginary headline in the air with her hands.

"It's corporal punishment," corrected Heidi, rolling her baby blue eyes. "Capital punishment is the death penalty."

Kelli shrugged. "Whatev," she said. Then she turned to me. "Okay. So, to help you get over the suffering you endured yesterday, I am personally going to do your makeup for Liz's party Saturday night. We. Are. Going. To. Look. Fabulous."

I smiled, but having spent the entire night lying in my bed and waiting for Amanda to call, I was way too tired to speak. I'd texted Amanda twice already since getting the money, but she hadn't gotten back to me. Now my phone was in my pocket on vibrate, but I wasn't exactly expecting it to ring.

"Are you okay?" asked Traci. She put her head on my shoulder and stroked my arm. "Did those freaks hurt poor Callie?"

"Yeah, you're acting really weird," said Heidi, irritated.

"No, I'm fine," I said, not wanting to piss off Heidi. Was this what Mr. Randolph had been talking about yesterday when he'd lectured us on entangling alliances? I made myself sit up straighter. "Really. I'm just sooo tired."

"Hey, Jake. Hey, Lee." Heidi was looking over my shoulder, and her voice was singsongy, the way it always gets when the guys are around. "Hey, Keith." A second later, Jake, Lee, and Keith appeared at the end of our table. Seeing Keith made me think of the fight with Nia yesterday, and I couldn't look at him.

Lee had on this Abercrombie jacket he wears a lot that looks really good on him and his cheeks were flushed, like maybe they were all just coming in from the fresh air. Sometimes I worried that, with his designer clothes and perfect body, Lee's totally out of my league and it was only a matter of time before he realized it.

"Ladies," said Jake, glancing around and smiling at us. Jake, Keith, and Lee have been friends forever, but while Keith and Lee have always been cute, Jake used to be kind of pudgy and short—I always thought of him more as Keith and Lee's side-kick than anything else. He'd gotten much taller lately, not as tall as Lee, but definitely not a shrimp, and he'd thinned out and gotten contact lenses. Suddenly he was Mr. Tall, Dark, and Handsome and the rumor about his family being some kind of royalty back in India, where both his parents were born, didn't seem terribly far-fetched. Sometimes Heidi joked about helping Jake's family reclaim their throne, and even though he'd explained about a million times that there *was* no throne, Heidi never completely dropped it. The truth was, if Heidi wanted for there to be a throne, I had the feeling that somehow there was going to be a throne.

"So are you guys going to Liz's tomorrow?" asked Heidi. It was a rhetorical question. Liz wasn't as popular as the I-Girls but she was pretty cool, and she lived in this huge house about a block away from Heidi's. Every year for her birthday she has a gigantic party, and everybody who's anybody in our grade goes. Even some older kids come because her brother's a year ahead of us, and he usually invites a bunch of his friends.

"Are you going to talk to us if we go?" asked Jake. "Or are you just going to ignore us and talk to all the older guys?" He was leaning over Heidi and she was looking up at him. I couldn't believe he hadn't asked her out yet.

"Well, maybe you should give us a reason to talk to you," Heidi answered, twirling a length of pale blond hair. "Make it worth our while."

"Is that a challenge, Heidi Bragg?" Keith was leaning toward Heidi, too, his football jacket hiding his thick neck. I wondered why people always describe the popular girl as a queen bee. It was more like she was a flower and all the *other* kids in the grade were bees, circling around and trying to get to her.

While I was watching Heidi talk to Keith and Jake, Lee had come around to my side of the table.

"How's it going?" he murmured. It was like he was asking about something a little bit secret.

"Okay," I said. It was only one word, but it felt like the biggest lie in the universe.

"I saw you yesterday, Callie." I still loved it when he said my name. "When you were washing that car." His brown eyes were almost gold in the sun streaming through the cafeteria windows, and again I was struck by how impossible it was that Lee Forrest could exist in the same universe as Amanda, Nia, and Hal, and that both universes were *my* universe.

"Yeah," I said. "I saw you, too." I remembered his waving to me and cheering and how good it made me feel. "Thanks for the support."

"No problem," said Lee. "What's the deal? Why did Thornhill make you clean his car? Do you know Amanda or something?"

That's the problem with lies: once you start telling one, you can't stop. "Not really. She's in my math class."

"Wow," said Lee. "So she must be, like, some kind of math genius."

Lee was always saying nice things like that.

"She is, actually," I said. After listening to the I-Girls trash her so much, I was glad to be able to say something honest and

complimentary about Amanda out loud that I said it again. "She's a real genius."

Amanda stopped being the topic of conversation as talk turned to the weekend and Liz's party, which was a relief. When the bell rang at the end of lunch, we all got up from the table together, and even though we hadn't been talking or anything, it just worked out that Keith and I walked out of the cafeteria together. When we got to the door of my bio class, Keith was in the middle of telling me something about his family's plans for spring break. I looked up and saw Hal and Nia.

They were coming down the hall, and Nia saw me but Hal didn't. She looked at me, looked at Keith, then looked away, as if she'd just laid eyes on the most revolting sight possible.

"Isn't that wild?" finished Keith.

"What?" I said, and then, to stop him from repeating himself, I just said, "I mean, yeah. Totally. It's totally wild."

"Gotta motor," said Keith. "Later."

"Later." I walked into the bio lab and dropped onto my seat, where I spent the next forty minutes staring blankly at the board, not understanding a word Dr. Moser uttered.

I'd called my dad when Amanda didn't show for math class and, as we had agreed, he picked me up in his truck after school. It looked like he might have slept in his clothes, but as far as I could tell, he was sober.

"We're returning this money," he said grimly, and I could tell he was angry.

"Oh," I said. When I'd left him last night, after telling him all about how I'd gotten the money, he'd said he wanted to sleep on it. Now that he'd made his decision, I couldn't help feeling a little bit proud of him. Sure, we might lose our house. But at least we weren't going to keep it by using possibly stolen goods.

"Now, where does Amanda live?"

I'd never actually been in Amanda's house, but once, when we were biking to get coffee after school up in the College Green part of Orion (it's called that because all of the streets are named after colleges and universities, not because there's an actual college there), Amanda had pointed to a really nice old Victorian house.

That's where I live."

She was a little bit ahead of me, and she didn't slow down or anything. I was kind of surprised.

"Don't you want to go inside?" I knew Amanda was living with her father's parents; her mom was an anthropologist who was doing field work in Uganda for the academic year, and her dad was traveling a lot because of the work he did for the United Nations—something with microloans in Latin America. I'd never met anyone who actually lived with guardians and not parents before, but in Amanda's case, it made total sense. There was something about Amanda that made it seem almost like she didn't have parents. It was like she was . . . I don't know, too removed from the average teenage stuff the rest of us have, like parents and curfews and fights about whether or not she'd done her homework or could have money to go to a movie. There was something about the whole setup that made me even more curious to see her house, to meet her grandparents.

"Not especially." She'd gotten a little farther ahead when I slowed down to look at the house, and now she had to shout for me to hear her. "Come on!"

Before I started pedaling faster, I got a good look at the front porch, where a really nice, old-fashioned swing hung. The door, which was a bright, sky blue, was slightly open, like it was inviting you to come inside. The house was old, but it was in pristine condition, and as I rode past, I realized that it reminded me of my house before my mom left. It was kind of cool that Amanda's house was so much like mine (or like mine used to be). Maybe our families would turn out to have all kinds of stuff in common. Maybe when my mom came back from wherever she was and my dad started acting normal again and Amanda's mom came back from Uganda and her dad finished traipsing around south of the border, they'd meet and like one another and the four of them would become friends.

It was such a nice picture (the six of us at a barbecue at our place or stringing popcorn on a Christmas tree at Amanda's) that I kept it in my head for the entire ride.

* * *

I'd thought I remembered which street was Amanda's, but when we turned onto it, I realized it couldn't possibly be the one because this street had a sidewalk and the one she and I had been riding on that day didn't. My dad had to drive around for almost twenty minutes before we hit the right block, and then we almost missed the house because they'd repainted the door red. The whole time we were driving, my dad was getting more and more agitated, but I didn't know if it was because he was having second thoughts about giving back the money or because he hadn't been sober at this time of day for months.

I called her from the car (again), and she didn't answer (again). In truth, I was a little nervous about seeing her face-to-face after everything that had happened since I last saw her. As much as I was dying to ask her what the hell was going on, a part of me was almost hoping she wouldn't be home, that I'd just meet her grandparents, give them the envelope with the money in it, and leave a message for her to call me.

My dad was a few feet ahead of me, and when we got to the door, he rang the bell, then knocked, as if he were too impatient to wait even a second for someone to answer. At first there was only silence from inside, but then we could hear footsteps, and a voice said, "I'm coming, I'm coming."

A minute later the door swung open and an elderly man in a wine-colored cardigan stood facing us. He had to have been at least eighty, which was older than I'd imagined her grandfather being.

"Hello," said my dad, and I was relieved that he didn't

sound angry or impatient.

"We're here to see Amanda."

The man smiled up at my dad, and despite his age and stooped posture, I sensed something vibrant in him. "I'm sorry, I don't hear as well as I should. Could you say that again?"

"We're here to see Amanda," said my dad, louder this time.

"Amanda?" asked the man. He was still smiling, like people showing up at his house and making demands was something he truly enjoyed.

"Amanda—" My dad looked over at me, and I supplied the word he wanted.

"Valentino," I said. Though considering she lived here, I couldn't see why her grandfather, no matter how old, would need to be reminded of her last name.

"I'm sorry," repeated the man. "Did you say Amanda Valentino?"

"Yes," answered Dad.

He shook his head. "I'm afraid there's nobody here by that name."

chapter 14

This wasn't possible. I looked around me. There was the swing I'd seen that day on our bikes. The wide porch. Even if the door was a different color, everything about the place was exactly the same.

Amanda had definitely said she lived in *this* house.

"Um, is it possible she *used* to live here?" We'd biked past in late November and now it was the middle of March. True, Amanda had never mentioned moving, but clearly there were a *lot* of things Amanda had never mentioned.

"Oh, I suppose it's possible." The man chuckled. "But that would have been a long time ago. My wife and I have lived here over fifty years."

This wasn't possible. "Amanda Valentino," I said, and after all my fears about my dad behaving badly, now it was my voice that sounded harsh and irritated. "She's a teenager, about my height. Beautiful. Changes her appearance a lot. She told me she lives here."

The man didn't seem to have heard the last sentence because he was distracted by an idea. "Are you by any chance looking for Callista? Callie?"

"What?" My dad's voice was a near shriek.

Again, the man didn't seem to notice. "Oh, that must be who you're talking about. A lovely girl. She helped my wife and me with some errands this winter, back when it was so icy in January. Honey!" he called over his shoulder to someone inside the house. "There are some nice people here, say they're looking for Callie."

I felt a wave of dizziness and I wondered if it were possible that I was actually going to faint. As I grabbed onto my dad for support, an elderly woman appeared by the man's side. She was as hunched over as he was and wearing a dress almost the same color as his sweater. I once read somewhere that married people come to look alike, and I wondered if that was what had happened with the two of them.

"Yes?" she said.

"Sweetheart, these people are friends of Callie's. They're looking for her."

The woman's face lit up, and she gave us an enormous smile. "Oh, she's a lovely girl. Did Harold tell you how she helped us this winter? I don't know what we would have done without her."

"Smart as a whip, too," continued the man. "Going to be an astrologer."

"Now, Harold." The woman gave him an affectionate look. "An astronomer." She turned back to us. "Her mother was an astronomer, you see. So that's why she was interested."

Now I felt my dad's arm starting to shake. When neither of us spoke, the woman's expression suddenly changed.

"Nothing's wrong, is it? She's not in any kind of trouble?"

Miraculously, I found my voice, though it was shakier than I would have liked. "No," I muttered. "No, nothing like that. I just thought she might be here. She's fine, though. Absolutely fine."

"Oh, that is *such* a relief," said the woman. "We haven't seen her in a while, but she said she'd come again."

"Would you care to come in for a cup of coffee?" asked the man.

"Or tea?" the woman added. "We have some lovely teas you might like."

We managed to decline the offer, say good-bye, get off the porch, and get into my dad's truck without my actually being conscious of any of those things happening. My dad pulled away from the curb so fast his tires squealed and I'm sure he left tracks on the pavement. When we got to the corner he made a left, then pulled over and slammed on the brakes.

"What kind of sick game are you playing, Callie?" He was breathing hard, and his face was red.

"Me? You think *I'm* playing some kind of game? Are you kidding?"

He leaned toward me and pointed his finger in my face.

"Did you take that money from somewhere? Is that what happened?"

"You think I *stole* the money and came up with a story about Amanda? Is that what you're saying?" My voice was stronger now, and I was yelling.

"I don't know what to think," said my dad. "I don't understand you at all."

"*You* don't understand *me*? You've got to be kidding." I could feel myself starting to cry, but I was too angry to care. "I'm not the one who's drunk half the day, Dad. I'm not the one who's filling up our house with the crazy redwood forest. I'm not the one who's losing his mind, okay? So don't you sit there and tell me that I'm a friggin' mystery to you when you're the one who's become a totally different person!"

I was breathing hard, and I turned my face away from him and looked out the window. We were parked in front of another Victorian house, not quite as nice as the one Amanda claimed she lived in, but still pretty nice, and for a minute I was overwhelmed by the desire to live in it. Or in any one of the houses that lined this street.

Or in any house but the one I actually lived in.

My dad and I sat there for a long minute, but neither of us said anything. Then he turned on the engine and pulled away from the curb, heading toward home.

We didn't speak the whole way back, but when my dad parked in front of the garage, I said, "Just keep the money, Dad. Who cares where it came from? Who cares what she did to get it? Just keep the money and save the house."

I didn't wait for him to respond, just got out, shutting the door behind me before going inside and heading up to my room. All I wanted was some time to myself, time to lie down and try to make sense of a world that had, over the course of the past thirty-six hours, gone utterly insane.

For a second when I opened the door to my room, I expected to see a new note from Amanda, but even though I pulled the comforter off my bed and dug around all the pillows, there was nothing there. I even opened my desk drawers. Nothing. As I lay down on my bed, I couldn't decide if I was relieved or disappointed.

Just as I closed my eyes, there was a tap at my door. Then another. "What?" I called. The last thing I felt like doing was hashing out everything with my dad.

No answer. Another tap.

"What?" I said again, louder this time.

Again no answer but two taps in quick succession.

Sighing loudly, I swung my feet to the floor and crossed the room.

"What?" I practically shouted as I swung the door wide.

But there was no one there.

"What the—"

Another tap made me realize the sound hadn't been coming from my door at all—it had been coming from the window. I walked over and looked down.

There, standing behind my house, was Hal Bennett.

CHAPTER FIFTEEN

As soon as he saw me, Hal said something, but I couldn't hear. I tried opening the window, but the storm window was stuck, so I couldn't lift it. Hal watched me struggle for a minute, then gestured for me to come down. I held up my index finger hoping Hal would recognize the universal symbol for *I'll be down in a minute*, then went out into the hallway. Heading downstairs, I wondered what I'd tell my dad if I passed him, but even though his truck was still parked in the driveway, he wasn't around. I didn't exactly mind. It was bad enough that Hal had seen the state of my lawn. I didn't need him seeing the state of my dad.

Hal waiting for me made me remember all the times when we were kids and would meet up in the woods—so even though it was weird that he was standing there, it also kind of wasn't.

Hal moved to Orion the summer before sixth grade, which was coincidentally the most boring summer of my life. All of my friends were away at camp or doing stuff with their families, so I had no one to hang out with, and I used to go exploring in the woods behind my house alone. One afternoon, while I was making my way across a stream via this really old, mossy log, I saw Hal. We talked for a while, and then we spent the day climbing trees and exploring this creepy cave he'd discovered earlier in the summer.

I didn't notice stuff like his haircut or his high-waisted pants. The truth is I was kind of a fashion disaster back then, too, with my baggy T-shirts and cargo shorts and my hair in two asymmetrical pigtails. Hal was fun—he didn't talk a lot then either, but he taught me how to fish and he was good at climbing the hills of rocks in the woods that were equidistant from each of our houses.

And then one day while Hal and I were making our way across that same log, I somehow lost my balance and fell and broke my arm. It was a pretty bad break (I had to have pins in it and surgery and everything), so I couldn't climb around in the woods anymore—instead, I started going to the bookstore at the Galleria for something to do. And that was where I ran into Heidi, Traci, and Kelli (not at the bookstore, of course, at the food court). They were shopping for school clothes and Heidi said hi to me, which was really surprising since the three of them were super popular and I . . . well, I wasn't a loser or anything, but I was definitely a neutral.

I couldn't believe it when Heidi invited me to come over to

her house and hang out with them poolside—it was like being invited to be on your favorite reality TV show or something. Their lives were just so cool. I couldn't swim because of my arm, but I could definitely enjoy lounging on the fancy white chairs that lined the pool and drinking the Oranginas her maid brought us in these fancy plastic glasses with little palm trees all around the base. That was the day Heidi pointed out that all of our names ended with *i* (except mine, but she was nice enough to let me drop the *e*) and she said we should be the I-Girls.

I'd never had a group of girlfriends like the I-Girls before. Heidi called me every morning and we'd either meet up at her house or go to the mall or the movies. When my other friends came back from their summer sojourns, I didn't make plans with them, and after a while they stopped calling. Meanwhile, I completely forgot about Hal. By the time school started, I looked like a completely different person. The I-Girls had taken me shopping for cool clothes, and I'd gotten my hair cut by the person who cut Heidi's and her mom's hair. Sometimes, when I passed Hal in the hallways and pretended not to recognize him, I wondered if maybe I'd been so transformed since our time together that he really didn't recognize me as the girl he used to meet in the woods.

"Hey," he said. He was wearing a cool suede jacket that could have been vintage. It made me think of Nia's jacket from the day before, and now I wondered if Amanda had taken *both* of them shopping for their clothes. For the millionth time in the past two days, thinking of Amanda made me feel left out and stupid, like the whole time I'd thought we were friends, she'd actually just been playing some ginormous joke on me.

"Hey," I said back. Then I wasn't sure what to say. Part of me wanted to tell Hal all about the money and about going to Amanda's house earlier (or going to *not* Amanda's house earlier), but part of me didn't want to tell him more about Amanda than he already knew.

"Feel like walking?" he asked.

"Um, sure." Anything was better than just standing there in silence.

I thought Hal would turn in the direction of the woods, but instead he went the other way, up to the right and toward Crab Apple Hill. Except for once, I hadn't been there since the last time I'd gone with my mom, back in late October when she'd woken me in the middle of the night to see a meteor shower.

As I walked with Hal, it was hard not to be aware of his extreme cuteness. And I couldn't help feeling like he was thinking really deep thoughts—not about Amanda, necessarily, but maybe about art. It made me feel awkward and self-conscious, like whatever I said was bound to sound shallow or stupid. That fear kept me from talking, which only made me more aware of the silence.

Even when we'd climbed to the top, neither of us said anything for a minute. Crab Apple Hill isn't exactly Mount Everest, but Orion isn't exactly Nepal, either. I mean, it's pretty flat, so you don't have to be all that high to get a good view of the surrounding lands. I almost never came up during the day, so it was kind of cool to look around at something other than the night sky. Off in the distance, I could make out the Endeavor football field and bleachers.

"My favorite run takes me right past here," said Hal, pointing out toward the east.

"I know." It wasn't until the words were out of my mouth that I realized what I'd just revealed.

"You know?" asked Hal, turning to me, a confused look on his face.

"I mean, I didn't know it was your favorite. I just . . ." Sometimes I blush so hard you can practically hear it spreading across my body. "I just come out here sometimes with my mom's telescope." Suddenly I realized what that sounded like. "To look at the stars!" I added quickly. "But once I saw you running by. Not with the telescope or anything. Just, you know, with the naked eye." As I spoke the word "naked," I had to fight the urge to turn and run at top speed back down Crab Apple Hill, not stopping until I'd gotten inside my house, bolted the front door, and buried my head under all ten of the pillows on my bed.

What, exactly, had been so bad about silence again?

"Oh." Hal did not seem to notice my humiliation. "Stargazing. That sounds like fun."

"It's great," I agreed eagerly. I didn't add that, with one exception, I hadn't done it in about six months.

"I haven't heard anything from Amanda," said Hal. "And

it's starting to freak me out. I really thought she'd be back at school today."

"I went by her house this afternoon." I continued to gaze around the landscape, anywhere but at Hal. "Well, what I *thought* was her house."

"What do you mean?" asked Hal. He sat down on a low, flat rock and squinted up at me.

I told him about having ridden past Amanda's house with her months ago.

"But she doesn't live on Princeton Avenue," he objected, when I mentioned the name of the street we'd biked on. "She lives downtown. It's an apartment building right by the tattoo place."

"What?" What was Hal talking about? "No she doesn't."

Hal wasn't at all affected by my telling him he was lying. "Yes she does," he insisted. "Those new condos they just built? She and her mom are living in the—what do you call it, the show apartment? The sample? Whatever, it's the one they decorate to let you see what it will be like. That's where they're living until theirs is finished."

"But—" A condo in town? I'd had such a sure picture of Amanda in the Victorian house. I couldn't replace it with some sterile, prefurnished apartment. Besides, her mom was in Uganda with the gorillas.

Hal seemed to feel bad for making me so confused. His voice was soft as he continued. "What happened is that when her dad died—"

Instead of making me feel better, I felt like I was being lectured by a crazy person.

"When her dad *died*? What do you mean, *when her dad died*? Her dad didn't *die*. He works for the UN."

Now it was Hal's turn to look at me like I was one taco short of a combination platter. "Her dad died a long time ago. When she was, like, three or something."

Okay, now I had proof that Hal was out of his mind. "Hal, no way did her dad die when she was three. He taught her quadratic equations, which, I can assure you, even a math genius like Amanda did *not* learn at the age of three. Her parents are both alive, and the reason she's here in Orion is because her mom's in Africa and her dad's in Latin America and she's living with her father's parents in that big Victorian house over on Princeton Avenue." But even as I spoke the words, I knew they were totally nuts. Or I was.

Or something.

chapter 16

Hal stood up. "How could she live with her father's parents when they were killed in a car crash on her sixth birthday?"

I took a step toward him and raised my voice a little, like volume was the thing that was going to convince him. "How could her father's parents have been killed in a car crash when they're her guardians?"

Hal took a step toward me and raised his voice a little, too. "How could they be her guardians when she doesn't have any family in the world except her mom?"

"But—" I was about to repeat the thing about her living with her grandparents when I realized the total stupidity of me and Hal standing there screaming at each other.

Hal must have realized it, too, because he just stood there, mouth slightly open, like he'd caught himself before he really got going.

"Something very, very weird is going on," he said finally. He sat back down and started digging in the mud with his stick.

"Tell me about it. And there's something else you should know." I squatted down a few feet away and told him about the money. I hoped he wouldn't ask why she'd given me money. I didn't like the idea of lying to Hal, but I wasn't sure I was ready to share all my family's dirty little (or not so little) secrets with him, either.

When I told him the amount of cash, Hal let out a long, slow whistle. "Wow."

"I know," I said.

He thought for a minute. "Do you think she . . ." He swallowed, like he couldn't quite bring himself to say the words. ". . . stole it?" he finished quietly.

I shook my head. "I don't know. I mean, Amanda's definitely . . ." How could I describe her in just a word or two?

"Unconventional?" Hal offered.

It was good enough for now. "Yeah," I said. "But I don't think she's, like, a *criminal* or anything."

"Still, that's a lot of money. I never thought of her as being especially rich."

Neither of us said anything for a minute, taking in what we'd just learned.

Hal spoke first. "I never met her mom. She talked about her a lot, but I never actually met her. Do you think that's weird?"

Who was I to say what was weird?

"What do you mean?" I asked.

"Well, like . . . I almost started to think . . ." Hal looked embarrassed, as if he was about to say something truly outrageous. "I almost started to think she didn't *have* a mom. That she was on her own. Does that sound crazy?"

I remembered my own sense that Amanda was somehow too cool to have regular parents, but I hadn't thought of living with her grandparents as being on her *own* exactly. It was a scary thought. I mean, I guess in some ways *I* was on my own, what with my mom being MIA and my dad being AWOL himself. But it wasn't like if something really big happened to me and I needed him, he wouldn't come through.

Was it?

Imagining what it really meant to be "on your own" was creeping me out.

"They must have a record or something," said Hal slowly. I could tell from the way he said it that he was talking to himself more than he was talking to me. Still, I couldn't help asking.

"Who? Who must have a record?"

"The school. The school must know where she lives. You have to provide proof when you register that you live in the district."

My legs were getting tired, so even though I knew the ground would be cold and damp, I sat down on it. "How do you know?" Sure enough, I could feel my butt getting chilled.

"When we moved here we had to wait until we got some kind of bill addressed to my parents to register me. My mom was really annoyed by it. She kept saying the whole system was too suspicious and paranoid." He smacked his leg with his fist. "God, I just wish we could get our hands on her file."

"Not to sound suspicious and paranoid myself," I said, "but couldn't she have just faked the documentation to fool the school? I mean, it's the kind of thing she would have done and Endeavor would have fallen for. They're not exactly Langley."

"Langley?" asked Hal. "Who's Langley?"

"Sorry, my dad's in the security business. Used to be, anyway. Langley, Virginia, is where the CIA headquarters are."

"Got it," said Hal. Then he cocked his head to the side and looked at me, only he wasn't looking *at* me so much as he was looking *through* me at his own idea. "Speaking of security, how does Thornhill know Amanda painted the graffiti?"

"What do you mean?" I asked. Thinking about it now made me realize I hadn't thought about it before. "I guess . . . you know, he must have seen her."

Hal shook his head. "But he couldn't have seen her or he would have stopped her."

Duh. "Right," I said. "Of course."

"And when did she do it?" asked Hal. He thought for a second. "It must have been in the evening, right before he left school for the day. He must have found it when he walked out of the building."

I shook my head, and not just because I'd been with Amanda all afternoon on Wednesday. "Impossible. It rained all day and all night on Wednesday, remember? If she'd done it any time Wednesday, it would have washed off."

"Oooh, excellent, Sherlock Holmes," said Hal, high-fiving me, with just a little too much enthusiasm.

I pretended to stick an imaginary pipe in my mouth. "Elementary, my dear Watson," I said.

Suddenly I remembered the purple envelope. Could that have been how Thornhill knew? But from the way it was slipped in between the papers on the front seat, it looked like it hadn't been moved from the time Amanda put it there (if she'd put it there, or if it was even there at all). *Should I tell Hal about the envelope now?* But then I'd have to admit that I hadn't told him and Nia about it earlier. Then again, was this really the time for keeping secrets?

Out of nowhere, Hal said, "She's the reason I went to New York, you know?"

I had no idea what he was talking about. Did this have something to do with Thornhill's car? "New York?" I repeated.

"I went to New York, remember? For that art contest?" Maybe because he was embarrassed to be talking about winning the contest, he leaned forward and toyed with his shoelace, retying what I was pretty sure had already been tied.

"Sure," I said. "That national contest you won. That was really cool."

When Hal lifted his head, his cheeks were bright red with embarrassment, but he didn't look away from me this time. "It was because of her that I even entered it. She got me to do that caricature of Thornhill for the paper. Then she gave it to Mr. Harper along with a few other drawings of mine that she, um,

'borrowed' from my portfolio." Mr. Harper was the head of the art department, but he didn't teach any freshman classes.

"Wow," I said. I could totally picture Amanda marching into Mr. Harper's office with a copy of *The Spirit* in one hand and a pile of art she'd stolen from Hal in the other, demanding he let Hal represent Endeavor.

Hal was looking off into space, almost like he wasn't talking to me anymore but was thinking out loud. "No one ever took my drawing that seriously before . . ." Suddenly he jerked his head in my direction and snapped his fingers. "Security cameras," he said. "He must have seen her on the surveillance tapes."

I was confused for a second and then I realized we were back on Thornhill's car. I'd totally forgotten about Endeavor having security cameras on all the entrances and both parking lots. The VP put them in last fall after a series of break-ins, although it turned out nothing was ever taken.

"Well, that security tape is something I wouldn't mind seeing for myself," I mused.

I didn't mean anything by saying it. I wasn't like, *If only there was a way we could actually watch Amanda decorating Thornhill's car.* I just kind of said it the way I'd say, *I wish I could find out where that cell phone I lost over the summer is*, or *I wish I could ask George Washington what his motivations for crossing the Delaware were instead of having to come up with them on my own for this stupid history paper.* What I meant was *I wish I lived in a parallel universe, one where we could view the tape of Amanda vandalizing the car. Too bad that isn't possible.*

116

But apparently what I said and what Hal heard were two very, very different things.

"That's what we'll do," he said.

"What? What will we do?"

"We've got to see the tape. And we've got to find out what address the school has for her, family details, whatever, anything concrete about her—just get that official school file."

"And how exactly are we supposed to do that?" I asked.

"Well, it can't be that hard," said Hal. "I mean, both her file and the tape must be in Thornhill's office, right?"

I pictured the big file cabinets against the wall. "Riiight . . . ," I admitted.

Hal pushed his fingers through his hair. "We could create a distraction. Get everyone out of the building."

"A distraction such as . . ."

"Pull the fire alarm?" suggested Hal.

I shook my head. "Remember what happened to Seth and Wyatt Hall?"

Hal winced. "Right. Good point." Seth and Wyatt Hall, twins, were seniors at Endeavor. Or, more accurately, had been seniors last semester. Right up until they were expelled for staging a fire alarm during first-semester finals.

"Bomb threat?" said Hal.

"I think that might be a federal offense."

Hal stood up and began pacing in small circles. "Okay, okay. This just can't be that difficult. We're not trying to perform open-heart surgery or anything. All we need is, like, ten minutes alone in Thornhill's office."

"Hal, that's like saying, 'All we need is a million dollars.' It's not really an 'all' kind of situation."

"Okay, okay." Hal suddenly stopped his pacing. "We're being stupid. Tomorrow we're going to be in the building. It's a Saturday morning, so the whole place is going to be deserted. We're talking about the *perfect* opportunity."

"Being in the building and being in Thornhill's office are two different things," I said, stating the obvious. "I mean, even assuming we could get to Thornhill's office from wherever we're having detention without anyone seeing us, we still have to get *into* the office."

"We could pick the lock. They do it all the time in the movies. I think you just need a credit card and one of those . . . you know . . ." He gestured at his head. "One of those hair thingamabobs."

"It's called a bobby pin. And have you ever *tried* to pick a lock?" I asked.

"Not exactly."

"Let's just say it's not as easy as it looks in the movies." Years ago, when my parents were redoing the kitchen, one of the workmen hadn't realized we don't lock the front door, and had locked it from the inside before leaving for the day. I'd had the brilliant "just pick the lock" idea, too, only about ten hours into my attempt, I accepted that you can't believe everything you see on TV and I gave up, climbing the apple tree that's outside my room and getting into the house through my open window instead.

"Oh," said Hal, and he plopped down on his rock again.

I felt bad about shooting down each of his plans without offering one of my own. But I wasn't exactly an expert at breaking and entering. I tried to think of anything my father had ever told me from his security days. "Um, what if we stole his keys? You know, tomorrow, while we're in detention. You could distract him while I get his keys." How, exactly, I was going to "get his keys" wasn't really clear to me, but Hal looked cheerier than he had before I started talking, so I kept going. Actually, just making up a plan, even one I knew would be impossible to execute, was kind of exciting. I stood up. "And don't they make keys at that hardware store next to Sal's Pizza?" I closed my eyes, picturing the three stores that made up a mini strip mall less than a mile from Endeavor. Could one of us get there and back in little enough time that Thornhill would believe we'd just gone to the bathroom or to get something from our locker? "We could steal his keys, bring them to the locksmith, get them copied—"

Now it was Hal who was shaking his head. "I was with you up to the part about getting them copied. But you can't copy school keys."

Maybe I'd started out thinking my plan was impossible, but now that I'd gotten kind of into it, Hal's criticism was annoying. I put my hands on my hips. "What do you mean you can't copy a school key? What are they, some special brand or something?" The key to my dad's new truck had this really fat top and if you lost it, you could only get a new one from the manufacturer. But I'd never noticed anything special about the keys to the school.

"Haven't you ever seen one up close?" asked Hal.

"A school key?" I tried to remember. "Just on the custodians and stuff."

"I locked my jacket in my homeroom once," said Hal. "And the custodian let me borrow his keys to let myself into the room. All the keys have a number on them and say DO NOT DUPLICATE. So unless we could, I don't know, maybe bribe a locksmith? He'd have to be willing to break the—"

But I wasn't listening to a word Hal was saying. My heart seemed to have stopped beating for a second, only to start pounding a million miles an hour. I remembered that wintry afternoon. Amanda's blond wig. The key. I thought of the person who had put the scarecrow in Thornhill's office over February break.

Squatting down, I put my hand on his arm. "Did you just say 'do not duplicate'?"

"Yeah, it means—"

I sat down, my head spinning. Was it possible? Could Amanda have actually . . . ?

Hal had stopped talking and now he was staring at me. "Are you okay?"

Was I okay? I couldn't tell. My pounding heart was making it hard for me to focus.

When I didn't answer, Hal leaned forward to look me in the face. "Seriously, Callie. What's the matter?"

I finally met his eyes. "I think I know how we're going to get into Thornhill's office."

CHAPTER 17

I'd felt really tough and confident when I told Hal we'd be using the key Amanda gave me to break into Thornhill's office, but sitting in the library with the vice principal staring at us, I couldn't help feeling like even *thinking* about breaking a school rule was a very, *very* bad idea. It didn't help my confidence that when Jason Phipps and Todd Markham walked in to serve their detention, Mr. Thornhill called them over to the desk at the front of the room and said something to them very quietly, something I'm pretty sure included the word *expelled*. Jason and Todd are juniors, and they hang out with this pretty rough group of kids who are always getting in trouble for throwing wild parties after the Enders win a game (a rare event, I'll grant you). I wondered what they were in for today, since football season was long over. Whatever it was that they'd done, could it be worse than breaking into the vice principal's office and going through his stuff in search of a student's classified folder and surveillance footage?

I highly doubted it.

And how could we be sure the key would even work? I'd lain awake half the night thinking of all the keys in the world stamped with DO NOT DUPLICATE. I mean, even if the key Amanda gave me *had* come from a school custodian, who was to say it came from a custodian at *Endeavor*? Amanda had said they'd moved around a lot. Maybe the key opened *another* vice principal's office, one at a high school in Minnesota or Missouri, a junior high in Oklahoma, an elementary school in Maine. How would Amanda have gotten a key to Thornhill's office? And why would she have given it to *me*? By the time the sky started to get light, my definite feeling that Amanda had somehow known I'd need a key to Thornhill's office someday and had therefore given me one (without, of course, telling me *what* she'd given me) was so wobbly it wasn't even funny. Or it was funny. I was too tired to be clear on the difference, but either way, there was one thing I *was* sure of: the key that had been sitting in the bowl on my dresser with my loose change and random hair bands for the past few weeks was definitely *not* the key to Thornhill's office. I'd put it in my backpack last night when I was still suffering from the delusion that Amanda had literally handed me the key to solving our problem. Now, I couldn't figure out why I'd bothered.

I'd planned to tell all of this to Hal and Nia outside the school first thing in the morning, planned to tell them that we needed to go back to square one and figure out a different way to get into Thornhill's office, but even though I arrived half an hour early, so had Mr. Thornhill. And when Nia and Hal showed up, there was no way to pull them aside to tell them I'd had a change of heart, especially with the vice principal standing right there and watching us like a hawk.

There were only five of us in detention, and Mr. Thornhill put us each at our own table in the quiet study area of the library: me behind Hal, Nia over to my left. Which meant even if I *did* have the key to Thornhill's office (which I so clearly did not), how were the three of us supposed to coordinate a break-in when we couldn't talk to one another? And did Nia even *know* about the plan? Hal had said he'd call her, but there was no way to know if he had.

I needed to get a note to Hal. I reached into my bag for my Scribble Book and flipped through it in search of a blank page. When I found one, I wrote,

Plan is off. Key's a dud.

Just writing it made me feel better. Calmer. We'd reconvene and figure out some other way to get our hands on the surveillance footage and her file. And maybe we didn't even need Amanda's school records. Maybe she really did live downtown in that condo, and I was the only one she'd lied to about her address. Thinking of Amanda lying to me but not to Hal made me feel bad. I made a little stick figure with a tie like Thornhill's. Then I drew a box with lines going up and down it, like a cage. Then I drew three little stick figures in the box. I looked at my watch. Five minutes had passed.

I-Girls know when to pass notes—it's what we do. The time was not yet ripe.

In front of me, Hal cleared his throat and I jerked my head up. Was he trying to communicate something? But as I watched him, he just sat there, flipping through his sketchbook. I watched the pages ripple past, and whenever he stopped at one, it always seemed to be a drawing of Amanda. He was a *really* good artist—he totally got her personality, or changing

personality. In one she was shown in profile, laughing, mouth wide-open, head thrown back. In the next one Amanda's back was to the viewer, but I recognized her by the dark purple cape she wore. The setting was unfamiliar, though, until Hal moved his head and I realized she was standing on a dock with the Baltimore skyline behind her. Had they actually been to Baltimore together? The city was almost an hour and a half by train—when had they gone there? I thought of all the days Amanda hadn't been in school and I'd assumed she was sick or doing something with her grandparents or just playing hooky. Could she have been with Hal?

Thinking of the two of them on the train together heading to spend a day wandering around the city, I couldn't help feeling a little jealous—but the weird thing was that it was hard to know who I was jealous *of*. As Hal thumbed through his sketchbook and picture after picture of Amanda flipped past, it started to feel like they'd spent a *lot* more time together than she and I ever had. Were they best friends? Were they going out?

It was weird—I mean, it wasn't like I liked Hal. As in, *liked* liked Hal.

Did I?

Just as I was trying to figure it out, a ball of paper landed in my lap. I jerked my head around, but Nia had her face buried in a book. Jason was behind me, but it seemed unlikely some random junior I didn't even know would have just passed me a note. And Todd had his head on the table in a way that definitely gave me the impression he was asleep.

Without looking down at the crumpled sheet, I unfolded it and smoothed it out against my Scribble Book, keeping a studied look of innocence on my face. To my ears, the crinkling paper sounded like a cannon going off, but no one else seemed to notice. Mr. Thornhill was reading a newspaper. Hal was still focused on his drawings.

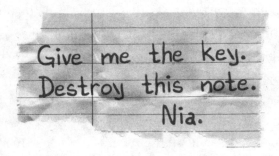

Give me the key.
Destroy this note.
Nia.

Oh, well, this was brilliant. I glanced at Nia, but she was still looking at her book. Okay, first of all, even if I thought it would open Thornhill's office, how was I supposed to *get* her the key? Just stand up, walk over, and hand it to her?

Mr. Thornhill: Callie, what are you doing?

Me: Oh, nothing, sir. Just handing Nia the master key to the school so she can break into your office.

Thornhill: Well, in that case, carry on.

Me: Thank you, sir. I'll do that.

I started ripping small shreds off the corner of the note. The first two times I tore off a piece, no one seemed to notice, but the third time, Mr. Thornhill looked up. "Could whoever is doing that to the paper please stop?" Noticing Todd's head on the table, he stood up and went over to him. "Todd?"

Todd stirred, but he didn't sit up. Mr. Thornhill slapped the desk, and Todd jerked his head up. "What?" he asked, looking around in a panic.

"Ah," said Mr. Thornhill. "Much better. Now, if you have nothing to do and nothing to read, I suggest you avail yourself of one of the marvelous texts that surround us in this most sacred of spaces, a library."

"Wha?" asked Todd, either because he was still asleep or because he didn't know what Mr. Thornhill was talking about.

"I said, do your homework or read a book, Markham. Or anticipate another Saturday like this one in your immediate future." Mr. Thornhill went back to his desk and Todd sat where he was for a minute. "I mean now, Todd!" Todd got up, walked over to a nearby shelf, and took a book off it. Then he sat down with the book on the table in front of him. Closed.

Before I could think about it, my hand shot up. Mr. Thornhill was looking at Todd and shaking his head, but he saw me. "Yes, Callie? You have something to tell me? Something that might get you and your friends dismissed sooner rather than later?"

"Sorry, Mr. Thornhill," I said. "I was just wondering if I could get a book, too. I thought I had one, but I must have left it at home."

Mr. Thornhill sighed. "Make it fast, Callie."

In a second, I'd scribbled on a slip of paper:

I'm afraid this key isn't going to work

Once I'd finished writing, it was all I could do not to make a beeline for Nia's chair, but I forced myself to examine the shelves closer to my table for a full minute, long enough for Mr. Thornhill to settle back into his paper. *Polio: The Race to the Cure. The Silent Measles Epidemic. So, You Want to Be a Doctor?* Hoping I looked like someone in search of a good read, I turned around and made my way across the aisle to the bookshelf nearest Nia. *W. H. Auden: America's Poet. The Collected Works of Emily Dickenson.* As if it were on fire, I could feel the outline of the key burning through my jeans and into my skin. *Colossus. Ariel.* As I squatted down, I slid the hand holding my note into my back pocket. Just as my fingers touched metal, Mr. Thornhill said, "Have a seat, Callie."

My fingers closed around the key and I slipped it out of my pocket. "I'm just looking for this one book," I said, grabbing a small blue book off the shelf. I stood up and, as I did, purposely dropped the book so it slid under Nia's table. Bending down to retrieve it, I put the key and the note on the floor right by her foot. She acted like she hadn't noticed and I wondered if maybe she really *hadn't*. Well, wouldn't that be just great. We could sit here all day with both Nia and Hal getting more and more pissed off at me for not having delivered the key to her when the whole time it would have been sitting on the floor next to her. Should I try to whisper to her? I could just hiss *floor* or something and maybe it would be enough to—

"Callista Leary, that is *enough*," boomed Mr. Thornhill. "Take your seat. *Now*."

I stood up. Nia gave no indication that she'd noticed anyone within a ten-foot radius of where she was sitting, much less that she'd felt or heard a small metal key fall next to her shoe. Could she really have that much focus, or was her failing to acknowledge my being right next to her proof that she *did* notice?

I went back to my seat, holding *The Collected Poems of W. B. Yeats* tightly in my hand. I sincerely hoped it was going to be interesting enough to distract me.

When fifteen minutes had passed, I was pretty sure Nia had no idea she had the key. When twenty had passed, I started wondering how I was going to phrase *and* get a second note to her. (*Nia, I'm sure the key doesn't work. But if you want to try it anyway, it's on the floor by your foot with a note that says basically the same thing. Oh, destroy this note. And that one, too.*)

Mr. Thornhill had finished his paper and was sniffing around our tables like a guard dog checking on his prisoners. My face was buried in something called "The Wild Swans at Coole," but I had no idea what the wild swans were doing or where Coole was.

"Mr. Thornhill, may I use the bathroom?" Nia's hand was in the air, but she didn't wait for him to call on her.

"Make it fast," said Mr. Thornhill. I turned to watch her slip her bag off the back of the chair and put it over her shoulder. Just as I was wondering whether Nia knew she had the key or whether she really did have to go to the bathroom, she passed by my table.

"Nice," she buzzed. She was so quiet that it took me a second to realize she'd said anything. And then the door to the library swung shut behind her and she was gone.

chapter 18

Is it possible for time to move backward? Backward. Absolutely. Backward. For a while, it seemed to me that the clock at the front of the room just wasn't moving at all, but then I looked up and it was *definitely* two minutes earlier than it had been when I'd last checked. Meanwhile, what could Nia possibly be doing? What was she going to say to Thornhill about being gone for so long? Even though I wasn't the one who was about to have to explain my absence to him, my heart was alternately pounding and stopping. If this went on for much longer, I was going to need one of those machines doctors have that zap a person's chest with ten thousand volts of electricity to bring him back to life.

For a long time I was sure Hal was as blissfully unaware of

Nia's absence as I was conscious of it. While I shifted around in my chair, glancing at the book in front of me before looking up to check the time again, he stayed focused on his sketchbook, calmly drawing the library. How could he just sit there like that? How could he be so *mellow*? But then Mr. Thornhill stood up and I saw Hal's hand go to his pocket. As the vice principal made his way toward the door of the library, Hal's hand closed around his cell phone. My heart was beating so hard I was sure everyone in the room could hear it. I could tell Hal was dialing a number, but then Mr. Thornhill took a stapler from the librarian's desk and headed back to sit down and Hal slid his hand from his pocket. I couldn't tell if he'd hit send or not.

Less than a minute later, the door flew open and Nia, breathless and red in the face, came in. If you'd have told me three days ago that I'd be this happy to see Nia Rivera, I'd have laughed in your face.

"That was longer than I would have liked a bathroom break to be, Nia," said Mr. Thornhill, not looking up from his project.

"Sorry," said Nia. "All the girls' bathrooms in this wing are locked. I had to go to the one by the theater."

Was she lying? If so, it was a bold lie—how easy would it be for Mr. Thornhill to check? But before I could decide whether he was likely to do that, Jason raised his hand.

"Mr. Thornhill, I gotta go to the bathroom, too."

Mr. Thornhill didn't look up. "I'm sure you can wait, Jason."

"No, seriously. Mr. Thornhill, I have this problem with my

bladder and it means that if I don't go to the bathroom at least once an hour I—"

"Be so kind as to spare us the details of your physiological disorders, Jason," said Mr. Thornhill. "Please come up here."

In spite of myself, I was kind of curious about what Jason was going to tell Mr. Thornhill. Were there really disorders where you *had* to go to the bathroom every hour? I heard Jason say the word "doctor" and Mr. Thornhill say "highly doubt" when suddenly Nia's hip bumped against my table, and in the middle of the wild swans was the familiar key and a tiny piece of folded-up paper.

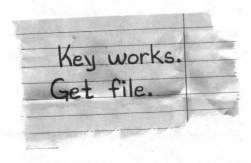

I looked up, but Nia was already sitting at her table. Only the fact that she was breathing a little rapidly made it possible for me to believe this was all happening. Had she really broken into Thornhill's office? Had she been able to get the footage? For a second I wondered why she hadn't just grabbed Amanda's file while she was in there, but then Mr. Thornhill said something to Jason and as Jason left the library, I realized it was time for me to focus on how I was going to get out of there, too.

Jason took almost as long in the bathroom as Nia had, and I couldn't help imagining that he, too, had broken into Thornhill's office. But it seemed unlikely that *everyone* serving detention had the same agenda. Mr. Thornhill didn't ask Jason why it had taken him so long, so I figured he'd probably believed Nia's story about the bathrooms being locked.

The clock ticked. I was sure I could feel Nia staring at me, but whenever I looked over at her, she was buried in her book. *Now,* I said to myself. *Do it now.* But I just continued to sit there. Then suddenly my hand was in the air like it had shot up by itself. My heart was racing so hard I felt dizzy, and the deep breath I took did nothing to calm me down.

"Five minutes, Callie," said Mr. Thornhill. He did not look up from what he was reading.

"Mr. Thornhill, may I—"

He raised his head. "I said, you have five minutes. Don't make me come looking for you."

Was it paranoia, or did he utter those words as if, were he to come looking for me, he would know exactly where to find me? I swung my bag off the table and headed toward the door of the library.

The vice principal's office was as far from the library as it was possible to be without actually leaving the school. No sooner had the door shut behind me than I started running, glad I'd thought to wear my sneakers instead of my boots, which would have clattered down the hall like a dozen horses. But even though I was really sprinting, it felt like it took at least five minutes just to *get* to the main office.

My hand was shaking so much I could barely work the key; it slipped around in my fingers and wouldn't go into the hole for so long that I thought Nia must have returned the wrong key to me. But just as I was about to confirm this one said DO NOT DUPLICATE, I felt the smooth slipping of metal on metal and the key was in the lock and the door was opening.

It was really weird to be in the main office all by myself, with none of the hustle and bustle of secretaries or phones or students filing in and out. I heard a noise and started, then realized it was just my own breathing—the sound was harsh and foreign. *Get a hold of yourself, Callie. You've got one chance to do this right.*

Mr. Thornhill's door squeaked slightly, and then it was open and I was standing alone in his office.

I went over to the filing cabinets along the wall. My hands were still shaking, and I was having trouble remembering the alphabet. Was Valentino before or after Valence? Valentine? I literally had to stand there humming the alphabet song, trying not to think about how it would look when I was apprehended, my ABCs on my lips. They weren't going to send me to jail; they were going to send me to kindergarten.

Valentine, Jane P. Velat, Richard M. Velez, Thomas J.

Wait a minute.

I went back to the first V folder and started making my way through them, more slowly this time. But when I got to

Richard Velat, there was no way around it—Amanda's file wasn't here.

Damn. Damn. Damn. Damn. Where was it? I spun around. Mr. Thornhill's desk was as clutter-free as it had been Thursday morning. Even the folders that had been there then had been put away, so there was nothing to disrupt the pristine green of the blotter that sat on the gray surface of his desk.

His desk. I went over to his desk and stood there, hesitant to open it. Was I really going to go through the vice principal's desk?

Callie, you're standing in his office, which you just broke into using a stolen key. You don't really think things are going to go worse for you if he finds out you went through his drawers, do you?

Suddenly it occurred to me that maybe Thornhill would have brought Amanda's letter (if the purple envelope I'd seen— or not seen—in his car was, in fact, a letter from Amanda) into his office with him this morning. I could picture him discovering it as he was getting out of the car, slipping it from between the newspapers, reading it on his way into the building. Then he would have put it . . . I looked at the blank surface of the desk again.

Where?

Slowly, carefully, as if not getting caught were all about being as silent as possible, I slid open the top, middle drawer of Mr. Thornhill's desk.

Amanda's file wasn't there, but pretty much everything else in the universe was. As messy as the interior of his car had

looked through the window, it had nothing on his desk drawer. There were thousands of pens and pencils, many just stubs, old, crumpled Post-its, erasers, stamps, paper clips. Toward the back, shoved under some of the detritus, was what looked like one of the manila folders from the drawer . . . Amanda's! It had to be Amanda's! Sweaty-palmed, I reached back and slid it out, but there was no name on the tab and there was nothing inside. I tried sliding the folder back into place, but it kept getting stuck on something. Now I was completely freaking out. I shoved as hard as I could, but whatever the folder was catching on wouldn't budge. Finally, I reached my hand into the back of the drawer and slid what turned out to be a plain, white envelope toward me.

Who would have guessed a little envelope could cause so much trouble? Now that it was out of the way, the folder slid back easily, but my hands were shaking so much that as I went to put the envelope back under the folder, I dropped it. I grabbed for it too hard, wrinkling the thin paper. Would he notice? I slid it toward me and flipped it over, planning on smoothing it out.

There, in the top left-hand corner was the familiar spinning red galaxy. And scrawled across the front of the envelope was one word, *Roger*, written in my mother's handwriting.

For a second I was sure I was wrong. I had to be. Maybe it just *looked* like my mother's handwriting. Because why would there possibly be an envelope from my mother in Mr. Thornhill's desk drawer?

I was sure I was going to be sick, and when my phone buzzed, I didn't recognize the sound at first. Without even looking at my cell, still staring at those five letters my mother had definitely written, I hit the center button and glanced at the screen of my phone.

CHAPTER NINETEEN

For a split second, I did not react. And then I was instinctively shoving the envelope into my pocket, slamming the drawer shut, and racing for the door of the office.

As I pulled the door open, I half-expected to find myself face-to-face with Mr. Thornhill, but the outer office was empty. I raced to the door and hurled myself through it, landing on the floor in a heap with the contents of my bag surrounding me.

And that's when I heard them.

". . . really not a problem, Jane."

"You have no idea how much I appreciate your helping me, Roger. If these financial aid applications aren't postmarked today, we're out of luck."

"We'll get those transcripts xeroxed for you."

I scrambled to my feet, sweeping my phone, lipstick, wallet, and half a dozen pens and pencils into my bag.

"It's lucky I thought to knock on the library window. I figured when I saw your car in the lot, you had to be somewhere in the building."

I could see the tip of Mr. Thornhill's shoe as I flung myself into the small alcove next to the door of the office, where the school's one pay phone was. My breathing was fast and shallow, and so loud I was positive Mr. Thornhill and this Jane person had to hear it. But then there was the click of the office door shutting behind them—I couldn't hear their voices anymore, so I shot down the corridor toward the library.

Nothing makes me have to pee worse than being scared. So it took me about one second after tumbling through the door of the library to realize I had to pee so bad I was going to wet my pants if I didn't get to the bathroom soon. I had time to register Nia's face looking up at me and Hal, half-standing, his phone in his hand. Nobody else really seemed to be awake, so I took the chance.

"Here," I called, chucking the key in his direction. "No file." Then I turned my back on them and raced out, hoping against hope that I wouldn't run into Thornhill and that Nia had been lying about the bathrooms being locked.

She had been. I sat on the toilet for what felt like a long, long time, holding the envelope on my lap and staring at the familiar writing. I wanted to open it. A few times I even started to, but then I stopped. What was I going to find when I read what was inside? Was it possible I was sitting here holding an old permission slip or late note, something no more significant than the rest of the junk I'd dug through in Thornhill's drawer? Or what if it were something from the opposite end of the spectrum—a suicide note or a love letter that would explain why my dad hated Thornhill so much? Was I really prepared to walk back into the library having just discovered that my mom was secretly in love with Mr. Thornhill? Um, no. I folded the envelope back up and shoved it deep into my pocket.

By the time I returned to the library, Hal was gone. I'd barely had time to sit down in my seat and turn to Nia to ask her where Hal was when the door opened and Mr. Thornhill came in. I fumbled with the strap of my bag, trying to look like that's all I was doing.

"Where is Hal Bennett?" Mr. Thornhill demanded.

"He said he'd be right back," said Nia, and I was again impressed by her chill tone. "He had to make a bathroom run."

"The theme of the day appears to be overactive bladders," sniffed Mr. Thornhill, taking his seat and looking down at the papers in front of him.

"Overactive somethings," I heard Nia whisper. And when I turned to look at her, her face was in her book, but she was smiling.

When Hal opened the door to the library, Mr. Thornhill immediately started dressing him down for not having waited for permission to go to the bathroom, so there was no way for

Hal to let us know what he had found. He sat back down in front of me, opened his sketchbook, and started drawing as calmly as if he hadn't just broken possibly the biggest school rule there is (not to mention the law). I glanced over at Nia, who also seemed to be nonchalantly reading. Was I the only one completely freaking out?

All signs pointed to yes.

The rest of detention passed without anyone asking to leave, and by the time Mr. Thornhill stood up and announced that we were dismissed, I was practically losing my mind. All I wanted was to be at home, alone in my room with the envelope open and my mom's letter in front of me.

I ran over to put the poetry book back on the shelf. As I passed her, Nia whispered, "Check your locker." I jerked my head around to look at her, but she was passing by Hal's table. I wondered if she was giving him the same message.

"Hal, Nia, Callista, I will see the three of you next Saturday at the same time unless you have some information you would like to share with me between now and then." He looked at the three of us as if he knew absolutely that we were up to no good.

I tried to make my face perfectly blank when I spoke. "Mr. Thornhill, that book I thought I had with me this morning must be in my locker, and I really need it for an assignment. Could I grab it on my way out?" I couldn't believe how effortlessly the lie rolled off my lips. This life of crime was scarily easy.

The vice principal looked at his watch. "I am going to

my office to get my briefcase, and I want everyone in front of the building in two minutes at which time I plan to turn on the security system. If you can't get what you need or use the bathroom"—he gave Jason a significant look—"before then, I suggest you wait until later."

I didn't like the idea of his going to his office before leaving the building. Suddenly half a dozen ways in which I might have left evidence of having been there occurred to me. What if I hadn't put that empty folder back in the drawer exactly where I'd found it? And what if for some reason Thornhill wanted to look back at the note from my mom? What would he do when he discovered it was missing? I would have to hope he would assume he lost it in that jumble of a drawer.

Thinking about the note made me wonder if, in my panic, I'd shut the desk drawer all the way. But if I hadn't, Hal would definitely have closed it when he left the office. Unless he'd found it open and thought Thornhill, not me, had left it that way.

The possibilities for detection seemed endless. If only he wasn't going to be in his office again until Monday, enough time to forget exactly how he'd left things. My palms, which had been relatively dry for the past two hours, suddenly felt damp again.

I was so distracted by these thoughts that at first I forgot to head in the direction of my locker—my only goal was to get out of the building as fast as possible. But then I remembered Nia's hissed command and the totem Amanda had stenciled on our lockers earlier in the week. Could she have left another drawing, one Thornhill and the custodial staff hadn't discovered yet? The possibility of a message from Amanda had me running toward my locker almost before I realized how desperate I was to hear from her.

This time I didn't have to be right in front of my locker to see what was there—the bright yellow piece of paper sticking out from between the vents was visible from several feet away. I slipped it out carefully, sure it would be a note, and I was right. My hands shook, but I could still see that the words on it had definitely been written by Amanda. *She had* was on one line and *think* was just beneath it.

She had think?! Was this supposed to mean something? Was it supposed to be some kind of message? Because if so, it wasn't exactly communicating much to me. Suddenly I felt a wave of frustration. *Why can't she just pick up the phone and call like a normal person?* I was so mad I kicked the locker below mine, and the searing pain that ran up my leg after my foot made contact with the metal surface only made me madder. For a second I was tempted to just crumple up the card and toss it. If Amanda had something she wanted to tell me, let her tell me. I was tired of her games, tired of not hearing from her (or not hearing from her in any of the ways you normally hear from people). I'd spent the morning serving detention. Why? Amanda. I'd broken into the vice principal's office and (for all I knew) was about to find out I'd been discovered and was facing expulsion. Why? Amanda. I'd come barreling through the halls of Endeavor like my life depended on it only to find at the end of my race that what awaited me was a scrap of paper that meant . . . nothing. And why?

Amanda.

Not to mention my toes, which were now throbbing with pain.

I was so mad I actually looked over my shoulder for a garbage can to toss what was, as far as I could tell, a useless piece of paper, but then I realized how long I'd been standing there. Great—not only was I going to get in trouble for all the crimes I'd committed this morning, but now I was going to be locked in the building until Monday. I shoved the worthless scrap into my back pocket and booked for the front door, wincing each time my right foot hit the linoleum.

CHAPTER 20

Outside, Mr. Thornhill, Nia, and Hal were waiting. Hal seemed out of breath. Apparently he'd made a run to his locker as well. I looked around but Jason and Todd were nowhere to be seen.

"Remind me, Callie," snapped Mr. Thornhill, looking meaningfully at his watch. "Were you *retrieving* a book or *writing* a book?"

"Sorry I took so long," I apologized. In the midst of my being so mad at Amanda, I could still breathe a sigh of relief that Mr. Thornhill didn't seem about to accuse us of having raided his office over the course of the morning.

"I'm not really interested in apologies from you." He drew a circle in the air as if to enclose the three of us in it. "From any of you, actually. What I *would* like is some information about your friend Amanda."

I looked down at my feet. In some ways, Mr. Thornhill's request was even more absurd than he realized. Clearly, if there was one thing I knew right now, it was that I didn't have any information about Amanda. Any *accurate* information, that is.

Mr. Thornhill waited a minute, then sighed. "I don't know who you think you're protecting her from. I am not her enemy."

Something in his voice made me jerk my head up and look at him. I'd expected to find him staring me down, but instead he was looking across the parking lot in the direction of his car, almost like he was picturing it the way it had looked on Thursday morning.

As if he, too, were surprised or unsettled by the softness in his tone, Mr. Thornhill bent down and picked up his briefcase. "Well, it looks like we will all have the dubious pleasure of sharing one another's company in one week's time. Unless, of course, other developments make that unnecessary." Again he waited, and again none of us said anything. Then he quickly turned and headed off in the direction of his car.

Even though there was no way he could have heard us talking, we were silent until he'd pulled out of the parking lot.

"Let me see what she left you," said Nia eagerly.

As Hal reached into his jacket pocket, I said, "I don't know what she left you guys, but what she left me makes absolutely no sense. It's this yellow piece of a—"

"Postcard," finished Nia, her hand held out to take it.

Surprised, I continued. "Right. With—"

"Part of a message on it," she said, still thrusting her hand

impatiently in my direction.

I was amazed. Maybe the rest of the note was on *Nia's* part of the postcard. Suddenly I wasn't mad at Amanda anymore, I was dying of curiosity. I fumbled in my pocket for the card as Hal held out his section for Nia to see.

In a second, Nia had put the three pieces of the postcard together, and we could see what was a picture of a yellow brick road, winding up to something that was ripped away at the top of the frame. Had Amanda kept that part for herself?

"What's written on the back?" I asked, almost grabbing for the card in my excitement.

Holding the three pieces together against her palm, Nia flipped her hand over so we could read Amanda's message.

Beneath the message was the single letter *M*, and the rest of the message was ripped off.

"Meg knew she had to search. Think about IT. M," Nia read aloud. Then she snorted. "Oh, that's helpful."

I read the message over Nia's shoulder several times, moving my lips as I did. Meg. Who was Meg?

"Isn't there that girl in our grade named Meg?" Hal squinted off into the distance.

"You mean Meg Horton?" Meg Horton had been one of the girls I hung out with before I became an I-Girl.

Hal shrugged. "Yeah, that could be her last name."

"She moved away at the end of eighth grade," I said. "Amanda wouldn't even have known her."

Nia put her hand over her forehead and held it there for a minute, then dropped both hands down to her side without letting go of the slips of paper. "This is maddening."

"We're going to figure it out," said Hal. "But you know what, if she left these, she is still around. She is here somewhere, which is something."

We all thought about that for a second. That did seem like a good thing.

Nia shook her head as if to clear it. "Okay, I need some time to think. Do you guys mind leaving me with your notes?"

A few minutes ago, I'd been so mad at Amanda's playing a trick on me that I'd almost thrown out my portion of the postcard. Now that I realized it was part of something bigger, that it really *was* some kind of a message, I felt sad at the idea of just giving it away. But there was something comforting, too, about handing it over to Nia. It was like she'd . . . I couldn't quite find the words I wanted, but it was as if I knew she'd take care of it for me. Like whatever this was, whatever it meant, was as important to Nia as it was to me.

And suddenly I felt an overwhelming urge to apologize to Nia for everything—for Heidi and Keith and the I-Girls

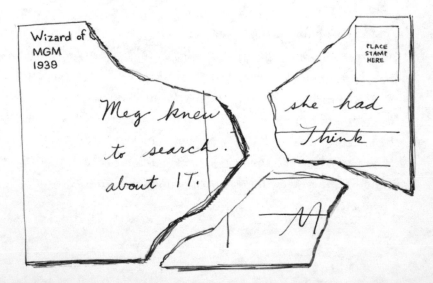

and . . . and for me. For just being who I was.

But how freaky would that have been? If I just suddenly blurted out, *Nia, I'm sorry I'm me!*

Instead, I held my hands up to indicate I didn't need my portion back. "Go for it." Then I turned to Hal. "Did you find her file?"

He shook his head. "I checked his desk drawers, his brief-case, and the closet. It's not there."

"Do you think she took it herself for some reason?" asked Nia, chewing on the nail of her index finger. "I mean, she *did* have the key to his office."

I remembered the pile of folders on the backseat of Thornhill's car. "Or could he have moved it?"

"Anything's possible," said Hal. "So maybe for now we should stick with what we know, like the addresses she gave us. One's *got* to be real. Callie's already gone to the Princeton Avenue house and that was a bust, so why don't we check out the condo downtown and the hotel she told Nia she was living in."

I turned to gape at Nia. "She told you she was living in a *hotel*?"

"The Comfort Inn out on Route 10." Nia nodded at the memory. "But she told me that when I first met her, and she said they were only staying there until they found a place to live. Her parents were going through a really ugly divorce and her mom grew up here in Orion." Nia shrugged. "That's what she told me anyway. That's why they'd moved here."

An ugly divorce. A dead father. Uganda. Latin America. There wasn't even a common *theme* to Amanda's lies, much less a consistent story.

"Did she ever mention having moved after that?" asked Hal. "Ever say they'd left the hotel?"

Nia raised her eyebrow. I noticed she did that when she thought a question was beneath her. "We didn't really have those kind of conversations." I knew what she meant. Amanda wasn't the kind of friend you asked, like, if she'd done the English reading or if she'd studied for the bio quiz or if she and her mom were still looking for a house to buy or rent.

Those were the types of conversations you had with everyone else. And Amanda was most definitely *not* everyone else.

"Look, I'm going to go home and see if I can figure out what this postcard means," said Nia. "I feel like it's important."

Hal and I nodded. "What about watching the surveillance footage?" Hal asked.

"If you guys want to, you could watch it at one of your houses tonight," said Nia, and she looked a little embarrassed. "But my parents will be all in our faces if I go out or have people over. Saturday's kind of our family night."

Saturday night was *family* night? I couldn't decide if I was jealous of Nia or felt sorry for her. Her pointing out that it was Saturday night reminded me that I was going to a party with the I-Girls in a few hours, but the strange thing was, right now I didn't feel excited about Liz's at all. There was no way around it: Callie Leary, I-Girl, was standing in front of Endeavor hoping Hal Bennett would say he and Nia Rivera and I could spend Saturday night at his house watching footage of the Endeavor parking lot.

Before I could even begin to analyze my feelings, much less formulate a story to tell my friends about why I wouldn't be at the party of the century, Hal said, "Um, my mom wasn't exactly a big fan of Amanda's." I noticed his cheeks were flushed and that he was looking beyond us, like the brick facade of Endeavor was so fascinating he couldn't take his eyes off it. "I'm not sure we should watch it at my place."

Despite my inexplicable disappointment, I stayed silent; it was one thing to have a fleeting wish that I could spend the evening with Hal and Nia solving the mysteries Amanda had created for us. It was another to issue an invitation that would involve having Hal and Nia over to witness my dad's post-cocktail hour behavior.

"What if you guys come over to my house tomorrow?" said Nia, obviously assuming from my silence that my mom, like Hal's, was no fan of Amanda's.

"Great." Hal clapped heartily. "What time?"

"I'll call you in the morning," said Nia. "I have to ask if it's okay and also what time we're getting home from church. Sometimes we stay for lunch or we have lunch company after."

Church? Family night? I was so not in Kansas anymore.

"Okay," I said. "So I guess we'll talk tomorrow, then."

"Yeah," agreed Nia, with her usual wariness. "Tomorrow."

"Tomorrow," said Hal.

"Tomorrow," I repeated.

chapter 21

The first thing I did when I got home was race upstairs, shut my door, and lock it—like I was being chased or something. Then I sat on my bed and stared at the envelope. Roger. There was the familiar downward swoop of the *R*, the little twist in the *g*. I'd never thought of my mom as having particularly distinctive writing, but now I realized just how familiar it was, like her voice or her face. It was unique. It was her.

I slid my finger under the flap. Maybe because it had gotten wet since being opened, the paper stuck a little and then tore. I wasn't worried about Thornhill noticing anymore, though—at some point I'd realized he was never going to be getting this back.

Inside was a single sheet of paper with the logo in the corner. It might have been torn from one of the thousands of identical pads we had all over our house—five-by-seven sheets of white paper we used for grocery lists and scrap paper everywhere.

Roger, I have to leave town and I need you to look after Callie. As you know, for her own safety, I can't tell her good-bye. I love her so much, Roger. If there is any way for you to keep an eye on her, to let her know how much I love her, I would be so grateful.

Underneath, my mother had signed her name, the broad *U* dwindling down to a jagged line as it ran almost to the edge of the page.

I raised my eyes, but my room, the most familiar place in the world to me, suddenly felt strange, like it was a place I'd never been before.

My mother was alive.

She was alive and she loved me.

She *had* had to leave town. *For her own safety, I can't tell her good-bye.* I wanted to run, singing, down the stairs, and into my dad's workshop. *She's alive, Dad! She's alive!*

I was off the bed and halfway across the room before I stopped. What would my dad's reaction to this note be? I pictured him, heading off to Thornhill's house or office and pounding on the door, demanding to be let in. My mom was

154

scared for my safety, and maybe even for her own. What would happen if my dad caused a scene and someone overheard, someone who wanted to know where she was?

For some reason my mom hadn't told my dad she was going. So maybe he needed to be protected, too. Maybe so protected he couldn't even know . . .

For a second I stood there, my eyes on the door, the note in my hand. If my mom hadn't wanted to tell my dad, was it okay for me to tell him? What if something really bad happened? What if he could get hurt, or she could? Slowly, I made my way into the hall and then into my parents' room, where I opened my mom's closet and stepped inside.

The first thing I noticed was the smell—my mom always wore the same perfume, Chanel No. 5, and every one of her shirts and sweaters must have had a touch of it. I stepped up to a wall of suits and blouses and breathed deeply—it was like she'd just taken them off.

She loved me. My mom loved me. She hadn't wanted to leave . . . she'd *had* to leave. As I touched first one shirt and then another, and then moved from shirts to sweaters to jackets to shoes, it felt like I was going through a photo album of my mother. *Snap!* Here she was dropping me off at school. *Snap!* Here she was coming in the door after work. *Snap!* Going out for dinner with my dad. *Snap!* Working in the garden. *Snap!* Cooking dinner. *Snap!* Dancing around the kitchen to some old, cheesy song on the radio. *Snap! Snap! Snap!*

It had been so long since I'd let myself think about my mom, I hadn't realized what a struggle it was to block her out of my mind until I stood there, crying, letting memories of her wash over me. For the first time since October, I felt truly happy. Because there was one thing that I knew for sure, and it was this: If my mother hadn't wanted to leave, that meant she would try to get back.

My good mood didn't last as long as I'd thought it would. By evening, my mind was full of all kinds of horrible thoughts. *Why* had my mom had to get away? Was she being chased? And, if she was being chased, did that mean she might already have been . . . caught? The thought made me literally ill, and a couple of times I was sure the images in my head were going to make me throw up.

When Kelli called at five to find out what I was wearing and to see if I had something green she could borrow, it was all I could do to hold up my end of the conversation. Mostly I just said "mmm" and "yeah" and "not really" while I tried to think of how to get out of going to Liz's party. I mean, how was I supposed to act normal when my brain was in the process of short-circuiting? But somehow my lips couldn't utter the sentence, *I think my mom is running for her life*, and I found myself agreeing to be at Kelli's by eight thirty, which is when Heidi's mom would be picking us up.

The sea-green T-shirt with the tight long sleeves that belled at the wrist I'd planned to wear to Liz's party to cover my tattoo was in the hamper, and none of my other green clothes were going to cut it. I had an old green sweater that was kind of bulky and that I wore sometimes on super cold days, but that wasn't exactly hip party wear. And I had a green tank top that was flattering but hardly warm enough for mid-March and would so not cover the little bear.

Should I just bag wearing green? As I stood in front of my dresser, the drawers spilling their contents over their sides from my frantic search for green clothing, it occurred to me just how stupid this whole we're-all-wearing-green thing was. I mean, me and Heidi and Traci and Kelli—we weren't a soccer team, we were a group of friends. Why should we wear the same color to a party just because Heidi thought it was a cool idea? Would it really matter if I showed up at Liz's party in red or blue or orange?

But then I thought about walking through Liz's front door with all the other I-Girls in green and me in not green. I thought about how people would think I wasn't on the inside—maybe they'd assume Heidi hadn't told me about the night's color scheme, had purposely shut me out because the three of them were planning to dump me. And what if Heidi was mad that I'd ignored her idea and she then decided to ignore me? And what if, because of how Heidi was acting, *everyone else* decided to ignore me?

Sometimes it's really, really hard to know if your response to a situation is realistic or paranoid. This was one of those times. Green it was.

There must have been over fifty people at Liz's house when we arrived, fashionably late. But even though so many people were already there talking, eating, and dancing in her darkened living room, it was hard not to feel that the party hadn't started until we arrived. That's the way it is when you're an I-Girl. No sooner had we pushed open the front door than it seemed like everyone came over to talk to us. Well, maybe not to *us*, but since Heidi could only talk to so many people at once, Traci, Kelli, and I found ourselves surrounded, too. It didn't take people long to notice that the four of us were all wearing green (I'd done the world's tiniest load of laundry that evening and washed my green shirt—drying it with the blow-dryer—which I wore with a green and blue plaid miniskirt and my Ugg boots. Basic), and within a few minutes, word had spread and the few girls who had coincidentally chosen to wear a green shirt or dress to Liz's had run over to show us that they, too, were wearing the official color of the night. Heidi hugged some of them and said it was "So awesome!" that they were wearing green, too. Others just got a lukewarm "Cool" or "Yeah, I see" when they pointed out to her that they were hip to the color scheme. Even though I've known her for years, I've never figured out if there's any logic to who gets the nod and who gets the deep freeze from Heidi. I wondered if Amanda could have come up with a program to run the numbers on *that*.

The three of us made our way to the den and set up camp on the Habers' sofa. Liz came over to say hi, and I felt a little bad. I mean, it was *her* party and *her* birthday; shouldn't we have been the ones to go over to her? But if anybody other than me thought it was weird that the hostess was paying court to someone else at her own party, they weren't indicating it, and Liz certainly wasn't complaining. Heidi launched into a funny story about a fan asking her mother for an autograph, and some-

158

one brought me a cup of Diet Coke. A bowl of chips appeared on the table in front of us, and soon more than half the party seemed to have moved into the den to sit near Heidi.

Even though I'd been so worried about my mom earlier when I was sitting there and obsessing about her, I started to feel okay. My mom wasn't the running-for-her-life type. My mom was the taking-care-of-business type. She'd gone off to do something, not have something done to her. She was going to do something, and when it was done, she'd come back and everything was going to be the way it had been. I was sure of that. I could *feel* it.

I finished my soda and whispered to Kelli that I'd be back in a few minutes.

Lee was in the kitchen wearing black jeans and a dark red rugby with a yellow stripe across the middle. I hadn't been looking for him, exactly, but when I saw him sitting on the counter, I got this warm feeling in my chest, like the night so far had been a question and he was the answer. Keith was talking, and while he listened, Lee threw a pretzel nugget up in the air and caught it with his mouth. Then he saw me and smiled, holding it between his teeth to show me what he'd done.

The smile I gave him felt lit with joy of my mom's note.

"Nice catch," I said.

He bowed his head, then gestured for me to come over to where he was sitting. He put his hands on my shoulders.

"Hey," he said. Lee has beautiful eyes, and sometimes he looks at me like the two of us are the only people on the planet.

Keith whistled. I noticed he was wearing a pale green sweater, and I wondered if Heidi had told the guys to wear green, too, only Lee hadn't obeyed her. "Get a room!" Keith said, and I could feel myself blush again. I turned around so Lee could casually drape his arms around my neck.

"Get a *life*, Harmon," Lee said.

I closed my eyes, leaning back against Lee and feeling relieved that I'd never told him how upset I was about my mom. Because a cute, popular guy like Lee probably isn't dying to have a girlfriend who's not only got semifrizzy hair and a body that, on a good day, is only so-so, but who's also an emotional wreck. And now the whole thing was moot—my mom was going to be okay, and Lee had never even had to know there was anything weird happening in my life.

When I opened my eyes, Lexa Booker and Maddy Harper came into the kitchen. "Hey," said Lexa. She didn't say it directly to me so much as she said it in my general direction. I knew she did that so if I ignored her, she wouldn't look stupid for having talked to me.

"Hey," I said back. The truth is, Lexa and Maddy can be kind of annoying sometimes. But I couldn't bring myself to ignore someone, even someone who was prepared for me to ignore her.

"I like your shirt," said Maddy.

It was just a glorified green T-shirt, but I didn't point that out. "Thanks," I said. Maddy was wearing a black, low-cut, paper-thin tee that I thought was kind of tacky, so I didn't return the compliment. She poured two cups of Diet Coke, then stood in the middle of the kitchen uncertainly, like she wanted to stay and talk but thought maybe she should go.

I knew Heidi would have let her just wait, feeling uncomfortable, until she finally got embarrassed enough to leave. And the truth was, I was kind of hoping she'd go away. But I couldn't just let her stand there.

"How's it going?" I asked.

"Okay," she said. I hadn't realized how clenched she'd been until she relaxed. Extending her leg and putting her hand on her hip, she stood where she was like she belonged there. "I saw you cleaning Thornhill's car on Thursday. That must have sucked."

Now I was sorry I hadn't let her stew in her own embarrassment until she vacated the premises. "Um, yeah," I said. What did she expect me to say, *No, Maddy, it was a total blast*?

"You sure looked cute doing it, though," said Lee, giving my shoulders a gentle massage. I could feel myself calming down in spite of Maddy's presence, and I leaned even more of my weight back against the counter.

"Do you know what I heard about her?" asked Maddy. "About Amanda, I mean."

Despite the low, low odds that this random, stupid girl knew the truth about Amanda, I found myself, for the first time all night, interested in hearing what someone had to say. What if it *did* turn out she knew something Hal, Nia, and I didn't?

But it would never do to look too eager. As I was debating how to find out what Maddy knew, Lexa jumped in. "What? What'd you hear, Maddy?" I noticed she'd straightened her naturally curly hair.

Maddy turned away from me slightly, as if she'd been addressing Lexa the whole time. "I heard she was in the witness protection plan. I heard her dad was big in the Mafia and then he turned against the leader of a New York family so they moved them here to Orion, only the mob caught up with them so they had to get her out of town in, like, a day!"

"No way!" shrieked Lexa.

"Way!" shrieked Maddy back, and when I didn't say anything, the two of them waited a second, then made their way out of the kitchen, still talking about Amanda.

Keith said something to Lee about a game they'd been watching before the party, and I wondered about Maddy's theory. On the one hand, it was so stupid it was laughable. Clearly Maddy watched way too much late-night TV.

On the other hand, was it any crazier than all of the stories Amanda had told us herself? The more I thought about it, the more embarrassed I was to have ever believed her. Her mom was in Uganda? Her dad worked for the UN? Why not say they were royalty and had to rule over their tiny European principality, unencumbered by children? Or astronauts who had left on a mission to Mars? For that matter, why come up with an elaborate story at all? If your friends are never going to meet your parents, why not just say they were run-of-the-mill people—a doctor and a lawyer, a teacher and an accountant, a chef and a personal trainer?

I wished I could call Hal and Nia and tell them what Maddy had said. I mean, if anything was possible, why *couldn't*

Amanda be in the witness protection program?

Just as I was thinking about stepping outside to make a couple of phone calls, Lee put his arms around my neck and gave me a squeeze, then kissed the top of my head. A second later, Kelli and Traci came racing into the kitchen. Seeing me and Lee, Kelli grinned.

"Oooooh! True love," she sang.

It was nice to imagine Lee's being in love with me, even though I didn't really think he was.

"Come on," said Traci. "Jake's setting up the karaoke machine."

Keith went over to Kelli and put his arm around her. "You might pass out when you hear me sing," he said. "I'm, like, that good."

"I bet," said Kelli, and she tossed her head to sweep the hair out of her face.

"Let's go!" said Traci, grabbing Kelli's arm but addressing all of us. "And don't say you're not singing."

Lee slid off the counter and took my hand, and I knew there was no way I could slip away to call Hal and Nia unnoticed. Besides, what did I even *want* to call them for? It wasn't like they were my friends exactly. My friends were here at the party with me. My I-will-be-bold-and-call-him-my-boyfriend was here at the party with me. Smiling with relief and confidence, I let Lee lead me out of the kitchen and toward the den, back into my real life.

CHAPTER TWENTY-TWO

I am running, running through the forest, but I am not me. Or I am myself, but somehow not me. I am covered in something soft and furry. I am in a fur coat. No, I am a fur coat. I am strong—my legs carry me effortlessly though I am running faster than I have ever run before. But I am not tired. I am whole. I am strong and brave. I am a bear, a gigantic black bear. I can reach up to the branches of trees and—

I hear screams. Terrified screams. Something is being terribly, terribly hurt. Only I can save it. My bear-self can save it. I'm coming, *I think.* Don't be afraid, I am coming. *But I can't find whatever is screaming. I am lost in the forest. The screams are getting so loud; I can't take it much longer.* Please, please. I am coming. *Suddenly there is a clearing. Lights. I see lights. A road. A highway. Blinding lights swirl around and the screams are the siren of an ambulance and there on the ground is the crushed, bloody body of a tiny, white bunny. My bear-heart is pounding. I must save it. But I can't get to it. The forest is too thick and it is holding me back.* No, please. No. I can help. I want to help. *But I can't think. The sirens are too loud; the forest is too strong.* Please. Please. I—

Brrring. Brrring. Brrring.

I bolted upright. It took me a long beat to realize I was at home, in my bed, and that my phone was ringing. How long had it been ringing? At first I couldn't get my legs to move the way I wanted them to, and I stumbled as I tried to cross the floor to where my phone lay on the edge of the rug.

"Hello?" My voice cracked. Through the wide-open shades that I hadn't bothered to close before I got into bed, I could see that it was morning.

"Callie?"

"This is Callie." I was pretty sure I didn't recognize the voice of the girl who was calling, but it was hard to concentrate through the dream that seemed to sit on my brain like a heavy, wet blanket.

"It's Nia."

"Oh, hi, Nia." Sitting upright was helping my focus. For example, I could tell that Nia wasn't exactly thrilled to be calling me. I'm not sure how I would have felt under normal circumstances, but given that her call seemed to be what had taken me out of my dream, I was feeling grateful to her.

"So, did I wake you? Big night last night?"

I squinted across the room at my alarm clock. Eight twenty.

Who called anyone at eight twenty on a Sunday morning?

"Um, not exactly," I wondered what Nia would have said if she could read my mind, if she could know how much I'd thought about her at Liz's party. "Not so big."

"Sorry if I woke you," she said, sounding anything but.

"No, it's fine." I tried to sound more alert than I felt. "What's up?"

"Well, I was talking to Hal, and he thought we should get together and make a plan. Maybe check out those addresses."

"Yeah, that makes sense." As I spoke, the dream panic became hazier, farther away. I leaned back against my chair. It was light. It was day. Everything was all right. "Do you want to go today? This morning?"

"I have church."

"Right," I said. "Church." Wasn't religion supposed to make you tolerant and loving? If so, maybe Nia ought to attend more than once a week.

"And we're going to watch the surveillance footage later. If you want to come over, I mean."

The funny thing was, I did. When I was with Lee and the I-Girls, Amanda and Hal and Nia felt like people in someone else's life. But now that Nia and I were on the phone and talking about watching the tape she'd stolen from Thornhill's office, I couldn't imagine spending my day with anyone but the two of them.

Was this a sign that I was becoming seriously schizophrenic?

"So why don't you come over around twelve? We could

watch and"—Nia lowered her voice—"I want to talk to you about the postcard."

"Did you figure it out? Is there a message in it?" My hand was suddenly shaking. What was Amanda trying to tell us?

"Well, all I know is—" Someone in the house yelled something and Nia called back, "Coming, Ma!" Then to me she said, "Look, I gotta go. I'll see you at twelve. I live at 12 Pinecrest Avenue, right off Maple Road. Do you know where that is?"

"Yeah, sure," I said. "I mean, I can find it." Maple Road was this fancy area not far from downtown. It wasn't fancy the way Heidi's neighborhood was fancy, with each house having a pool and the whole community being built around a golf course. Not "new development" fancy. Maple Road was older and elegant, with huge lawns shadowed by ancient, enormous oak trees and houses built around the same time as ours.

I had a feeling that their being built within a year of each other was going to be all my house and Nia's house had in common. I mean, what were the odds that one of her parents had filled their turn-of-the-century home with hundreds of dead branches or that the family was on the verge of being evicted?

"Okay," said Nia. "I'll see you at twelve."

"See you at twelve," I agreed. As I made my way down the hall and waited for the shower to get hot, I tried not to be jealous that there were people in the world who could actually have friends over.

I couldn't believe what Nia was wearing when she opened the door. Her navy blue dress had a tight bodice with rows of tiny buttons and a pleated skirt, and she'd paired it with pattern tights and ankle boots. The whole combo was completely fab, as was her hair, which was swept back into a low ponytail at the base of her neck. Suddenly *I* was the one dressed like a social outcast in my ancient hoodie and jeans. What had transformed Nia into a 1940s fashion maven?

What. Or should I say "who"?

"Hey," I said. I thought about complimenting her outfit but wasn't in the mood to be greeted with Nia's typical condescension. Instead, I complimented her on something else.

"What's that amazing smell?" Back in the day, both of my parents had been pretty good cooks, but nothing either of them had ever made smelled as delicious as whatever was cooking in Nia's house.

"It's nothing," said Nia, leading me from the front hallway into the modern, stainless steel kitchen where her mom was standing at the stove stirring a gigantic pan of something. "It's just my mom."

"Just my mom, just my mom," echoed Nia's mother. "How about, 'It's my *wonderful* mom'? 'My *miraculous* mom?'" She gave a final stir and turned to face me and Nia. "Hello," she said. "You must be Callie."

"Hi, Mrs. Rivera," I said.

A lot of parents you meet, if you call them by their last name, they'll say, *Please, call me Beth* or *Linda* or whatever. I had the feeling Mrs. Rivera wasn't the *Please call me* type, and I was right. She didn't give me her first name. But she gave my hand a really warm squeeze and kissed me on both cheeks with such enthusiasm that it made me believe her when she said, "I'm so pleased to meet you."

"Me too," I said. Maybe because I knew she and her husband were so strict about church and family night and stuff, I'd pictured Mrs. Rivera as older, more like a grandmother than a mom. I'd imagined her in a housecoat and slippers, speaking broken English and eyeing me, an outsider, with suspicion. Now that I was actually talking to her, I realized how narrow-minded I'd been. Nia's mom was really young-looking and pretty, with jet-black hair and creamy white skin. She *was* wearing an apron, but under it was a stylish black dress, and the heels on her feet were so high I couldn't believe she could walk a straight line in them.

The doorbell rang. "That must be Hal," said Nia.

"Aah, the famous Hal." And Mrs. Rivera winked at me in a way that made me pretty sure she thought I was in on some private joke.

"Hey, Ma, have you seen the keys to my car?" Nia's brother, Cisco, came into the kitchen minus his shirt. I didn't want to stare, but I couldn't help sneaking a peek at one of the hottest guys at Endeavor shirtless.

"Hey, Francisco," said Mrs. Rivera, echoing his tone, "how about you having some clothes on when we have guests?"

"Oh, hey, sorry, Ma. I didn't know anyone was here," said Cisco. He looked genuinely embarrassed, like he wasn't the kind of guy who regularly walked around shirtless in the hopes that random girls would admire his body. For a second we made eye contact. Then we both looked away, blushing.

Mrs. Rivera made a shooing motion with her hands. "Sorry yourself upstairs and fix it," she said.

"Right," said Cisco, turning around. "See you later, Callie."

OMG. Cisco Rivera knew my name. How cool was that?

As he left, he nearly crashed into a tall, handsome man who I figured must be Mr. Rivera, and who saw me about the same time he saw his son.

"How about a shirt there, mister?" said Mr. Rivera to Cisco. Then he smiled at me. "Hi, I'm Nia's dad."

"I'm going, I'm going," said Cisco. "Have you seen my car keys?"

"You didn't lock them in the car again, did you?" asked Mr. Rivera.

"Let's just say it's not impossible," said Cisco. "But if I did it's not my fault! If you guys would get me something other than a hundred-year-old Accord, I wouldn't always—"

"Francisco Rivera!" said Mr. Rivera, and his voice made me glad *I* wasn't the one who had locked my keys in the car. "Tell me a young man who was given a car for his birthday is not complaining about such a generous gift."

"No, Dad, I'm just saying—"

"You're just saying in the future you're going to be more careful with your car keys, right?"

"Right," said Cisco, looking down at the floor. "Of course."

"I think that thingy you got at the hardware store to open it is in the garage by Nia's bike," said Mrs. Rivera.

Mr. Rivera shook his head. "Now put some clothes on."

"I heard you, I heard you!" Sorry as I was to see Cisco disappear, I figured it was probably for the best. No way could I act natural around Nia's parents if her Greek god of a brother was wandering around without his shirt.

"I'm Callie," I said to Mr. Rivera, hoping he hadn't noticed me staring at his son.

"It's nice to meet you, Callie," he said. Mr. Rivera was such a cliché of tall, dark, and handsome I was almost embarrassed to look at him. For a second I wondered if he was a movie star or something, but then I remembered that he was the CEO of some big company. Still, he and his wife were definitely one of the most glamorous couples I'd ever seen outside of a magazine. Luckily when he came over and shook my hand, he didn't kiss me like Nia's mom had. I wasn't sure I would have been able to handle it.

He turned to his wife. "Sweetheart, did you move that printout that was on the dining room table?"

"The article?" She had her back to her husband and her spoon in the pan again. When she stirred it, whatever was cooking gave off an even richer smell.

"Mmm," said Mr. Rivera. "What is that?" He walked over to the stove and she held up the spoon she'd been using for him to taste.

"Oh, Ramona," he said. Then he kissed the tips of his fingers. "¡Delicioso!" He tried to take the spoon from her hand and dip it back into the pan, but she pushed him away. "Out! Out! Go read your article."

"Wait, now I want to eat lunch." He laughed and reached for the spoon. She laughed, too, and pushed him away. Then she said something in Spanish that I couldn't understand and he said something back. Seeing the two of them together joking around like that made me think of my parents, and along with the familiar lump rising in my throat, I felt a wave of hope wash over me, too.

It was a relief when Nia came back into the kitchen followed by Hal, and I felt even better when she introduced him to her parents, and I realized he'd never been to her house before. Somehow I'd imagined they'd been hanging out together for months, maybe with Amanda, maybe both knowing just *they* were friends with Amanda. It made me feel kind of good to see that he was a stranger here, too, like the three of us were on more equal footing than I'd thought.

"We're going to go into the den, okay?" said Nia. "To do that research."

"Are your friends staying for lunch?"

I was surprised that Nia didn't hesitate. "Yes," she said, and she gestured for us to follow her.

The den was way less modern than the kitchen—cozy, with walls of pale green and two huge, comfy sofas facing a gigantic flat-screen TV. My parents are really down on television, so we have a screen that's about the size of a credit card. This one would have been acceptable in a movie theater.

Nia pressed open the door of a wooden entertainment center and flipped a switch. The TV glowed blue and a console of lights on the DVD player came on.

"Okay, I think this is going to work," said Nia. "I hacked into the surveillance footage history, downloaded the footage from the front parking lot and just burned it onto a DVD, but it should play on this machine."

I was glad I hadn't been the one whose job it was to retrieve the surveillance footage—I can't even save stuff onto a flash drive. "You had to *hack* into the surveillance footage history and burn a DVD?" I couldn't believe I'd been irritated that Nia hadn't taken the time to look for Amanda's file in Thornhill's office. "How did you even know how to do that?"

"It wasn't that hard." Nia shrugged. "The whole security system is just cameras that dump what they record onto a hard drive. All I had to do was enter the date and time we wanted to see and download it. The computer seems to be on in Thornhill's office all the time—I didn't even have to enter a password or anything."

My mind was still reeling from the fact that Nia knew how to hack into a computer system. I mean, I can barely work my cell phone, and whenever I want to upload a song onto my iPod, I have to ask Traci to remind me how to do it.

I wanted to ask Nia more, but suddenly the screen was filled with the empty parking lot at Endeavor. The picture was slightly distorted, like we were looking through the bottom of a glass bowl. The timer on the lower right-hand corner of the screen read 5:00:00.

"I didn't know what time he'd arrived, so I just figured I'd start at five A.M.," explained Nia. She picked up a remote control and came over to sit on the couch with us.

At first, we just watched the screen, but as 5:00:00 became 5:03:08 and then 5:07:15, she suddenly hit the fast-forward button, exclaiming, "Oh, wait, this is so stupid." The screen grew slightly blurry but the basic picture didn't change.

"Wait!" said Hal. A car was pulling into the parking lot. The counter read 6:25:19.

Nia stopped fast-forwarding and the speed slowed to normal. As we watched, Vice Principal Thornhill parked his car and got out, locking the doors. It was weird to see him this way—I felt like we were spying (which, I suppose, we kind of were).

Nothing happened on screen, but no one suggested fast-forwarding. And then, suddenly, a figure in jeans and a hooded sweatshirt appeared at the rear of the car.

"It's Amanda!" I shouted.

"Is it?" Nia leaned forward. "I can't tell."

I realized I'd been assuming it was Amanda, but just as she leaned over the trunk of the car, the hood of the sweatshirt fell back, revealing her profile. It was far away. It was a low-resolution image. But it was also most definitely Amanda. She took what looked like a pouch out of the pocket of her hoodie, bent over the trunk of the car, and started drawing.

"I think—" said Hal.

"Oh my god, there's someone else!" Nia gasped.

She was right. A second figure, dressed identically, joined Amanda, but this time I had no idea who it was. We were all leaning so far off the couch toward the TV we could easily have tipped over onto the floor. Nia kept taking off her glasses and

putting them back on, and Hal and I were both squinting at the screen. Still, there was no way to know who that second person was.

It took less than half an hour for the car to be covered in the elaborate designs we would later spend an afternoon washing off, and then, just as the counter hit 7:04:11, the unknown person gestured to Amanda. Amanda stood where she was briefly, then took something out of her back pocket and slid it between the door frame and the window of the passenger-side door before taking off after her mysterious partner, on foot, out of the frame of the camera. That was it.

"I knew it!" Hal exclaimed.

"Shh!" whispered Nia, and we watched in silence as a car pulled into the parking lot a row away from Thornhill's. The driver got out, examined the vice principal's car, and walked toward the school. For the next half an hour, the same scene was repeated about fifty times, but neither of the hooded figures reappeared. Finally, when the clock said 7:43:08, Nia hit the stop button.

"So it *was* definitely Amanda," said Nia. "But what did she slip in his car?"

"She slipped him a note." In his excitement, Hal had stood up, and now he started pacing back and forth between the coffee table and the TV.

"I saw it!" I jumped up, too. "I mean, in the car. It was stuck in a pile of newspapers."

"You think she wrote to him?!" Nia's expression was a perfect blend of scorn and amazement. "You're trying to tell me that Amanda Valentino graffitied Vice Principal Thornhill's car and then left him a note? What'd it say, 'Dry Clean Only'?"

"I'm telling you, I saw a note from her in his car." Hal stopped in front of Nia and stared pointedly down at her.

I stared along with him. "I saw it, too, Nia." Suddenly it occurred to me that it was kind of strange how two people I knew had disappeared after writing notes to Vice Principal Thornhill. Should I tell them about my mom? But if I was keeping it a secret from my dad, was I really going to tell Hal and Nia? Besides, I still had not told them anything about her disappearance. I decided not to start now.

"I'd give anything to see that note," said Hal as he plopped back down on the couch, and I remembered his saying the same thing about the surveillance footage. If he suggested we break into Thornhill's car, was I going to have the courage to say yes?

Was I going to have the courage to say no?

"Okay, well, I guess this explains why he was so certain she did it. Anyway, speaking of notes . . ." Nia walked over to a stack of papers on the bookcase by the window and took something off the top of it. When she came back, I saw she was holding the now taped-together postcard from our lockers. "I didn't have any grand discovery while I was Scotch-taping this."

The three of us sat on the sofa, Hal and I on either side of Nia, staring at the postcard like it was just a matter of time before it revealed its message to us.

I broke the silence. "Um, do you think Meg is the person who painted the car with Amanda?" Hal shrugged.

"But why did Amanda keep part of the card?" Hal pointed to the section that was missing. "M—what? Do you think it said something else about this Meg person?"

"Think about it. Think about IT," I repeated, half to myself. "Well, whatever 'it' is, it's clearly important because she capitalized the whole word."

"Let's see the front of the card." Hal took the card from Nia and flipped it over. "This is important, too."

"The yellow brick road." Nia shrugged. "We know she loves *The Wizard of Oz*. Maybe she just had this card lying around."

Hal shook his head. "Nope, everything means something to her. What do you do with the yellow brick road?"

"Follow, follow, follow, follow the yellow brick road," I sang, in spite of myself.

"Thank you, Judy Garland," snickered Nia.

Sometimes it felt like the only proper response to Nia was to stick my tongue out at her, but I managed to restrain myself.

"So she's telling us to follow her," said Hal.

"Oh, *that's* clear as a bell." Nia rolled her eyes.

"But where? Where are we supposed to follow her?" It was hard not to be frustrated when every plausible answer just created another question.

"I know!" Nia snapped her fingers, her face the picture of mock enthusiasm. "OZ!"

"You're hilarious," I said.

"This is insane," Nia insisted. "Follow the yellow brick road? 'Think about it?' This is information?"

"Think about IT," corrected Hal, his voice, amused, rising on the last word. "And don't forget, we need to take a page from Meg's book and search." He experimented with changing his inflection. "Take a page from MEG's book. No, Meg isn't capitalized."

Suddenly it was like they'd switched roles—Hal was joking, Nia was intent and dead serious. "Wait a second—'Take a page from Meg's book.'" She slapped her forehead. "Oh my god! I know what the note means."

"What?" I couldn't believe she'd figured it out when I was still completely in the dark.

"Wait a second!" She dashed out of the room and almost before she was gone, she was back, carrying a book. "Meg. It. IT." She looked from me to Hal. "Don't you get it?"

I still had no idea what she was talking about, but Hal was smiling. "Nia, you're a genius."

She shot him a flirtatious grin. "I know."

"Okay, would one of you geniuses mind filling me in here?"

Nia held up the book so I could see the title. "*A Wrinkle in Time,*" I read off the cover. "By Madeleine L'Engle."

"Which is what the *M* is for," Nia explained. "Before the card got ripped, it must have said Madeleine L'Engle."

When neither she nor Hal elaborated, I said, "And . . ."

Nia flipped through to the end of the book. "Meg and her brother go to search for their missing father. He's being held hostage by this enormous brain on an alien planet."

"Um, you're saying Amanda's being held hostage by an

178

enormous brain on another planet and she wants us to search for her?" Was I the only one who found this interpretation of her note just a little ridiculous?

Nia looked up from the book. "You're kidding, right? I mean, tell me you can see that you're being just a tad literal."

"But it *is* a message that we're supposed to search for her," said Hal. "I'm sure of it. Follow the yellow brick road. Think about IT. Meg knew she had to search. All signs point to Amanda wanting us to look for her. I can't believe I didn't figure it out earlier." He shook his head at his own blindness. "Some guide I am."

I felt the blood freeze in my veins. "What? What did you just say?" I noticed Nia, too, was staring at Hal, though she hadn't said anything.

"Um . . ." Normally unflappable Hal looked uncomfortable, and as he spoke, he stared at the coffee table so he didn't have to make eye contact with either of us. "Okay, the thing is, Amanda kind of asked me to do this thing for her. To, like, guide her through—"

Nia interrupted him. "Through life at Endeavor. She asked you to be her guide?"

Now Hal turned to look at Nia. "How did you—oh my god," he said, suddenly realizing. "She asked you, too?"

I couldn't believe this was happening. "But she said she only had *one* guide," I said. "She told me that she picked one guide and it was—"

And at the same time, all three of us finished my sentence with the identical word. "Me."

For a second, the word seemed to shimmer in the air.

"Well," said Nia sarcastically. "Now that we all know just how special we *weren't* . . ."

I was reeling from the fact that Amanda hadn't chosen me out of the crowd so much as she'd chosen a crowd.

Had she ever seen anything special in me at all?

"So what do we do now? We need to *think*," continued Nia. "We need to think *like Amanda*."

I laughed and so did Hal. "Okay, that's only, like, impossible," I said.

"Is it?" Nia fingered the card.

"Callie's right," said Hal. "Her thinking was totally original. It seemed random, but it made a deep kind of sense. There were layers upon layers upon layers of shifting meaning. Like, did you ever see her diary?"

Nia and I both nodded, which didn't surprise me. Amanda's diary was as much a part of her as her costumes, her quotes, and her crazy hairstyles. She actually had several diaries. She always had one of them with her and she was always writing stuff down. It was because she'd shown me her diary that I'd shown her my Scribble Book.

"Well, how can anyone else follow that kind of . . . random logic?" said Hal.

"I don't know," said Nia, "but we'd better figure it out."

"Isn't this beautiful?"

We were sitting in the window seat of the library downtown. Amanda's hair was long and straight, parted in the middle, and she was wearing a headband with a peace symbol in the center of it around her forehead, and a long-fringed, beaded shirt. She held a tiny piece of yellow glass in her hand, and when I held mine out, she dropped the glass onto my palm. It felt smooth and warm.

"I love the color," I said.

"I wonder whence it came," Amanda mused.

"Don't you know? I mean, where did you find it?" I asked.

"No, I mean in the grand scheme of things. What was it before it was a piece of sea glass?"

I held up the small nugget of yellow and tried to imagine it as part of something bigger. "A necklace?"

"Mmmm, I like that. Maybe an ancient necklace passed down from one generation to another. Mother to daughter for hundreds of years."

"My mom has a necklace that she got from her mom," I said, picturing the small shamrock my mom always wore around her neck. "She got it for her sixteenth birthday." I didn't add what I was thinking, which was that I was supposed to get it from my mom for my sixteenth birthday.

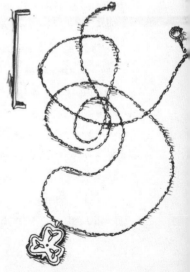

Assuming, of course, that I ever saw my mother again.

As if she could read my mind, Amanda reached over and touched my knee gently, comfortingly. "I bet you'll look great in that necklace."

Neither of us said anything for a minute, and then Amanda reached into her bag, rummaging past Oracle cards and keys, rejected lipsticks and eyeliners, pens and costume jewelry before laying her hand on what she wanted. "Look! I was able to mix this exact shade of yellow."

Amanda's diary that day was just a regular marble composition notebook decorated with strips of different ribbons and buttons glued on, but it was so full of stuff that it couldn't lie flat. There were drawings, photos torn from magazines, page after page covered in writing that flew by too fast for me to catch more than the occasional word: *rain*; *after we*; *can't ever*. When Amanda finally got to the page she wanted, she held the piece of glass against it. "See!"

I leaned over her book where several bold dashes of yellow paint in slightly different shades covered the page. Sure enough, one was the exact color of the glass.

"Nice," I agreed.

"Harder than it might look," she said. "But worth it. I like a challenge. And check this out." She pointed to the next page where a picture that seemed to be from a kid's book was pasted. Two animals, a bird and a cat, were sitting in a boat with their back to the viewer. "Isn't that cool?" said Amanda, running her finger over the drawing.

"Um, yeah. Sure." I waited a second for her to explain, then finally asked, "What is it?"

Amanda was still staring at the page. "It's the owl and the pussycat."

When she didn't continue, I prompted, "And . . . ?"

Reciting from memory, Amanda went on, "The owl and the pussycat went to sea / In a beautiful pea-green boat."

I'd heard of the owl and the pussycat, but I didn't see what a pea-green boat had to do with a piece of yellow sea glass. I shook my head. "Okay, you've totally lost me."

"Do you remember how it ends?" asked Amanda.

When I said I didn't, Amanda recited what I guess was the end of the poem. "And hand in hand on the edge of the sand, / They danced by the light of the moon, / The moon, / The moon, / They danced by the light of the moon."

She raised her head and looked up at me. "This yellow is the exact color I always pictured the sand in the moonlight. Don't you think?"

"Um, I never really thought about it," I said. "But either way, it's a beautiful color." I looked from the glass to the splashes of paint and back again.

"Really, everything's beautiful." Amanda was still staring at the illustration. "If you look at it the right way."

"I have to be honest—it would defy all the odds for me to think like Amanda," I said.

"I agree," chimed in Nia, her head resting on her hands.

Suddenly I remembered something from last night. "Hey, can I ask you guys a really weird question?"

"Now *that's* thinking like Amanda." Hal touched his nose with his index finger. "She was queen of the weird question."

"This one isn't *weird*," I said. "It's more . . . stupid. Or semi-stupid. Or just *Law and Order* stupid. Do you think Amanda could have been in the witness protection program?"

"Oh my god, who said *that*?" asked Nia.

I felt myself bristle. "Hey, I *said* it was a stupid question."

Before Nia could offer up another comment, Hal said, "Witness protection doesn't fit with my sense of who Amanda is." He paused for a second, then continued. "And even if it did, if you're in the witness protection program, aren't you supposed to be . . . I don't know, inconspicuous? Like, blending in with the scenery?"

"Good point," I said. "Amanda was the opposite of inconspicuous."

"It feels like we are going backward," sighed Hal.

"Well, at least now we know she wants us to look for her," I pointed out. "That's a pretty big step forward."

"Yeah, but why does she want us to look for her?" wondered Nia, counting off the question on her index finger.

"And where?" Hal held up two fingers.

"And what's with the missing section of the postcard?" Nia

waved three fingers in the air.

"And where did she get twenty-five hundred dollars?" I held four fingers up, spread wide.

"What?" said Nia.

I realized I'd only told Hal, not Nia, about the money.

"I have to tell you something else she did." But before I could tell her anything, her mom appeared at the door of the den.

"Lunch, everyone," said Mrs. Rivera.

"Mom, we're—" said Nia.

But Mrs. Rivera clearly did not brook the answer no. "Come," she insisted.

And as we walked past Nia's mom and filed into the dining room, I tried to reassure myself that Hal was wrong about our going backward. Now that we knew Amanda wanted us to look for her, we'd definitely taken a step in the right direction.

The question was, right direction or not, how many steps 'til we got to the end of this particular yellow brick road?

CHAPTER 23

I'd thought we'd get to talk more about Amanda after lunch, but Nia's mom made it clear that Sunday afternoon was designated homework time. Hal and I were welcome to eat as much as we liked and then clear out. So by the time we said good-bye, we hadn't made any plans for what I was starting to think of as Project Amanda.

On Monday, as I was leaving the cafeteria, I saw Hal and Nia ahead of me down the humanities corridor, and I started walking faster so I could catch up with them. I'd passed by them earlier, sitting at a table alone and talking, and I'd wanted more than anything to join them. Lately it seemed like the only time I felt okay, like I wasn't pretending to be someone or something I wasn't, was when I was with Hal and Nia and we were talking about Amanda. But Lee was sitting next to Kelli, who was already waving me over to our usual table—there was no way I could pretend I hadn't seen them, so I passed Hal and Nia and joined the group.

It was some consolation that Lee's face lit up when I sat down, like he was really glad to see me. When he leaned toward me and said, "Saturday night was awesome, wasn't it?" I tried to be glad I'd made the choice to sit where I had, even if my *"Totally!"* was basically a one-hundred-percent lie.

When lunch ended my friends were headed in the opposite direction, so it was easy to take off after Hal and Nia. As I made my way toward them, I passed Bea Rossiter, and my stomach turned over as it always did.

I walked faster, leaving her far behind. When I tapped Hal on the shoulder, his enthusiastic greeting erased all thoughts of Bea. "Hey! I was just going to text you." He lowered his voice. "After school we were going to meet up and check out those addresses of Amanda's. It seems like the best way to try and find her. Do you want to come?"

"I'm sure she has way better things to do, Hal," said Nia, refusing to make eye contact. And the way she said it made me wonder if she'd seen me walk by their table earlier or if she'd decided to turn on me for some other totally random reason. When I left her house yesterday, I thought things were better between us; apparently that was optimistic.

"No, actually, I don't," I objected.

"Great." Hal was either choosing to ignore the sparks flying between me and Nia or was truly clueless about them. "Let's start at the condos downtown. You know the ones I mean, right? The Riviera."

I'd passed the billboard advertising Orion's new luxury condos about ten thousand times. "'The Riviera: Not just a place to live, a lifestyle,'" I quoted.

Hal laughed and, in spite of herself, Nia smirked, too. "Do you want to meet there at four?" said Hal.

I had a history test tomorrow that was going to require at least three hours of cramming plus a million pages of English reading to catch up on. "Perfect," I said brightly. "I'll see you at four."

The Riviera was nothing like the other buildings in downtown Orion. The town's main street (which is actually *called* Main Street) is mostly wood and brick buildings, and none are more than four or five stories tall. There was a huge zoning fight when the town council originally heard the proposal for The Riviera, which was supposed to be a glass and steel tower of, I think, ten stories. My mom was really involved. She called the building "The New York-ization of Orion," but if you asked me, the idea that one building could turn Orion into New York City was completely hilarious, considering the two have about as much in common as I have with a megababe.

Ultimately, the developers had to satisfy themselves with a five-story glass tower that looks even weirder than a ten-story one would have. It's like someone started to build a sexy, cool Manhattan skyscraper and then, at the last second, changed his mind and just put a roof on a short glass building.

Basically, you feel as if you're looking at a teensy, shrunken supermodel.

Nia was already there when I pulled up on my bike, leaning against a parking meter where she'd locked her bike. My stomach sank. If only Hal were there first.

"Hey," I called, pulling up to her and hopping off my bike.

"Oh, hey." She didn't say anything else.

I stood the silence for about ten seconds, then started babbling. "My mom hated this building." Then, realizing what tense I'd used, I rushed to correct myself. "Hates. She hates it."

If Nia thought there were something weird about my difficulty differentiating between past and present, she didn't mention it.

"So does mine," she said.

Were we friends now? Were we getting along? It was so weird how sometimes she was totally cool with me and sometimes she wasn't. I decided not to push my luck by saying anything else, which Hal made easier by arriving a minute later. He was riding a bike that was way too small for him and that, I noticed as he leaped off it, was pink.

"Sorry I'm late," he said, breathing hard. "I had a flat and I couldn't find the pump."

"I take it this is your sister's bike?" asked Nia, eyebrow arched.

"I feel I'm man enough to ride a girl's bike." Hal stepped back to admire the white basket and tassels hanging off the handlebars.

"Absolutely." I nodded. "If anyone could carry off a girl's bike, it would be you."

"Thanks, Callie," said Hal. He patted me on the shoulder. "I appreciate your vote of confidence."

"Notice she said *if*," Nia reminded him.

"Point taken," said Hal, and he locked the bike to a pole.

The three of us turned and stood there, looking up at The Riviera. Finally, Nia broke the silence. "Okay, you said she was living with her mom in the model apartment until their apartment was ready for them to move in."

"Right," said Hal. "They ordered all kinds of special fixtures from Europe or something."

We started walking toward the building. Sliding glass doors opened silently, revealing a lobby even fancier than I'd imagined. A ginormous chandelier with about ten thousand pieces of tinkling glass hung from the ceiling, and the floor was a dark pink marble. My mom had wrinkled her nose and said how tacky it was, but I couldn't help thinking it would have been kind of cool to live there. They even had a gym and a rooftop pool!

There was a man sitting behind a wooden desk with a small gold plate that said CONCIERGE on it, and suddenly I wondered how we were even supposed to get up to see if Amanda did, in fact, live here.

Since I'd been in the lead, I got to the guy's desk first, and Hal and Nia came up behind me a second later. The man looked up at us like the only things he liked less than muddy shoes on his marble floors were teenagers.

"Um, hi," I offered.

"Hello," he said. Even though I could tell he wasn't happy about the three of us showing up in his pristine lobby, he gave us a toothy smile. I wondered if that was something they taught in concierge school.

"We're, ah—"

"We're here to see the model apartment." Nia used her official, legalistic tone, like she had in Thornhill's office.

"Are the three of you in the market for an apartment?" asked the man condescendingly.

"Our parents are," said Hal quickly. "We're meeting them here."

"I see," said the man. And to my tremendous relief, he pointed to his left. "In that case, take the elevator on your right. It's the fourth floor, Apartment D."

The elevator was as swanky as the lobby, with wood-paneled walls and its own minichandelier. When the doors opened at the fourth floor, I was a little disappointed in the hallway, which, with its stucco walls and industrial carpeting, felt more like a hotel corridor than a posh New York address. Apartment D was two doors down from the elevator, and the door was slightly ajar. Suddenly I realized that we might be seconds away from seeing where Amanda *actually* lived, and my heart started to beat really fast. Was the mystery about to be solved?

We'd barely pushed the door open when I had my answer.

No.

The model was like a cross between an office and a still life. The glass walls provided a really sick view—you could see all of Orion and past the town into the mountains south of the city. There was super modern furniture everywhere—a living room with a flat-screen TV almost as big as the one at Nia's house and a dining room table elaborately set for dinner. There were even some magazines casually scattered on the beige sofa, as if someone who lived there had only just finished reading them. But next to the front door was a desk with a fax machine and a pile of brochures with *The Riviera: Not Just a Place to Live, a Lifestyle* printed under a photograph of the building all lit up at night. Every surface was immaculate; there wasn't so much as a takeout coffee cup on the desk.

The idea that anyone could actually have lived here was nothing short of laughable.

"Hello?" called a voice, and a second later a very attractive blond woman in a tight black skirt and cream-colored sweater came around the corner of the apartment.

"Hi," said Hal.

"Well, hello there," said the woman, her voice perky. "Looking for an apartment?"

"Not exactly," admitted Hal. "We're kind of here under false pretenses."

"How intriguing," the woman practically purred. "A mystery."

"Yes. Exactly." Nia took over. "We're looking for our friend, and she suggested she lived here."

"In The Riviera? I'm sure I can help you find her," the woman gave us a big smile, as if she didn't mind our being too simple-minded to do something like, oh, say, use a building directory to locate our friend. I found myself growing annoyed with her.

"In this apartment," I broke in.

"I don't . . . I don't understand." The woman looked from me to Hal to Nia. You could tell she'd gone from finding us amusing to wishing her colleague downstairs ran a tighter ship. "She said she lived in Apartment 4-D? But no one lives here. This is the *model apartment*." She emphasized the last two words and spoke them slowly, as if perhaps our problems stemmed from our lack of command of the English language.

Despite being annoyed by how condescending she was, even I couldn't ignore how absurd we sounded. I turned to go. "Come on, guys," I said. "This is stupid."

"Wait a minute." Hal took a step toward the woman. "She was our age, really friendly. Wore kind of crazy outfits sometimes."

To my surprise, the woman's face lit up. "You must mean Chloe. I think she said her name was something like that. Blue wig? Oh, and a platinum blond one?"

Okay, this was too weird. There couldn't be *another* girl walking around Orion with different wigs. So then why . . . "But her name is—" I started to say, but Nia cut me off.

"So you *did* know Chloe," said Nia, emphasizing the name and giving me a look.

Her perkiness restored, the woman perched on the edge of

the desk, swinging her well-toned leg and smiling at us. "Oh, I wouldn't say that I *knew* her. But she and her mom were considering buying an apartment here."

"You met her *mom*?" asked Hal eagerly.

"Yes, of course I—" she started to say, but then she cut herself off and looked out into the distance for a second. "Wait, now that you mention it, both times she was here her mom called while we were talking. She couldn't make it. Chloe took a brochure for . . . I think it was the penthouse? She was such a dear. The second time she came she brought me a little cookie. Isn't that lovely?"

"Lovely," said Nia wryly. "And she never said anything about coming back with her mom or why her mom couldn't make it?"

"Sorry." The woman shook her head. "I can't remember. Work, maybe? No, I might just be making that up. Why? Is something wrong?"

"No, nothing," said Nia quickly.

"Oh, I'm sure you misunderstood what she'd said." The woman stood up and clapped her hands together once as if to applaud our having solved this mystery. "She must have told you she was *looking* at the model apartment because she and her mom *might* live here. But she meant here in the *building*, not here in this actual apartment." She giggled and gestured toward the immaculate surroundings. "You can see what I mean, of course."

"Of course, it *is* completely clear now," said Nia, her voice dripping sarcasm. "Well, thank you."

"Oh, it was my pleasure to meet you." The woman shook each of our hands. "Maybe if your friend and her mom move in, I'll see you again."

"Maybe," I said.

Nia and I waved good-bye, but Hal was clearly too thrown by what had happened to be polite. When we got to the elevator, he jabbed angrily at the down arrow, and he didn't speak a word as we crossed the lobby and left the building. When we got to our bikes, he just tossed his leg over his sister's pink frame and shouted, "Comfort Inn" before shooting off down the street.

The ride was flat enough that it wasn't hard, but Hal set a fast pace, so we were all panting by the time we arrived in the parking lot of the Comfort Inn. I'd driven by the place a million times, but I'd never been this close, and it was definitely way seedier than I'd pictured. Honestly, if Amanda *were* living here, I almost didn't want to know.

"I don't think I can go inside," said Nia, taking in the bruised-looking paint of the building and the scraggly weeds breaking through the asphalt. "It's too depressing."

To my relief, Hal suggested Nia and I just wait outside while he went in to talk to the manager. Five minutes later, when Hal came out shaking his head, I couldn't decide if I was relieved or disappointed that we'd hit yet another dead end.

"The guy thought I was joking," he said. "I get the feeling this isn't exactly a family inn."

"Did you describe her to him?" asked Nia.

"Oh no, I never thought of that." If he'd been frustrated by our experience at The Riviera, now he was totally pissed off. "I only said a girl named Amanda Valentino and refused to tell him anything else."

"I just thought maybe—"

"Forget it, Nia," said Hal. "She was totally full of it, okay? She was just messing with us. We're idiots for thinking *anything* she ever said or did meant *anything*!"

"Hal, don't—" I'd been about to tell him not to take his frustration out on Nia, but before I could finish my sentence, he cut me off.

"Forget it, guys. Forget I said anything. And forget Amanda, too. Because that's what I'm planning to do."

And a second later, he was pumping his legs and flying down Route 10 faster than I would have thought a little pink bike could go.

"Wow." Nia watched him disappear into the horizon.

"Wow," I repeated. "He's upset."

"I'll say."

"You don't think, I mean . . ." I faltered for a minute, thinking of all those drawings of Amanda in Hal's sketchbook. "You don't think there was anything going on between them . . ."

"No, I can't really picture her as anyone's girlfriend, but I kind of know . . ." Nia's voice trailed off, and I turned around to face her. She was rubbing her finger along the handlebar of her bicycle, studying it as if she'd never seen anything as fascinating as the grip she was holding.

"What?" I asked when she didn't finish her sentence.

"I kind of know how he feels." Once she'd uttered the sentence, Nia seemed able to relax and meet my eyes. "I don't want to go back to my life before Amanda."

We were talking about way more than a wardrobe make-over here. Nia's statement was so raw that I was afraid to respond. I was positive if I said, *I know just how you feel*, she'd say something like, *How could* you *possibly know how* I *feel?* I didn't want to blow it.

I settled on, "Yeah."

Nia put a foot on the pedal of her bike. "You don't know anyone named Chloe, do you?"

I went through my classes and shook my head. "I don't think there's anyone named Chloe in our whole grade."

"Well, I should get home," she said. "It's pretty late."

I thought of Nia's house, her parents laughing and flirting, her cute brother, the delicious dinner that awaited her.

"Yeah," I said. "I should get home, too." I wondered if the heat was even on at my house.

"Well, um, bye," said Nia. She stood up on her pedals and headed off.

"Bye." As I pedaled out after her, I thought about how neither one of us had said anything about looking for Amanda together anymore.

But really, what was there to say?

When I got home, the house was cold but there was the smell of heat, so I knew that at least the furnace was working today.

There was a light coming from under the basement door, but I did not have it in me to deal with my dad—I just headed upstairs to my room, overwhelmed by all the studying I still had to do and by how totally useless the afternoon had proven to be. Amanda had told so many lies that if not for Hal and Nia, I might start to wonder if I had made her up entirely—I might start to worry not that she had disappeared but that she had never existed in the first place.

At the top of the stairs, I saw that a little bit of light was coming from my room, and I felt a wave of irritation at myself for having forgotten to turn off my reading lamp. My dad did not need a gigantic electric bill. It was one thing for us to have no heat now that spring was coming. It was another for us to have no *light*.

But when I pushed open the door of my room, I saw that the light wasn't coming from my reading lamp; it was coming from a tiny, illuminated aluminum Christmas tree right in the middle of my bed. I gasped. Because there, under the tree, was a purple envelope with a coyote in the upper left-hand corner.

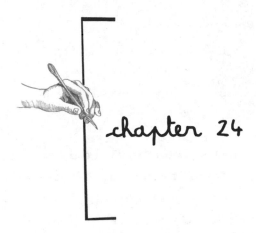

chapter 24

Hands shaking, I opened the envelope. Inside was a folded-up piece of paper, and when I spread it out, half a dozen pressed leaves and flower petals fell on the bed. On the paper was a collage of drawings of plants and pieces of plants intertwining and forming a border around a quote written in large, beautifully calligraphed letters, which read:

All that is necessary for evil to triumph is for good men to do nothing

Underneath, in Amanda's bold script, it said:

The quote is from Edmund Burke, but the drawings are all Beatrix Potter's. Like Beatrix (Beatrice, Bellatrix), we warriors fall, but so too do we rise.

And for the first time since Vice Principal Thornhill had called me into his office, I felt really, truly afraid. My heart pounded in my chest, and my brain could only form one thought over and over again.

How does she know? How does she know? How does she know?

It was raining so hard that night, December 21, the longest night of the year. Icy rain coated the apple tree branches in the yard until they knocked against the windows of my room as if they wanted to come in. I used to love cold, rainy December nights. My dad would light a fire in the living room and make mulled cider and we'd all sit downstairs and wait for the power to go off. (If you live in the country, you get used to power failures during winter storms.) When it did, we'd light candles and read or watch a DVD on my mom's laptop until it got late, then go upstairs with our candles like we were characters out of *Little House on the Prairie*.

But for the past two months my house had been creepy enough without the lights being off, and sitting in my room with a candle and trying to read only made me think of what life was going to be like if my dad really did get fired. (He still had a job back then, but he was missing work a lot and sometimes I heard him having shouting matches on the phone with his boss when I came home from school.) So when I heard someone pounding at the front door, my first thought was (and I know this is completely insane, but if you'd been there and felt the creepiness of the night, you might have thought this, too) that I'd heard a ghost.

But then the person must have realized the door was unlocked and less than a minute later, I heard someone calling, "Callie! Callie! Callie!" and crying, and I took my candle and ran downstairs thinking, *Mom*! Instead there was Heidi, soaking wet and sobbing, and she threw her arms around me and just kept saying my name.

I'd never seen Heidi hysterical like that. Even when she cut her finger really bad on an X-Acto blade in art class, she just calmly walked over to Mrs. Rose—holding her left hand, which was literally gushing blood—and asked if she could please go to the nurse. So the combination of her sobbing and seeming to barely realize where she was made me think someone must have died, and I just hugged her and rocked her back and forth like my mother did with me and said everything was going to be okay even though I really didn't know what "everything" was yet.

Finally she pulled away from me and walked toward the dark living room. Still crying, she said, "Oh my god, Callie, you have to help me." She had a tissue in her hand, and she ripped it as she walked.

"What happened?" I asked, my arms cold and wet from the icy water on Heidi's coat.

She perched on the edge of the couch, but instead of answering me, she looked around. I followed her eyes, and even though it wasn't like I hadn't seen my living room, it was different to see it through Heidi's appraising eyes.

There were no lights on because of the power failure, but my dad had left candles burning on the dining room table. Their light plus the light from the candle I'd brought down illuminated the room just enough for anyone to see that something was pretty messed up in my house.

Not long after my mom left, my dad had gotten drunk and fired the woman who'd cleaned our house and sometimes cooked for us when he and my mom had to work late. Since she'd been gone, no one had cleaned or even really aired out the place, so there was a sort of musty smell to it. More recently, my dad had stopped opening or even sorting most of the mail, so the coffee table next to the sofa was piled high with bills and magazines and letters about frequent flyer miles and free credit card offers and catalogs. I'd been trying to keep up with the dishes, but there were at least two wineglasses on the floor and another one on the dining room table along with an empty bottle of wine. And even though the worst of the foliage didn't make its way across our threshold until much later, there were already some oddly shaped tree branches leaning against the walls and a bunch of wooden planks stacked up by the (dark) fireplace.

"Heidi, what happened?" I asked again, though this time it was as much because I didn't want her looking around at my house as because I wanted to know.

Finally dry-eyed, Heidi spoke without turning to face me. "There was an accident."

I thought of Heidi's mom and dad, her little brother. Could one of them be . . . "Oh my god, Heidi, is everyone okay?"

"I don't know," she said, and now she did turn to me. "I didn't stop to check."

"Wait, what?" I'd assumed she meant a car accident, but of course Heidi didn't drive, so she wouldn't have been the one to stop and check anything. Could something have happened in their house? But in that case, why wouldn't Heidi have called instead of coming all the way over? "I'm sorry, Heidi, I'm so confused. What kind of accident?"

Her gaze level, Heidi said, "I took my dad's car out and I went for a drive."

"You took his car?" My voice was a shriek. I pictured Heidi behind the wheel of her dad's BMW two-seater.

"Don't be such a goody-goody, Callie! It's not like I've never driven before. And I'll have my permit next year anyway. I'm a good driver, okay?" Heidi's eyes flashed with anger and I shrank back against the couch.

"Sure," I said quickly. "I'm sure you are."

"It wasn't my fault. It was really dark and the road must have been icy from the storm and the car kind of . . . skidded and I tried to pull the wheel the other way and then . . . that's when it happened."

Heidi started to sob again, and now that she was crying and not giving me that scary, angry look, I felt bad for her. How many times had my mom or dad barely managed to swerve to avoid a dog or even a deer? How many dead animals had we passed lying in the road? I'd always wondered what that awful moment would feel like, that instant when you heard the bump and felt the thump of a tiny, furry creature under the tires of your car. My

eyes prickled. Poor Heidi.

"Oh, Heidi, I'm so sorry," I said, guilty that I'd been so obviously shocked by her taking the car. Heidi was my friend. She needed my understanding, not my judgment. I slid closer to her and put my arm around her, resting my chin on her shoulder. "I'm really, really sorry. You must have totally freaked."

Heidi was still crying, crying hard enough that I wasn't even sure she'd heard what I said. I was about to repeat myself when I realized that between sobs she was trying to get words out.

"I . . . I . . . I . . . ," Heidi hiccupped.

"You what?" I squeezed her shoulder, then patted her back.

"I think she saw the car," said Heidi, and saying it made her practically wail with horror. "I think she recognized the car."

"But how could—" And suddenly, the end of my sentence died in my mouth. Because fuzzy animals don't recognize the cars that hit them.

"Heidi, what did you hit?" My voice was calm and slow. I drew my arm back to my side, shivering slightly from the cold water seeping through my sweater.

Maybe because she heard the change in my voice, Heidi sat up straighter. "I hit Beatrice Rossiter. She was riding her bike, probably home from one of those geek clubs she belongs to, and I hit her and I think she might have seen."

This wasn't happening. Heidi wasn't really telling me that she'd hit somebody and kept driving. People didn't really do things like that.

Did they?

"Heidi, we have to call someone. We have to call nine-one-

one and you'll tell them where to find her. We don't even have to give our names." I couldn't believe how calm and practical I was being.

Heidi stood up. "Are you crazy? Are you completely insane? You think they won't trace a call like that? I could go to jail, Callie. Is that what you want? You want me to spend my life in jail just because—"

The ice that had formed around me cracked, and I was screaming right back at her. "They're going to find out anyway, Heidi. They don't need phone calls to trace stuff like that. They can check . . . dents and, and . . . paint and marks."

Now it was Heidi who seemed icy. "The car's fine. I checked. It's back in the garage. You can't tell at all. Nobody is going to trace anything."

"But what if Bea's . . ." I couldn't finish the sentence, but Heidi could.

"She's not, okay?"

"How do you—"

"She's just not. So drop it. I'm sure she's fine. She probably just got a bump on her head and rode home and put an ice pack on it or something. And I'm not going to not get my permit or my license or worse because of some stupid, pointless accident!"

Heidi snarled the last part of the sentence, and the look on her face scared me. I'd stood up when she did, and now I took a step back.

"Why did you come here?"

"I need you to cover for me, Callie. If anyone asks, I need you to say I was here all afternoon and all night."

I thought about how much closer Kelli and Traci lived to Heidi, how easily she could have gone to one of their houses and asked them to cover for her. She'd walked or biked over three miles to get from her house to mine. Why?

I couldn't not ask. "Why me, Heidi?"

And even in the dim light, even though I could just barely make out her face, I knew. She'd figured it out. She'd figured out something weird was going on with my family, that my mom wasn't always just "too busy" to pick me up from her house, that there was a reason we never came over to my house anymore, a reason the lawn looked the way it did the few times she and her mom came to pick me up or drop me off. She'd never once mentioned anything to me, never once asked me if something was up, if I was okay. But she'd filed away the information and now that she needed it, she was using it. Because how could she have burst into Kelli's or Traci's house hysterical and dripping wet and gone unnoticed by their parents?

Neither of us said anything. Heidi glanced around the room one last time before looking back at me. "We're best friends, Callie," she said. "That's what best friends do. They help each other." She walked across the room, put her arms around me, and squeezed. "Thanks, Callie," she said. "You're the greatest."

And then she was gone.

Without realizing what I was doing, I'd shredded the collage, and now I dropped it in the trash can as if Beatrix Potter's drawings were burning my fingers.

How could Amanda possibly have figured out that Heidi was the one whose car hit Beatrice Rossiter? Nobody knew but me and Heidi, and sometimes the way Heidi talked about Bea made me wonder if even *she* remembered what she'd done.

I looked back at the quote. *All it takes for evil to triumph* . . . What Heidi had done was evil. It was. But what I had done was evil, too. If Amanda was looking for a good person in this scenario, she'd have to look beyond me—I was in way too deep to be good.

And why was Amanda talking about Bellatrix? The only Bellatrix I knew had nothing to do with Beatrice Rossiter *or* Beatrix Potter. It was the third brightest star in the constellation Orion, and its name meant "female warrior"—

Suddenly I thought of something. Heart pounding, I got up and raced over to my desk, digging frantically through the messy top drawer for my planisphere. Could it be? Was it possible?

I spun the outer wheel until I got today's date. But there was nothing about Orion or Bellatrix.

"What are you trying to tell me?" I shouted to the empty room.

This was so frustrating. I went back to my bed, spinning the planisphere forward and back, forward and back, looking at the stars as they rose and fell. All the stars that weren't Bellatrix appearing and disappearing, rising and falling.

The third time I pushed the circle forward, I went a bit too far, landing on tomorrow night, not tonight. Tomorrow night, when, between eleven and twelve o'clock, Bellatrix was going to vanish below the western horizon.

And I knew exactly where I was going to find Amanda.

CHAPTER TWENTY-FIVE

In November we had to memorize Juliet's speech in English class. "Gallop apace, you fiery-footed steeds, toward Phoebus's lodging." It's all about how she just wants night to come because she can't wait to be with Romeo. Lee got his hands on my book and he wrote, *LF and CL = R and J*, in the margin and drew a heart around it. That day, waiting impatiently for Friday to come so I could go to the movies with Lee, I'd thought I understood how Juliet felt.

But clearly I hadn't understood anything.

Every second of Tuesday seemed to last an hour. Every hour seemed to last a month. Normally I never have enough time to finish a bio quiz, but today, I swear, I had time to finish it, check it over, and check it over again.

Twelve more hours. Nine more hours. When I saw Nia and Hal in the hallway on the way to gym, I was actually glad that we didn't talk to one another in school, and it wasn't because I was afraid that being seen talking to them would equal social suicide. Trying to pretend I was worried about where Amanda was when I *knew* where she was (or where she was going to be in just a few short hours) felt almost as impossible as telling them my plans for later that night. Because part of what made tonight so exciting was that *I* was going to see Amanda. *I*, not we. She'd left *me* a message, and even if it was petty and immature, I couldn't help being proud that I was the one she'd singled out. Okay, she'd been friends with Nia and Hal, too; I wasn't trying to deny that. We were all her so-called guides. Maybe she'd cut school to spend the day with Hal in Baltimore or prowl cool shops with Nia for great vintage clothes. But when push came to shove, she and I *did* have something special, something she didn't have with anyone else.

All day the sun had been playing hide-and-seek with the clouds, but by dusk the sky was thick with gray, and I was sure I was going to be spending my night sitting on Crab Apple Hill in the pouring rain. I decided I wasn't even going to bother bringing my telescope if that happened—let's face it, I wasn't exactly planning on stargazing anyway. Right around seven it started to drizzle, then pour, and I made a mental note to get my mom's big yellow slicker out of the front hallway. But within half an hour the sky had cleared, and when I poked my head out the back door, the stars were twinkling in the pristine sky over our house, like they had a message for me.

Which, in a way, they did.

I'd heard my dad moving around in his workshop when I got home, but I didn't go down. Before our fight the previous week at Amanda's "not" house, we'd seemed to run into each other around our place a whole lot more than we did now, but whether he'd decided he wanted to avoid me or I'd decided I wanted to avoid him, I couldn't say. The result was the same either way, though: We were staying out of each other's way. The only shocking thing about this night as opposed to all the other nights of our living on opposite sides of a private demilitarized zone was that when I went downstairs to make myself a peanut-butter-and-jelly sandwich at around nine, there was some food on the stove. At first I thought it was just a dirty pot, but I hadn't seen it when I made myself breakfast in the morning, so if it was dirty, it was recently dirty. It was also half-full of macaroni and cheese. I tried to remember the last time we'd had macaroni and cheese in the house—tried to remember the last time we'd had *anything* that required perishable ingredients like milk and eggs, but I couldn't.

For a while after my mom left, friends and neighbors dropped in with care packages—casseroles, bags of groceries, cakes, and cookies. It was kind of like they'd gotten together and decided the easiest thing to do was to act as if my mom had died rather than taken off. But then this one neighbor, Cara Marks, asked my dad one too many questions when she came to drop off a bean salad, and the next thing I knew, he was throwing Cara and her Pyrex dish out the front door.

Needless to say, the offerings dropped off pretty fast after that.

Apparently they'd started up again, but I didn't really feel like analyzing why. Instead, I scarfed down the food and headed back upstairs. I still had hours before I had to meet Amanda, but I wasn't taking any chances. She'd only read a planisphere once—that night in January we went stargazing. For all I knew she'd misread the time or not realized just how quickly a star disappears over the horizon. I checked my backpack. Flashlight. Planisphere. Phone. Key. As long as I had Amanda in person, I was going to be asking her about everything.

Everything.

I had put the kettle on to boil, and by the time I was downstairs again, it was whistling. I'd thrown an extra sweater into the backpack along with my mom's slicker, just in case it decided to start raining again. I filled the thermos with water, added hot cocoa mix, and spun the top on, then threw the thermos into the bag and hitched the bag over my shoulder. My body was practically humming with anticipation and excitement. As I picked up my mom's telescope, I wondered if I should leave my dad a note. I mean, just because he hadn't seemed to care one iota about my whereabouts for the past several months, it wasn't *impossible* that he would come into my room to check on me.

Was it?

Then again, there was no way I was going to tell him where I was (*Dear Dad, Gone to sit alone on a hill at midnight. Don't wait up. Love, Callie*), and I really didn't like the idea of lying to him. So what, exactly, was I supposed to put in a note?

The telescope was heavy, and it was digging into my shoulder. This internal debate was taking way, way too long. I decided the last thing I needed was the area around my house swarming with the cops my dad called in a panic because the one time in months he chose to take a paternal interest in his daughter, he discovered her missing. The note I dashed off and left on the kitchen table seemed truthful (if vague) enough.

Dad, I'm with a friend. I'll be home late.

C.

After I'd written it, I stood there rereading my words for a minute, wondering if anyone seeing the note would think it was weird, or if they'd be able to tell from that simple sentence just how far apart my dad and I had grown over the last few months. For a second I considered adding something (Love, C, maybe?), but then I decided to bag it. My dad and I had so many problems—what was one word (or one note) going to matter?

The rain had left everything smelling rich and earthy; I felt I could sense all the seeds and flowers underground getting ready to push themselves up through the damp soil. My head felt full of an unfamiliar buzz, and even the weight of the telescope and my backpack couldn't slow my step. It was almost nine o'clock.

Two hours left.

At the top of
Crab Apple Hill, I
set up the telescope.
It took me a lot longer
to get Bellatrix in my
sights than it should have—I
was out of practice. But when I
found her, her white, almost bluish light shimmering in the
clear night sky, I felt a surge of joy unlike anything I'd felt
in months. It was as if Bellatrix spoke to me, like her bright,
bright light were a promise. *She's coming. She's coming.*

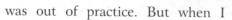

Twice over the next hour, I was sure I smelled Amanda's
perfume on the air. Once I even stood up and called out,
"Amanda!" but there was no answer. By ten fifteen, I was starting to get a little creeped out. I mean, I'm not one to be afraid
of the dark, far from it, but it *was* late at night, and I *was* out in
the middle of nowhere all by myself. If this weren't an invitation to foul play, what was?

And then, suddenly, I heard someone coming up the hill.
Someone moving fast, and for a second I felt my heart hammering in my throat.

I spun around toward where the noise was coming from.
"Amanda!" I yelled.

A head appeared over the crest of the hill. But it wasn't
Amanda's.

It was Hal's.

"Callie?" he said. He was wearing a heavy sweater, like he,
too, had planned to be out in the cold night air for a while.

"Hal?" Disappointment made my voice harsh. "What are you doing here?"

"I . . ." He looked around almost frantically. "I'm supposed to meet—"

But before he could finish his sentence, we both heard someone picking a careful way up the other side of the hill. Flooded with relief, I again turned to face the sound. Maybe this wasn't the private reunion I'd hoped for, but at least she was coming.

"Amanda?" called a voice.

A voice that clearly was not Amanda's.

A second later, Hal, Nia, and I stood on the top of Crab Apple Hill staring at one another.

"She told me to . . ." Nia was panting from her climb.

"She called you?" asked Hal.

Nia shook her head, gulping air. Hal turned to me.

"What did she tell you?" he asked. He sounded, if possible, even more disappointed than I was, and for a second I wondered again if they had been more than friends.

"She told me to meet her here," I said. I was so frustrated I could have cried. "When Bellatrix dropped down over the horizon."

"What is this *Bellatrix*?" asked Nia, her voice restored. "Her note was all about the enduring mystery of Bellatrix. I don't even know what that is." Nia was angry, too, and she slashed at a nearby bush with her arm.

"She—" My voice faltered, and I had to clear my throat before I could finish. "She told you if you came here you'd solve the mystery of Bellatrix?"

"What the hell is going on?" asked Hal. When no one said anything, he repeated himself. "What the *hell* is going on? Where the hell *is* she?"

As Hal, Nia, and I stared at one another, I realized in a flash that Amanda wasn't coming. The knowledge was as clear and sharp as Bellatrix had been; it shimmered in the center of my brain with the same bluish white intensity.

Amanda hadn't brought us here so we could see her. She'd brought us here so Nia and Hal could see *me*.

I dropped to the soggy ground. "She isn't coming," I said.

"What?" hissed Nia.

"She isn't coming," I said again.

"Did you leave me this note?" asked Nia, and she took a step toward me and waved a piece of paper in my face.

"Oh, chill out, Nia," said Hal. "You know Amanda left you that note."

"But what *for*?" asked Nia, and for a second I thought she was going to cry. "What's the point of leaving us notes and telling us about some stupid mystery we're supposed to solve and then not even showing up?"

"It's not Amanda's mystery," I said, my voice dull and tired-sounding.

"What?" said Nia. "What are you talking about?"

"It's not Amanda's mystery," I repeated. "It's mine. It's my mystery and Amanda found out about it, and now she wants me to do something about it, and she wants you to be my witnesses." As crazy as the words sounded, I knew as soon as I'd

215

spoken them that they were true.

"So, what, you're going to solve the mystery of Bellatrix?" Nia's tone was venomous.

I looked up at her, and this time my voice was stronger than it had been a minute ago. "No," I said. "Not Bellatrix. Beatrice. I'm going to solve the mystery of Bea Rossiter."

When I'd finished telling the story, neither Hal nor Nia said anything for a long, long minute. Then Hal let out a long whistle. "Jeez."

"How did Amanda find out?" asked Nia.

"I have no idea." I raised my head from my hands briefly.

"You know you have to go to the police, don't you?" said Nia. "I mean, we're talking about a *serious* crime here. And you're . . . you're practically an accomplice. God, Callie, what were you *thinking*?"

"Thanks for your support." I lowered my head again.

Nia had been sharp and jabbing as usual, but Hal's voice was quiet and gentle. "What do you want to do now?"

"I don't know what I'm supposed to do," I said. "I don't know if I'm supposed to go to the police. Maybe Amanda had something else in mind."

"This is *so* screwed up!" said Nia.

"Chill out, Nia," said Hal. The whole time I'd been talking, he'd been looking away from me, out at the night sky, like he was listening but also waiting for Amanda to show up. Now he turned around and came over and sat down next to me. "I'm really sorry this happened. I'm sorry this happened to you."

Nia snorted. "It didn't exactly happen to her. It happened to Bea."

"Nia, just shut up, okay?" said Hal. And to my surprise, Nia did.

Hal was sitting so close to me that our knees were touching. I hadn't even realized I was crying until he reached out and touched my cheek with his hand, spreading a slight dampness as he did so. "Look," he said quietly, "you're going to do the right thing."

Now it was my turn to snort. "Yeah. Too bad I have no idea what that is."

"You'll figure it out," said Hal. Then, his voice sharper, he said, "Won't she, Nia?"

"Why are you including me in this condolence-fest?" asked Nia. "I don't know." When Hal and I continued to sit there, she added, "Yeah, you'll figure something out, Callie." There was another silence and then Nia said, more quietly, "That must have been rough when she showed up at your house. That must have really been rough."

I nodded. "It was," I said. "It really was." And a second later, to my surprise, I felt Nia's hand squeezing my shoulder.

The three of us stayed there, not saying anything, for a while. Then Hal finally broke the silence. "I'm glad you told us."

"Well, she made me tell you," I said.

Nia's voice was disembodied in the darkness. "I know what you mean. She wanted you to feel like you could trust us, so she kind of *made* you trust us."

"Not that we made it easy for you," said Hal, and even in the dark I could feel his smile.

"Well, maybe some of us made it easier than others," said Nia, and I could hear the smile in her voice, too.

"Maybe," I agreed, and we stayed there, still silent, but in a good way.

"Let's go down." Hal stood up and brushed off his jeans. "She's not coming tonight." From his voice, I could tell he'd only just accepted the truth—she really wasn't coming.

"Yeah, this is starting to creep me out," said Nia. To my surprise, she reached down to pull me up.

I took her hand and followed them for a couple of steps, then stopped. "You know what, guys, I think I need a minute."

"Are you okay?" asked Hal.

I nodded. "I just . . . I just have to be here by myself for a sec."

Nia took a step toward me and peered into my face. "You're not going to do anything stupid, are you?"

"What, like jump off Crab Apple Hill?"

She shrugged. "Maybe."

I shook my head. "No. I need to think for a minute, but it's nothing like that."

"Okay." She dropped my hand as abruptly as she'd taken it. Well, she was trying.

"Okay," said Hal. "But we're here if you need us, you know? Call anytime."

"Thanks," I said. "I know."

A minute later they disappeared over the edge of the hill.

* * *

I've never stayed up all night," I admitted. "Much less out."

"Really? I do it all the time."

The sun was just coming up over the horizon, and in the pale light of dawn, I could see the outline of Amanda's face and the landscape beyond Crab Apple Hill. There were some crumbs on her lips from the chips we'd been eating.

"Don't your parents tell you to go to bed?" I asked. I pulled the sleeping bag closer around my shoulders, shivering. Even though it was oddly balmy for January, the air was still cold enough for me to see my breath.

"They're night owls, too," said Amanda. "Once in a while we run into each other at, like, four A.M. because none of us has been able to fall asleep."

Sometimes Amanda's life sounded so strange. It was like she'd been raised on another planet, not in another city. I tried to picture the Valentinos running into one another in the hallway of their house like all-night bumper cars. But then I remembered that Amanda wasn't living with her parents now. When had these late nights happened? I was about to ask when Amanda pointed at the telescope. "It's a good thing I came along and spotted this or you would never have taken it out of the closet. I still can't believe you stopped using it for so long."

I yawned. "Yeah, well . . ." My voice trailed off as the yawn intensified; then I continued. "It wasn't like I was so eager to relive all the good times I had with my mom now that she's gone, you know?"

Amanda had been lying down but now she shot up so fast

the sleeping bag slipped off her top half; she must have been freezing in her thin shirt and tank top. "No! You can't think that way." Her voice was intense. "It's up to you to keep her alive. To keep her around. That way, when she comes back, it will be like she never left."

I laughed. "Yeah, right." I didn't know which was more absurd—the idea that I could ever feel like my mom hadn't left or the idea that she'd be back.

Amanda's face was serious as she leaned toward me. "I mean it, Callie. All that stuff you taught me tonight—finding stars and the planisphere and how to do longitude and everything. That's your mom. That's your mom in you. You're the little bear, she's the big bear. You're one." She put her hands together, one embracing the fist of the other. "She's only gone if you let her go."

Something about how tightly Amanda's hands were gripping each other made me feel like she was trying to say more than she was able, but before I could ask her about it, she saw something down below.

"Look!"

I followed the line of her finger, pointing out to the west.

Down below us, Hal Bennett was running by. His legs flew out behind him and his arms pumped, but somehow, maybe because he was so far away that we couldn't hear him or maybe just because he was such a talented runner, he seemed not to be exerting himself at all. It was like he was effortlessly sailing right above the earth.

"What?" asked Amanda.

I hadn't realized I'd been smiling until Amanda poked me in the side. "What, what?" I asked, unable to prevent my smile from growing.

"What's with the smile?"

Since I was now practically grinning from ear to ear, my "What smile?" sounded even more ridiculous.

"Nothing!" I said. "I'm just . . ." I shrugged.

"You're intrigued," said Amanda.

I loved how she said that. Not, *You're crushed out*, which is what Heidi or Traci or Kelli would have said. Not, *You like him.*

You're intrigued.

I nodded, still smiling. "I'm intrigued," I admitted.

"Why?" asked Amanda. "What intrigues you about him?"

"I don't know," I said. "He's just . . ." I closed my eyes and again saw Hal running by. "He's just . . . he's so his own person, you know? You didn't meet him before, when we were in middle school, but he was this enormous . . . dork, really. And then he comes back this year and he's a total hottie and there's all this buzz about him and it's like he doesn't care. It's like he doesn't even know!" I opened my eyes, finally, and looked at the space where Hal had been. "I'd like to be like that."

"A total hottie everyone's buzzing about?" asked Amanda, laughing. But the way she said it I knew that she knew that wasn't what I meant.

"My own person," I said quietly. "I'd like to be my own person."

There was a pause and then Amanda reached over and

squeezed my fingers. "You know what I think, Callie? I think your time has come to shine, and all your dreams are on their way."

"That's nice," I said. "Did you just make that up?"

She shook her head, reached into the bag, and took out two chips, handing one to me and popping the other one in her mouth. "Paul Simon. Here, have some breakfast." She bit off a corner of her chip. "It's the most important meal of the day."

I sat there chewing. As I reached for a second chip, I said, "So, do you know him?"

But there was no answer. I looked over at Amanda and saw that her sleeping bag was pulled halfway over her face, and she was fast asleep.

Somehow I'd missed Bellatrix dropping over the horizon. But instead of feeling sad, I knew it didn't matter. I could practically hear Amanda's voice in my ear. *Better to see it rise.*

I stood up and brushed off my jeans, then grabbed the telescope and folded it up far more expertly than I'd taken it apart a few hours ago. The sharp clicking of the legs snapping into place felt like the physical manifestation of the sharp decisions I was making in my mind, and by the time I'd finished dismantling it and thrown the strap over my shoulder, I knew what I had to do and how I was going to do it.

CHAPTER 26

Heidi's house is one of about fifty identical McMansions in The Acres, a development that's been there as long as I can remember. I'm pretty sure the only thing my mom hated more than racism, homophobia, light pollution, and The Riviera was The Acres. Whenever I hung out at Heidi's, I tried to have my dad pick me up or one of the Braggs drop me off because I swear, something happened to my mom the minute she had to drive in there. She became practically possessed, and for at least half the ride home, I had to hear about how horrible ten-thousand-square-foot houses are for the environment, and how anyone who would want to live in such a soulless community must also be soulless, and how if one of the people who lived in one of the houses accidentally walked into the wrong one some night (which wouldn't have surprised her, since they all looked exactly the same), he probably wouldn't even notice since the families inside the houses were as identical and one-dimensional as the buildings themselves.

As I rode my bike along the perfectly paved roads of The Acres, I got an inkling of what my mother had felt, as if the sprinklers dousing the emerald green lawns were spraying out not water but blood.

Heidi had paid a price for living her parents' dream in somewhere as protected and perfect as The Acres, and that price was nothing less than her very soul.

I rode past Heidi's block and turned onto the next street, Magnolia Way, where I stopped in front of a random house that, sure enough, looked very much like Heidi's. I checked my watch—right on time; Heidi's dad should be leaving the house with Heidi and Evan in the next minute or two, while her mom wouldn't leave for the studio for at least another hour. Just to be on the safe side, I rode around for about ten minutes, steering clear of Laurel Lane until I was sure everyone would be gone besides her mom. Then I circled back to Heidi's, coasting into her driveway and leaning my bike against the garage door.

The doorbell at Heidi's chimes out the first few bars of a song called Pachelbel's Canon, which I'd always thought was really pretty but that made my mom roll her eyes. I listened to the chimes echo in the vast interior for what felt like a long time, and then I started to get nervous. My plan had seemed so perfect, but what if I'd gotten my timing wrong? I hadn't been spending all that much time at Heidi's lately—could her mom's schedule have changed?

This was completely insane. What was I *doing* here? Last night it had all seemed so obvious—Mr. Bragg was the chief of police, and a conversation with him would need to be all about witnesses and proof. My word against Heidi's wasn't going to cut it with Chief Bragg, and the slight possibility that he'd believe me only made Nia's words echo in my head. *You're practically an accomplice.*

That was the main reason I'd decided to tell Brittney Bragg, but it wasn't the only one. Brittney *knew* her daughter, and the more I'd thought about it, the more I'd been convinced that anyone who knew Heidi, really *knew* her, would know the story I was telling was true. It might take her a little while, but if I could get her alone and explain everything to her carefully, Brittney was sure to believe my story. Thus this early morning ambush.

Only now my perfect plan wasn't feeling so perfect. Why wouldn't the wife of the police chief realize I was an accomplice just as surely as her husband would? There had to be a better way. An anonymous note? Better yet, a note from *Amanda*! I mean, this *had* been kind of her idea.

If the door hadn't opened right at that moment, I'm not sure what I would have done, but it did, and I found myself face-to-face with Brittney Bragg, Heidi's mom.

She wore an irritated expression as she opened the door, but when she saw it was me, her face softened, which was kind of ironic given what I was about to say.

"Callie. What a nice surprise. Are you looking for Heidi? You *just* missed her!" Brittney Bragg always delivered even the most mundane information like it was a piece of breaking news; I could practically hear the cameras whirring as she told me Heidi had left for school—the next words out of her mouth could have been, *Back to you, Chuck.*

"Actually, I was hoping to talk to you," I said.

Her hand fluttered to her throat, as if she were so flattered or surprised she didn't quite know what to say. She was probably just totally confused, but she would never have shown it. Brittney is even more unflappable than Heidi.

"In that case, come in," she said. As I stepped inside, she shut the door behind me, then led the way into the kitchen.

I'd tried to dress in a way that seemed serious, almost professional, but my black wool skirt and off-white cardigan just seemed fussy compared with Brittney's no-frills yoga pants and tank top. It didn't help that even though she was way older than me, she has a perfect body, perfect skin, and perfect hair. Whenever she saw Heidi's mom, my mom inevitably made at least one snide comment afterward about how much they could do with silicone; I'd always thought she was just being critical, but walking behind Brittney Bragg and seeing how flawless and sculpted every part of her body was, I couldn't help wondering if my mom was right. Could all the yoga in the world possibly make a person look that much like a Barbie?

There were a few dishes on the counter and a frying pan on the stove, so I knew the housekeeper hadn't arrived yet.

"Well, Callie, what can I do for you?" asked Brittney,

sitting down at the table and gesturing for me to do the same. She glanced briefly at the clock I knew was over the stove, and I heard the tiniest hint of impatience in her voice.

I'd rehearsed what I was going to say since deciding to say it, and now I launched into my presentation. "I have to tell you something, and it may be hard for you to believe." I kept my hands on the table as I spoke because I remembered how Heidi's dad had once told us that, when you're interrogating someone, the first thing you want to watch is his hands. According to Chief Bragg, if he's hiding his hands, he's hiding something else, too.

"You don't cover the news for ten years without learning that truth is often stranger than fiction." Then she leaned toward me, all the impatience gone from her voice. "Now, tell me. Does this have something to do with your mom?"

As I'd run through what I planned to say, I'd thought I'd anticipated everything that could happen this morning, but Heidi's mom's question completely threw me off my game. "What? No!" I spluttered.

Still leaning forward, she put her hand on my knee. "Whatever it is, I'll keep it in the strictest confidence."

Was it my imagination, or was there a glimmer in Brittney's eye? "Seriously, it's not about her," I said, and too late I realized I'd dropped my hands onto my lap and was twisting my fingers around themselves. I forced myself to put them up on the arms of the chair. Maybe I *was* guilty, but if so, I was here in an attempt to pay my debt to society.

Looking a little disappointed, Brittney sat back in her

chair. "Okay, then," she said, "what can I do for you?"

"I have to tell you something about Heidi."

"Heidi?" said Brittney, and now she seemed puzzled. "What about Heidi? Is she in some kind of trouble?"

If only. If only I was about to tell Heidi's mom that Heidi was pregnant or anorexic or a drug addict. The movie *A Cry for Help* that we seemed to watch in health class every year flashed in front of my eyes. *If your friend is in trouble, it's up to you to tell an adult.*

Too bad the film never bothered to address vehicular assault.

I took a deep breath and squeezed the arms of the chair tightly. "Brittney, on December twenty-first, Heidi took out one of your cars and went for a drive. While she was driving, she accidentally hit Bea Rossiter. That's how Bea got those injuries. Heidi didn't stop. She drove the car back home and didn't tell anyone but me."

I didn't breathe once during my speech, and by the time I got to the end, I was feeling a little light-headed. I thought it was from lack of oxygen, but even after I took a breath, the sensation persisted.

I'd expected Brittney to gasp or shout, *No!* or start asking me a million questions, but to my surprise, she just sat there, staring at me, like I hadn't said anything at all. Then, when it became clear that I was finished, she shook her head slightly as if she'd drifted off for a second and was now focusing again.

"I'm sorry, Callie, but what are you talking about?" Her voice was completely calm. Even as someone who'd always known her to be a rock, I was impressed.

"Um . . ." Did she want me to tell her the whole story again? I took a deep breath. "On December twenty-first—"

Brittney waved her hand between us as if there were cigarette smoke blocking our view of each other and she was trying to clear it away. "Yes, I heard you the first time."

"Then what—"

"Callie, are you . . . do you honestly expect me to believe that my daughter . . . that my daughter actually . . ." She stood up and crossed over to the island in the middle of the room, where she picked up a glass of water, went to take a sip, then put it down without touching it to her lips.

"I am so, so sorry," I said. "I know this must come as a total shock." I wasn't sure if I should walk over to her or just stay where I was.

But Heidi's mom didn't seem to be listening to a word I was saying. "A total—Callie Leary, this is the most revolting lie I have ever heard in my life! How dare you come to my home and start spewing such outrageous stories about my daughter!" She'd spun around to face me and the hand she pointed at my face was shaking violently. It felt like she could barely contain herself from flying across the kitchen and scratching at my face with her perfect, oval nails.

I stood up. "You can't really think I'd lie about something like this. Why would I?" I'd expected her to be shocked, but it had never occurred to me that she'd think I was making the whole thing up.

"Why would you? I have no idea! Because you're clearly

a very, very disturbed young woman, that's why. First your mother abandons her family, then your father goes crazy—"

"My father is *not* crazy!" I shouted.

Heidi's mom kept talking, like I hadn't said a word. "—those parents that it's no wonder you'd spew such *horrible*, such *outrageous*—" I'd never seen anyone so mad. There were flecks of saliva at the corners of her mouth, and her eyes were little more than slits.

"Leave my parents out of it!" I shouted. "And we're talking about your daughter, who stole your car and ran a totally innocent girl off the road and nearly killed her!"

"Get out of my house!" Brittney was pointing at the door and taking deep breaths, but if they were meant to calm her, they weren't doing a very good job. "Get out of here! Get out of here, you little monster!"

"I am not a monster!" I yelled. "Your daughter is the monster!" And with that, I raced for the front door, threw it open, and hurled myself onto my bike, riding so fast I almost collided with a FedEx truck that was pulling onto the block. The loud honking of the driver's truck seemed like the punctuation to Heidi's mom's accusations, and it took the entire ride to school for the sound of both to fade.

CHAPTER TWENTY-SEVEN

So it had all been for nothing. Amanda's note, talking with Nia and Hal, my plea to Heidi's mom. All of it had accomplished exactly nothing. Brittney was just going to dismiss everything I'd said as the ravings of a disturbed child-lunatic. And what was I supposed to do now, go to the police? If Brittney Bragg had thrown me out of her house, what was Chief Bragg going to do, run me out of town? Arrest me for slandering his daughter?

And what about Heidi? If she'd socially destroyed Nia for turning her in for cheating, what was she going to do to the girl who'd tried to reveal her criminal actions? All through the rest of my morning classes, I kept expecting to get a text message from her, like *You are so dead*, but my phone didn't buzz once between the time I slid into the bio lab and when the bell rang for lunch.

Out of habit, my feet turned in the direction of the cafeteria, but just as I got to the door, I realized what I was doing. Had I completely lost my mind? If there was ever, ever a place to be avoided at all costs today, it was the cafeteria. I needed to get out of the building, to get out of town. I had to move somewhere and assume a fake identity. Maybe with Amanda. Or my mom. My head spinning, I turned around and literally bumped into Heidi.

"Hel-*lo!*" she said.

"Where have you *been*?" said Traci. "We haven't seen you in, like, forever."

"Yeah," said Heidi. "Are you hiding from us or something?"

"I—I—" And suddenly I realized that Heidi had no idea what I'd done. For some reason, her mother hadn't told her anything about our confrontation that morning. Yet.

"*You* have got to hear about this sick, *sick* sale we're going to after school," said Kelli, linking her arm through mine and pulling me along with her into the cafeteria.

"Seriously," said Traci. "My mom's taking us and we're buying, like, *everything* for spring."

Kelli reached into her bag and pulled out a magazine. "Turquoise is the new black!" she announced.

Was this real? Was I actually supposed to just be here with Traci and Kelli and Heidi like the conversation with Brittney had never happened? Like the *accident* had never happened?

"And don't say you're not coming," said Kelli, plopping down at our usual table.

"Yeah, attendance is not optional," said Traci, sitting down across from her.

Heidi sat down, too, and now the only person still standing was me.

"Aren't you going to sit?" asked Traci, gesturing to an empty chair.

Heidi scowled at me. "What is *up* with you lately?"

Could I tell them? Could I really tell them? Could I say that I didn't have the money to go shopping with them because my mom had abandoned us and my dad had lost his job? Could I say that I spent all of my waking hours trying to solve the mysterious disappearance of the girl they considered the world's biggest freak? Could I tell them how adrift I felt whenever I wasn't with Hal Bennett and Nia Rivera?

Could I be honest and still be an I-Girl?

I already knew the answer.

But I also knew there was no way I could spend another lunch period pretending to be Callie Leary: Happy-go-lucky I-Girl. "I just need to go now," I said. "I'll catch up with you later." And with that, I turned around and headed out of the cafeteria.

If I'd thought my day had kicked off bizarrely, that was nothing compared to the shock I got when I pedaled up our driveway after school. For a split second, I wondered if I'd come to the wrong house. The lawn was freshly mowed, and the twigs and mud that had littered the front porch for months had been swept away.

I leaned my bike against the front of the house and pushed open the front door.

"Hello?" I called.

"Hello?" It was my dad, and it sounded like he was in the dining room. "Callie?"

I couldn't tell whether he'd been drinking. "Yeah, it's me," I said, positive that I sounded as shocked as I felt.

All of the wood that had been piled up in the entryway and living room was gone. The two-by-fours, the branches—everything. And instead of its usual musty smell, the house smelled of lemons and pine, like someone had spent the day cleaning. I walked through the living room where, instead of a crumbling tower of junk mail and catalogs collapsing over the edge of the coffee table, I saw a few small piles of letters, each of which had a Post-it on top.

Through the archway between the living room and the dining room I saw my dad. He was sitting next to the place where, as recently as that morning, the dining room table had sat. Now, however, ten chairs sat in a circle around an empty space.

What was going on here?

"I see you're redecorating." Through the open doorway leading to the kitchen, I got a glimpse of Joanna, the cleaning woman my dad had fired back in the fall. At the sound of my voice, she turned around and gave me a little wave.

"Hi, Joanna," I called, giving her a bewildered little wave back.

"Have a seat, Callie." My dad patted the chair next to him.

Now that we were sitting so close to each other, I saw that he had shaved that morning, and his flannel shirt and jeans smelled as fresh and laundered as the house. His skin was still pale, but his eyes weren't so red and bleary, and his breath smelled of the coffee he was drinking, not wine.

"Um, hi," I said, sitting down uncertainly.

And all of a sudden I understood exactly what was happening, and with my understanding came a blinding wave of joy. He'd heard from my mom. She was coming back!

I half-stood as if expecting to hear her step in the hallway, and as I did, my dad put his hand on my arm. I don't know if his words were a lucky guess or if my thoughts were written on my face, but he said softly, "She isn't coming back, Callie."

The joy I'd felt a second ago was washed away by a rush of panic. Was she . . . had he heard she'd . . .

He shook his head, reading my thoughts again. "I don't know any more than I did this morning or a week ago or a month ago. I haven't heard from her, and I don't know if we ever will."

I slumped back in my seat, overwhelmed by the bouncing ball of my emotions.

Why couldn't life have a pause button?

My dad took a deep breath, then exhaled slowly, like he understood I needed a minute to calm down. I noticed his hands were shaking slightly. "Callie, things are going to change around here. We're not going to live the way we've been living. I'm going to try to take better care of you."

But I was too numb from having my hopes raised and dashed to process what he'd said. Instead, I pointed to the empty space in front of me. "Where's the table?" I'd heard about companies that came and repossessed stuff, but my dad hadn't bought the table, he'd made it. And why would they have repossessed the table but given him enough money to hire Joanna back?

"I sold it," he said. "Remember Dr. Montgomery's wife?" he asked. Making his voice high and thin, my dad continued. *"I'll give you two thousand for it. I'll give you five thousand for it. Name your price . . ."* He switched back to his regular voice. "Well, I named my price."

"You sold the table, Dad? Your table? Mom's table?" In spite of how happy I'd been just a few minutes ago to see the house looking more or less normal again, I felt my eyes stinging. Now that I was sure my mom would be coming back, I wasn't happy about the idea of her returning to find her table gone.

My dad took my hand in his unsteady one. "It was just a table. I can make another one."

I shook my head. "But what about . . . why not just keep our table and use Amanda's money?"

Letting go of my hand, my dad stood up and went into the kitchen, reappearing a minute later with an official-looking envelope that said Bank of Orion in red letters in the top, left-hand corner. "This is the paperwork your friend will need when she shows up and wants her money back. I opened a bank account in your name and put the money in it and listed her as a cosigner. It was all I could do since I didn't have any of her official information." He handed me the envelope, and without thinking, I let my fingers fold around the cool, smooth paper.

"She wanted to help," I said, my voice dull.

My dad crossed his arms and frowned. "Honey, I know that. And I appreciate it. But I'm a grown man, and I really can't take money from a kid."

"Okay." I wanted so much to tell him, to tell him that he was right to step up and cope because my mom *was* going to come back to us and she *hadn't* wanted to leave. But fear of what he would do if he knew all I knew kept me silent.

"Now, I've got work to do, okay?" he asked. "I've got a lot to make up for."

I took a deep breath and nodded. "Okay," I repeated.

My dad stood up. For a second I thought he was about to say something more, but then he just brushed the hair off my forehead with his fingers and said "okay" once more before heading downstairs to his workshop.

chapter 28

"OMG, have you heard?" Traci, apparently writing off my behavior at lunch yesterday to PMS, was jumping up and down with excitement about her news, and I tried to feign at least mild interest. Even under the best of circumstances, I wasn't one for jumping up and down over anything before nine A.M. And my life lately was most definitely way too confusing to qualify as the best of circumstances.

"Heard what?" All around us the population of Endeavor was slowly starting its day, but it seemed to me there were more than the usual number of people whispering in small groups and talking in hushed voices. I perked up at the possibility that it might have something to do with Amanda but then realized the odds of Traci hearing something about her before I did were so low as to be nonexistent.

"Okay, you know Bea Rossiter?" She lowered her voice on Bea's name.

I felt a sudden wave of dizziness and reached for the nearby wall of lockers. Luckily, Traci was too pumped to notice.

"Well, these really fancy plastic surgeons at Johns Hopkins have *donated* their time to her case. Can you believe it?" Traci ran her hand through her hair as if it weren't already flawlessly framing her face. "They're going to, like, rebuild her face. Like that girl on . . . what was that soap we used to watch, the one with the hot doctor?" Traci squished up her nose in concentration, then shook her head. "Whatever—anyhoo, she's about to go from super-freak to super-chic!"

"Wow, that is so . . . amazing!" My mind was racing. Was it just a coincidence that this was happening the day after my conversation with Heidi's mom? Could Brittney and her husband have anonymously donated the money for Bea's surgeries?

Suddenly I thought of something—maybe the reason the unflappable Brittney Bragg had gotten so hysterical about what I'd told her wasn't because she *didn't* believe me but because . . . she did.

I grabbed Traci's arm. "Who told you this?"

I was so sure I knew what Traci's answer would be that I almost didn't hear what she said. "Um, Kevin maybe? Or . . . wait, no, Kelli texted me this morning. Or did Kevin tell me first? I can't remember." She shrugged.

"But not Heidi?"

Traci shook her head. "I haven't even seen her yet today. Look, I gotta motor. We'll talk at lunch, okay? And I have to tell you about this super-hot dress I got at Lollipop yesterday. You're going to *flip*." And with that, she turned and was swept up into the crowd.

The whole morning passed in a haze. I heard more details about Bea's surgeries (she wasn't in school because they'd already brought her to Baltimore to be evaluated; the Rossiters had been so shocked when they got the call that Mrs. Rossiter fainted; no one knew if the surgeons would rebuild her face exactly as it had been or if she'd look completely different when the surgery was over), but never the one fact I wanted to hear: Was this a donation from Johns Hopkins or was it a donation from a more local source?

We had a sub in history, and the woman was a witch with eyes in the back of her head, so there was no way for me and Heidi to exchange a word much less a note. Still, the way she waved hello to me indicated that her mother had said nothing about our conversation yesterday morning. At first I was confused, and then, as the period went on, I found myself getting angry. Okay, so maybe the story had a happy ending, but the beginning and middle hadn't been so pretty. Bea had spent months walking the corridors of Endeavor like the living dead and was now going to have to endure what were probably painful surgeries just to look halfway normal again. I'd been hiding a terrible secret, only to be called a liar and a freak by my friend's mom when I did the right thing and told the truth.

And Heidi had—what? I sincerely doubted the girl had so much as lost a night's sleep over the entire incident.

The sub turned to talk to Lexa for a minute and Heidi took a tube of lip gloss out of her bag, gesturing it toward me. *Look,* she mouthed. *New.*

I felt my blood boiling.

When I got to the cafeteria, Heidi, Traci, and Kelli were sitting at our usual table with Lee and Jake sitting across from them. Out of habit I started making my way toward them. But as I got closer and closer, my pace slowed until I wasn't walking at all, just standing there as if I were lost.

But the thing was, I wasn't lost. I knew exactly where I was, and I knew exactly what would happen if I kept going where I was headed. We'd talk about Bea's mysterious surgery, Heidi commenting on it as if the whole thing was as far away from her as Bosnia. We'd talk about Heidi, Kelli, and Traci's shopping spree. We'd make plans for the weekend, maybe agree to do some more shopping or go to a movie. I'd smile and nod and make jokes and flirt with Lee. It would be the way it always was because that was what being an I-Girl was all about.

Only the whole time, it would feel like I was trying not to scream.

Out of the corner of my eye, I saw Hal and Nia sitting alone at the same table they'd sat at the day last week when Thornhill first called us into his office. Nia was nodding; Hal was talking and gesturing behind him. I looked back the other way. Heidi was lifting her hair off the back of her neck and holding it so the ends fell just below her jaw, turning her head from side to side, like she wanted Kelli and Traci to evaluate what she'd look like with hair of a different length. Traci and Kelli nodded, then Kelli held her hair the same way and, almost instantly, so did Traci.

And suddenly I knew. I knew why Amanda had wanted me to tell Hal and Nia about the accident. Yes, she wanted me to do the right thing, to get some justice for Bea. But more than that, she wanted me to be free. To rise up and protect myself and those around me. Maybe even to protect Amanda herself.

Okay, Amanda hadn't chosen me as her only guide. But she *had* chosen me. She *needed* me. And she needed me strong and brave. Because let's face it: What good is a guide who's a pushover?

I stood where I was for a minute, remembering the final thing Amanda had taught me about bears: They hibernate. Which means they sleep for a long, long time.

But not forever.

And this little bear was waking up.

As if I hadn't so much made a choice right there as I'd accepted a choice I'd made a long time ago, I walked to the far end of the cafeteria and stood by Hal and Nia's table. Hal stopped talking and they both looked up at me—Hal like he was glad to see me, Nia with some suspicion in her eyes.

"Hey," said Hal.

"Hey," I said.

"Did you take a wrong turn? I think your table's

over there," said Nia, and she gestured in the direction of the I-Girls.

"You're not really going to give me a hard time about sitting here, are you, Nia?" I asked, and I held her look.

Nia seemed uncomfortable, like she'd expected a nasty response and wasn't sure what to do now that she hadn't gotten one. "I just . . . I mean, are you for real or are you just a tourist or something? Because sometimes it feels like you want it both ways."

I knew what she meant, and to prove I was serious, I did the only thing I could. I pulled out a chair and sat down. "I'm for real."

Nia looked at me for a long minute, then slowly nodded. "Well, okay then."

"Well, okay then," I repeated. We were still staring at one another.

"Well, okay then," said Hal, and he did such a good imitation of our serious tone that we both burst out laughing.

We were still laughing a minute later when Heidi, Traci, and Kelli stalked up to our table.

"Is this opposite day? Are you lost?" demanded Heidi, staring at me with her face wrinkled with disgust. "Or have these losers brainwashed you?"

In spite of my earlier determination to stand up for myself, it was disconcerting to have Heidi stare at me with such revulsion. I opened my mouth to respond, but Nia beat me to the punch. "What would someone without a brain know about brainwashing?"

"Ha, ha," Heidi snickered. "You're so smart you'd think you could not be such a *loser*."

"Oh, yeah, Heidi," retorted Nia. "If only I were cool enough to pick my friends by the last letter of their *names*."

"Like you even *have* friends," said Heidi.

"Well, I seem to have some of yours," Nia snapped back.

"Hey, guys, knock it off." I held up my hand to signal they should stop and, without getting out of my seat, turned toward the I-Girls. "Look, Heidi, just . . . I want to have lunch with Hal and Nia today. I know you don't really like them but they're my friends."

"They're your *friends*?" Traci looked sincerely shocked. "Since when?"

I felt a little bad. I mean, what had Traci and Kelli ever done to me?

"People can have a lot of different friends, Traci."

Traci gave a nasty laugh. "Um, I don't think so, Callie. We're not friends with people who are friends with freaks and losers."

And suddenly I didn't feel so bad after all. "Well"—I took a deep breath—"then I guess you're not friends with me."

"Are you seriously telling me that you're choosing these two freakazoid weirdos over us?" asked Heidi.

I looked at Hal and Nia. Hal was smiling encouragingly at me, but Nia's face was blank, as if she couldn't have cared less what I said next, as if it wouldn't have mattered if I stood up and said, *Psych!* and headed off with the I-Girls.

Only now I knew Nia. And I knew the only reason she was

looking at me like she didn't care what I did next was because she did.

"Yes, Heidi," I said. "I am seriously telling you that I'm choosing Hal and Nia over you."

"That is messed up," said Kelli. "That is *seriously* messed up."

"I hope you realize that Lee is totally going to dump you now," said Heidi. "You are dead to us. What is he going to do with a girlfriend who never gets invited to any parties?"

For the first time, I felt the weight of my decision to abandon the I-Girls. I hadn't counted on giving up Lee along with everything else. But then I looked into Heidi's snarling face and realized the only thing sadder than breaking up with Lee would be not breaking up with Heidi, Traci, and Kelli.

"Good-bye, Heidi," I said.

There was a moment of silence as the three of them stared at me. Then Heidi turned on her heel and, holding up her hand, said, "You'll regret this," before marching off. A second later, Kelli and Traci followed suit. I thought they might have looked a little sad, but maybe that was just wishful thinking.

Nia and Hal and I sat for a minute without saying anything until Hal finally broke the silence. "Your friends are certainly . . . opinionated."

"Yeah," I said. "Though you'll notice they tend to share the same opinion."

"I'll say. Like they share a brain," said Nia, and she reached into her bag and took out an enormous sandwich. "Anyone want half of this roast beef? My mom always sends me with enough food for about ten people." Her words broke the tension; I could practically see her mother pressing the food upon her in the morning.

"I'm good," said Hal, taking a sandwich out of his own bag.

"Callie?"

I had twenty dollars in my pocket that my dad had given me that morning, muttering something about a girl needing "mad money." But Nia's mom's sandwich looked way better than anything I was going to find in the cafeteria. And there was something about the way Nia was holding it toward me that made it feel like she was offering me more than a sandwich.

"Love some." I nodded, and, as I'd expected it would be, Nia's mom's sandwich was delicious.

"Okay," said Nia, pushing up the sleeves of her pale gray sweater and settling her elbows on the table, "just to catch you up, Hal and I were talking about getting the envelope you two think you saw in Thornhill's car."

I nearly choked on my roast beef. "You're talking about breaking into Thornhill's car?"

"We need to see that note." Nia's voice was even but there was the undercurrent of a threat in it, too.

"The note could be anywhere," I pointed out. "It could even be in his *house*." The possibility of having to ransack Thornhill's house was a little more than I'd bargained for.

As if he could read my mind, Hal said, "Let's not borrow trouble. Occam's razor says if it *was* in his car then it *is* in his car. Let's start there."

"Please, do you *have* to bring up Occam's razor?" I asked.

"Occam's razor is great, it's handy—" Hal started.

"You know what I've been thinking about lately?" inter-rupted Nia. "Amanda's other friends. What luck have they had in finding her?" She was looking off into the distance in a way that made me realize she hadn't heard the last couple of things Hal and I had been saying.

"Amanda's other . . . what are you talking about? Amanda didn't have other friends," I said.

Nia smiled at me and patted my hand. "Right. Like *you* thought she didn't have other friends and *I* thought she didn't have other friends and *Hal* thought . . ."

"Okay, okay." I bowed my head in her direction. "Point taken."

As I was trying to figure out how we were supposed to even *find* Amanda's other friends, much less get them to work with us on finding her, Hal's little sister, Cornelia, materialized at our table. Even though I hadn't seen her in years, I recognized her immediately—she was much taller than she'd been the summer Hal and I hung out, but she still had the same straight red hair up in a high ponytail and the same serious expression I remembered from the few times she'd joined me and Hal in the woods.

"Hey, Cornelia," said Hal. "What's up?"

"The sky," she said. It was weird to see a little kid here; the middle school has its own cafeteria and the younger kids basically never came into ours.

"Mom put my lunch in your bag," announced Cornelia somberly.

"She did?" said Hal, reaching for his backpack. "Why didn't I see it?"

"I don't know," said Cornelia. "Why didn't you?"

His head almost buried in his bag, Hal said, "Callie, you remember my sister, Cornelia. Nia, this is Cornelia. Cornelia, Nia."

"Hi," said Cornelia, who didn't seem remotely intimidated by standing in the high school cafeteria or being introduced to two high school girls, one of whom she didn't know.

"Hi, Cornelia," I said.

"Hi," said Nia. Then she turned to me. "What about distributing flyers?"

"You want to paper the school with flyers? Saying what, exactly?" I said.

"I don't see it," said Hal, emerging from his bag.

"Saying . . . I don't know, like, *If you know anything about Amanda Valentino's whereabouts, please contact* . . . Then we could put our names and numbers at the bottom."

"You're eating it." Cornelia pointed at the remains of her lunch.

"That's *my* sandwich," protested Hal, looking down at the half-eaten sandwich in front of him.

"Let's think about how long it would take Thornhill to rip those down *and* make us tell him everything we know about Amanda's life and lies," I said.

"It's not your sandwich," said Cornelia. "It's almond-butter and jelly. It's my sandwich. Mom gave you money for lunch today. She didn't make you a sandwich."

"No she—" Hal thought for a second. "Oh."

"Okay, okay, so no flyers," said Nia.

"What about a Facebook page?" I said suddenly. "We could make Amanda a Facebook page and see if people visit it. I mean, she could have friends all over the country." I'd been really surprised when I found out Amanda didn't already have one given how much she moved around and how many people she must have wanted to keep in touch with. Now, of course, her response to my asking her about it (*"I like my reality to be real, not virtual"*) seemed a lot less "real" than it had at the time.

"She must have friends all over the *world*," mused Nia.

"Right," I said. "And you can't exactly post flyers in Hong Kong, you know?"

"Well, what if I just give you the money Mom gave me so you can buy your lunch and I'll finish the sandwich?" said Hal.

"Okay." Cornelia shrugged. "Works for me."

"What if we built a website?" I said.

Nia assumed a fake, chipper tone. "Yeah, good thought." She dropped back to her regular voice. "Too bad none of us knows *how* to build a website."

I thought of how now that I wasn't friends with the I-Girls anymore I wasn't even going to be able to upload music to my iPod. "Wait, aren't you, like, Miss Computer Genius? Didn't you hack into the school's surveillance footage history and burn it to a DVD?"

"Two bucks," said Cornelia.

"Two bucks?" said Hal.

"Hacking into the school's system and building a website aren't exactly the same thing. You have to know that computer language to build a website. That . . . what's it called, um—"

"HTML." Cornelia, who was holding out her hand, palm up, toward Hal, never looked in our direction.

"Excuse me?" said Nia.

"HTML," repeated Cornelia, palm still raised. "It stands for HyperText Markup Language. But it's only one of several computer languages you can use to build a website."

"I've only got a dollar seventy-five," complained Hal.

I reached into my pocket. "Here," I said. "I've got a quarter." Cornelia took the money from Hal, then added my quarter to the ones already on her palm. "How do you know that . . . about computers, I mean?"

"Oh, Cornelia's a total computer genius," said Hal. "These kids today."

"Really?" I asked. "You could, like, build a website?"

Cornelia shrugged. "It's no biggie," she said.

"I don't know," said Nia. "I mean, what are the odds Amanda's not going to be back before we could even *start* building a website?"

"You can build a website in a day," offered Cornelia.

We all turned and looked at her. "Are you serious?" said Nia.

Cornelia shrugged again. "I'm telling you, it's really easy."

Hal snorted. "Yeah, easy for you."

"Could you, like, get a website . . . ready? And not, um . . ." I couldn't believe how little computer lingo I knew. It was kind of embarrassing.

"Not launch it," Cornelia finished for me.

"Thank you," I said. "Yes, not launch it."

"Sure," she said. "First I'll have to register a domain name and secure a host."

"You've lost me," said Hal. "But if it's really easy, I want you to do that. Register that . . . name host thing."

"Domain name. And host. And it costs like thirty bucks," she said.

"I'll cover it," said Hal.

"We'll split it," I said, thinking of the twenty dollars in my pocket and glad that I *could* say it.

"What do you want to call it?" asked Cornelia. "The name has to be available."

"Amanda.com?" I suggested.

"Chances are it's already taken," said Cornelia. "Most first names are."

"What about amandavalentino.com?" said Hal.

"We could put photos of her on it. And your drawings," I said to Hal.

His face reddened when I suggested we include his drawings, but he didn't say no. "We should post the name she gave to the woman at The Riviera and even your name." His enthusiasm built as he thought of something else. "Maybe she's used them as aliases before?"

"Not to be a major buzz kill or anything, but this all sounds to me like Major Useless Projects 101," said Nia, crumbling up the bag her sandwich had been in for emphasis.

"Be that as it may," said Hal, "I'd feel better getting prepared."

Something in his voice, how low and serious it was, made me uneasy. I looked at him. "You think . . . you think we're going to need it, don't you?" I asked.

He met my gaze across the table, but he didn't smile or change his tone at all. "Like I said, I'd just feel better getting prepared."

CHAPTER TWENTY-NINE

Friday morning Heidi made a big show of turning her back to me and talking to Lexa Booker as soon as I walked into history class. I wondered if they were talking about me. I wondered if soon Lexa was going to be Lexi.

I was on my way from science to English when I looked up and saw Lee walking with Keith and Jake. We made eye contact, and I remembered how he'd kissed my head at Liz's party Saturday night, how he'd said I looked cute washing Thornhill's car. Could someone so nice really care what someone as mean as Heidi thought about his girlfriend?

"Hey," I said, and it wasn't until the word was out of my mouth that I realized he hadn't slowed down at all.

He hesitated for a second, then brushed his hand through his hair and said "Hey" without looking me in the eyes.

"Later," said Keith and Jake, and they kept walking, neither of them acknowledging me.

Lee and I stood in the crowded hallway while students headed to class swarmed around us. It was weird how a space could be so noisy yet feel so silent.

"I'm not an I-Girl anymore," I blurted out.

"Yeah," he said. "That's what they tell me."

I waited to see if he was going to say anything else. *Who cares if you're an I-Girl—you're* my *girl.*

"I've been hanging out with Nia Rivera," I said.

"Her brother's a pretty cool guy," said Lee. He still wasn't really looking at me.

"Right," I said. My eyes burned.

Lee shifted his backpack uneasily on his shoulder.

I took a deep breath. "So are we still—"

The warning bell rang. "I should get going." He edged away. "Don't want to be late for Monster Masterson."

"Sure," I agreed. "Don't let me keep you."

"I won't," said Lee, and I knew I wasn't imagining the look of relief on his face when he turned to go. "See you around," he called over his shoulder.

"Yeah." I brushed quickly at the traitorous tear that was slipping down my cheek. "See you around."

I was so glad to see Nia and Hal at lunch that I could have seriously bawled.

The second I joined them, Hal started up. "I've got a plan. Amanda wants us to search for her, so let's search. I want each of us to come up with a list of places Amanda could possibly be on a Friday night. We'll all pick . . . let's say three places. And then tonight, we'll hit all of them and try to find her."

"You think she's still in Orion?" Nia asked, passing me a bite of another one of her mom's amazing sandwiches, Genoa salami and provolone this time.

"Well, she keeps leaving us messages," Hal pointed out.

"Yeah, except for all we know, she could be in Paris by now," I said. "Or Rome. Or maybe she left to go meet her dad in Latin America."

"Except that her dad's dead," Hal reminded us.

"Except that he's not," I said.

"Okay," Nia broke in. "Glad we got that one worked out. Now, Hal, back to your plan. Nine places is a *lot* of places. How are we going to get to all of them?"

"That's the thing." Hal leaned forward, his excitement at his plan mounting. "It won't be nine places. I bet if we each come up with three places, we're all going to have at least two of the same places on our list. I'd be surprised if there are more than three or four places we need to go tonight."

I thought about what Hal was saying. Where *would* Amanda go on a Friday night? Was it possible she had a whole different group of friends in Orion, people she was hanging out with right now instead of us?

"Do you think she could have, like, a whole separate identity?" I asked. The thought made my stomach sink.

"You mean like a French spy?" asked Nia. "If anyone could

pull that off, it would be Amanda."

"I wasn't going quite that far. More . . . I mean, what if she's at some other high school right now sitting with her friends there? Like a parallel universe."

"I wonder if I wear glasses in that universe," mused Nia, twirling a strand of her hair.

"Ha, ha," I said. "I'm serious."

Hal pressed his fingertips against his forehead and groaned. "If that's the case, we'll never find her."

"That's what I'm saying," I said.

"I don't think that's what happened." Nia became purposeful. "I mean, she had a *life* here. Yeah, she ditched school *sometimes*, but not more than . . . what, once a week? Twice at most? Which means she would have been cutting at her other school *four or five times* a week."

I thought about how, after we were up all night stargazing, Amanda and I just ditched school and slept, then went for café mochas at Just Desserts and to see a matinee of *2001: A Space Odyssey*. And there were those pictures Hal had drawn of Amanda at the docks in Baltimore; maybe they'd cut school together, too. Nia didn't seem the type to cut so much as a class, but if anyone could have gotten her to break the rules, surely it would have been Amanda.

That meant there were at least three days she wasn't cutting Endeavor to go to another school.

"It does seem like a lot of trouble to go through, to register at two high schools and try attending both," agreed Hal. And then, as if he were reading my mind, he added, "Especially if you're not *always* at one or the other."

The bell rang and the three of us stood up and slowly gathered our stuff. "So what's the plan?" I asked as we made our way out of the cafeteria.

"Let's meet at four on the town green," suggested Nia. "It's central enough, right?"

"Sure." I nodded. "Sounds good." We were passing the main office, and just as we walked by, the door opened and Mr. Thornhill walked out, talking to a parent and student I didn't recognize. He shook the boy's hand, said something to the mom, and turned to go back inside when he saw us.

"Aaah," he said, making a slight bow. "Mr. Bennett, Miss Rivera, and Miss Leary. Who, I might add, have been spending a *lot* of time together for three people so emphatic about their non-friendship."

"Mr. Thornhill." Nia was brilliantly frosty.

I glanced his way briefly, then looked away. I hadn't actually laid eyes on him since I'd read my mother's note, and it was impossible not to see him differently now that I knew she'd asked him to look after me. Why him, of all people? What did he know about my mother, about my family, about *me* that I didn't know?

His voice was mild and amused as he replied to Nia's greeting. "I trust you're looking forward to our morning together tomorrow."

Ugh. Detention again. Had it been only a week since the last one? So much had happened. I'd completely forgotten that wasn't a one-shot deal.

Without missing a beat, Nia confirmed, "Wouldn't miss it, sir."

Hal gave a mock salute. "Great way to spend a Saturday morning, sir."

"Been looking forward to it all week," I said, my voice equally perky.

A small smile seemed to be playing around the corners of Mr. Thornhill's lips, but he didn't let it escape. "I haven't heard word one from your missing friend," he said. "This is a record, even for me. I'm sincerely hoping one or all of you will be able to enlighten me as to her whereabouts in the near future."

"That *would* be nice," said Nia, meeting his gaze easily. "If only she *were* our friend, maybe we could help you." Was there anyone as bold as Nia? I sincerely doubted it.

"If it were in the near enough future, you could all sleep in tomorrow morning," said Mr. Thornhill, ignoring her assertion that we weren't friends with Amanda.

"Anything can happen," said Hal.

"You never know," I agreed.

"Hmmm," said Mr. Thornhill. "Well, good day to all of you." And with that, he turned and disappeared into his office.

Nia shrugged when we glared at her. "Well, worth a shot."

Hal, Nia, and I said good-bye, and I spent as much of the afternoon thinking about Mr. Thornhill as I did trying to figure out where Amanda might be if she were still in Orion. As far as I knew, the vice principal had never once suspended

Amanda, even though she'd constantly flaunted his every rule. And wasn't it a little weird that if he was so desperate to know where she was he didn't call her parents? What did her official files say? Why force three kids he seemed to know were innocent to sit in detention for a month of Saturdays? Was *this* his idea of looking after me?

For the millionth time, I wondered about the note Hal and I had seen in his car and wished, more than anything, that I could know what it said.

CHAPTER 30

Four o'clock found me and my bike at the town green. I hadn't been able to come up with a list of any special places besides Just Desserts, but she *had* said it was her favorite place to get a Frappuccino, so that was something. Then there was the tattoo place where we'd all gotten henna tattoos, but I hadn't gotten the feeling Amanda was, like, a regular there. One time we'd gone for a ride through Peak Park, and Amanda had said she absolutely loved being in this little gazebo by the lake at sunset, so that and Just Desserts were the two places I'd decided we might possibly find her. It was a beautiful, clear day with a hint of spring in the air. If ever there was going to be an evening to enjoy a cup of coffee alfresco while appreciating a beautiful sunset, it was tonight.

I almost didn't recognize Nia when she pulled up next to

me on her bike. She was wearing a short, vintage black dress, a black sweater, high heels, and serious cat-eye glasses, and she had a long cigarette-less cigarette holder between her bright red lips. I had no idea how she'd been able to bike in that getup.

"Hi." She managed a fairly elegant dismount, I had to admit.

"Hi," I said. "What's with the duds?"

"Audrey Hepburn film festival at The Villa," said Nia, naming Orion's art cinema where Amanda and I had seen *2001*. "No way would she miss that if she's still here." Nia's skin was the color of caramel, and her eyes, outlined in kohl, popped behind her snazzy glasses. When, exactly, had Nia Rivera gotten so pretty?

Apparently when no one was looking.

I, meanwhile, had on an old pair of jeans and hiking boots in case we decided to hide out in the bushes and wait for Amanda at the gazebo. And just to make it lovelier, I had tucked my jeans into a plaid sock on one side for biking, and my sweatshirt had a huge shamrock on the front and said *Bill's Tavern* on the back. If Nia looked like Audrey Hepburn, I looked like Audrey Hepburn's leprechaun, fashion-impaired sister.

A minute later, Hal pulled up on his bike. I recognized him, but he was dressed almost as oddly as Nia.

"*Bonsoir*." He tipped his beret at us. He had on a black turtleneck and black jeans.

"Bonsoir," said Nia, and now it was her turn to ask, "What's with the duds?"

"Poetry slam tonight at Aqua," said Hal. "It was her favorite coffee shop."

"Aqua?" I said. "She never mentioned Aqua to me. Just Desserts was her favorite coffee place."

"She didn't even drink coffee," protested Nia, taking the cigarette holder out of her mouth. "She said caffeine is poison."

"You're joking, right?" Hal adjusted his beret. "That girl would down a double latte before you could say fair-trade organic roast."

"Look, whatever else we do, we need to be in Peak Park at sunset," I intervened. "She had this place she liked to go to watch the sunset whenever she had the chance."

Shockingly, neither Nia nor Hal had a competing sunset location.

"Sun should set around six." Hal shrugged. "So we have time to go someplace else before then."

"Play It Again, Sam," Nia asserted, forcefully as usual.

"Excuse me?" said Hal.

"Play It Again, Sam," said Nia again. "Her favorite vintage clothing store."

"Anyone got an alternative favorite vintage store?" asked Hal, and when I shook my head, the three of us got on our bikes and followed Nia off the green and down Main Street. Within a few blocks, she'd pulled off Main and made half a dozen turns until even I, who'd lived in Orion my whole life, was feeling lost. How had Amanda even *found* this store?

Play It Again, Sam turned out to be an old Victorian house not unlike the one Amanda had told me she lived in, only much shabbier and painted in outrageous, peeling shades of pinks and purples. Nia dismounted and the three of us leaned our bikes against the porch.

But when we pushed open the door of the shop, the sound of the tinkling bell was drowned out by a woman bellowing, "Sorry, we're closed!"

"Hi!" called Nia, either because she hadn't heard what the woman said or because she'd decided to ignore it.

"Closed," repeated the voice, and now I could see it was emanating from a tall black woman standing at the back of the store. I'd never seen such a tightly packed room—there was literally clothing everywhere: the floors, the walls. Dresses and shoes even hung from the ceiling, and as I tried to make my way in, I was clocked in the head by a pair of shiny white platform boots.

"Hi!" called Nia again. "We were hoping you could help us."

The woman came forward, brushing at her nearly shaved head as if the store were as dusty as it was cluttered. She was wearing a tight-fitting, Sgt. Pepper–style red jacket on top and billowy silk jodhpurs in sapphire on the bottom. On her feet were gold slippers that curled up at pom-pom toes.

"I'd be happy to," said the woman. "But not today. I'm doing inventory. Come by tomorrow."

Inventory? How could you possibly do inventory in such a

chaotic place. And in a *day*? Looking around, I calculated that ten people working twenty-four-hour days could not inventory the store in a month.

"We're actually not looking for clothes; we're looking for a friend," said Nia.

The woman looked Nia up and down, taking in her vintage outfit and the faux cigarette holder. She even reached out her hand and touched the sleeve of Nia's black sweater.

"I sold a sweater just like that not long ago," mused the woman. "Chanel."

"That's this sweater!" said Nia, excited. "My friend gave it to me. We're looking for her."

"Well, she's not here," said the woman, gesturing around the room with her arm.

Given how crowded the store was, I didn't see how the woman could claim with such confidence that Amanda or anyone else wasn't there somewhere.

"Do you remember the last time you saw her?" asked Hal eagerly. "Has she been by recently?"

Again the woman took in what Hal was wearing before she answered. Given how twenty-first-century American my jeans and sweatshirt were, I figured I'd better not call attention to myself.

"Ooooh," she sighed, rubbing the side of her nose. "She's in a lot."

"Do you remember when the last time was?" pressed Hal. "This week, last week?"

She thought for a minute, then shook her head. "Sorry,

can't really remember. Now, if you'll excuse me, I've got to get back to work."

"Did she ever give you an address?" I asked suddenly. "Or charge something on a credit card?"

As I'd anticipated, my wardrobe evaluation didn't go as swimmingly as Hal's and Nia's. The woman gave me a quick once-over, then shook her head. She was obviously not impressed. "I really can't recall. And I'm not sure I'd tell you if I could."

"Well, thank you so much," said Nia quickly. "You've been tremendously helpful."

"Yeah, thanks," said Hal. He'd taken off his beret when he was talking to her, but now he put it back on. Even someone as cute as Hal looks pretty dorky in a beret, and I hoped he wasn't coming to like it.

"Well, so much for that," said Nia as the door shut behind us. "Sunset?"

"Sunset," said Hal.

I don't know quite what I'd been expecting to find, but when we got to the gazebo, it was deserted. Over the next hour, while we sat on a bench watching, half a dozen elderly people and two families came by. While the kids fed the ducks, Nia, Hal, and I tried to figure out how to make the best use of tonight.

"We've got to divide and conquer," said Hal. "I'll go to the poetry slam. Callie, you check out Just Desserts. Nia, you go to the film festival."

"I think there are three movies playing at a time," said Nia.

"So rather than go into one of them, I'll just lurk around the lobby and hope to catch her there." She looked at her wrist. "I should probably go soon," she said. "I think they had a movie that started already. Should we synchronize watches or anything before I leave?"

We checked that our watches were all more or less the same, then agreed that I would wait until the sun had completely set before heading to Just Desserts. Since Nia had to be home by ten, Hal and I would get to the theater by nine thirty and meet up with her, then we'd wait for the last movie to get out.

Not surprisingly, Amanda didn't show up at the park, and when I got to Just Desserts, which was packed with college kids, she wasn't there either. I bought a cappuccino and drank it as slowly as I possibly could, but I was still finished with it long before seven. My stomach growling, I ordered another one, wondering how I was going to survive on nothing but caffeinated beverages and biscotti for the next two-and-a-half hours.

I don't know if it was the caffeine or the fact that I'd come in the hopes of seeing Amanda, but by eight o'clock, I was as itchy and impatient for her to show up as I would have been if we'd actually agreed to meet at Just Desserts and she was late. I kept checking my watch and looking around; as eight became nine, I found myself leaning forward each time the door opened and sitting back, disappointed, when the person who came in wasn't Amanda.

I waited until nine fifteen before I left, so sizzled from all the coffee I was a little worried my heart wasn't beating properly. I made it to The Villa in less than ten minutes, which no doubt was an all-time record for someone going from the hill to downtown. I wasn't completely sure my wheels actually touched pavement more than once or twice during the ride down.

I spotted Nia in front of the theater immediately. She was pacing back and forth under the marquee, checking her watch and the doors every second or so. When I called her name, she practically fell into my arms.

"Oh my god, this is *impossible!*" she said.

"What?" I asked. My whole body was shaking. I needed to eat something or I was going to start levitating soon.

"For all I know she's here and I missed her," said Nia, throwing up her arms in frustration.

"Seriously? Nia, what are you jabbering about?"

She grabbed me by the arm and handed me a ticket. "Look."

I followed Nia into the packed lobby, and within a minute, I knew exactly what she meant.

Inside, The Villa was wall-to-wall Audrey Hepburn. The guys who were there were dressed regularly, maybe a few more than usual in slightly dated suits, but almost every single woman was wearing a wig or a vintage dress or holding a cigarette holder, with or without a cigarette. The room was smoky and noisy, and I realized there was a bar set up at one end, which they don't usually have at The Villa. It was like we'd dropped into one of the parties in *Breakfast at Tiffany's*.

I took a few steps away from Nia, and when I turned around, I couldn't find her anywhere at first. Then I saw her, standing with her back to me by a poster for *Charade*.

"Hey," I said, touching the sleeve of her black sweater. "Thought I'd lost you."

But instead of Nia, some woman I'd never seen before turned to face me.

"I'm sorry?" she said. She was way older than Nia, and her cigarette holder had a lit cigarette in it. A cloud of smoke blew in my face.

"No, I'm sorry," I said, coughing and backing away from her.

A second later there was a tug at my sleeve, and I looked over to see the real Nia standing next to me.

"It's you, right?" I said.

"See what I mean?" she asked. "This is absurd. And I have to get home soon."

"Okay, okay." I tried to stay calm even as the caffeine urged the opposite "Don't panic. You go outside and wait for me and Hal there. I'm going to circle the lobby."

"Remember, there are still people *inside* the theater. This is only probably a third of the audience. They're waiting to see the nine-fifty show."

"Outside," I said firmly, feeling her panic starting to spread through my already jittery body.

I watched Nia leave through the glass doors, then started to make my way through the lobby looking for Amanda. It was like a bad dream—everywhere I looked there was a woman or a girl (and once even someone I realized was a guy in drag) who could have been Amanda dressed as Audrey Hepburn. The lobby was so crowded I'd barely managed to circle it once when people started pouring out of the theater on the second floor. I couldn't believe it—I was supposed to navigate a *bigger* crowd? I was actually relieved when I looked at my watch and realized if I didn't head outside, I was going to miss Nia.

She and Hal were on the sidewalk facing the lobby doors, both of them with defeated looks on their faces. As I walked toward them, I turned slightly to face the lobby and I could see why they looked the way they did—if anything, the crowd looked even denser and more impenetrable from here than it felt inside.

"Hey," I said.

"Poetry slam was a bust," said Hal.

"I've gotta go," said Nia. "I'm really sorry."

Hal waved away her apology. "Don't sweat it," he said. "We can take over from here."

But "take over" clearly translated into "fail satisfactorily." By ten forty-five, when the last movie got out, we were no closer to finding Amanda than before.

Hal and I looked at each other as the last stragglers exited the theater.

"Bust," I announced glumly.

Hal nodded.

"I told my dad I'd be home by midnight," I said. When I'd left the house, he hadn't asked for a time I'd be home, but since he was staying sober and giving me spending money, I figured the least I could do was let him know my ETA. He'd just called up *Have fun!* from his workshop, but I hoped he'd appreciated the gesture nonetheless.

"She once mentioned seeing a band at Arcadia," said Hal. "You know that all-ages club downtown?"

"Want to try it?" I asked.

Hal shrugged. "Nothing to lose." We unlocked our bikes and I followed Hal out onto the street.

"Oh, and, Hal?" He put his foot back on the sidewalk and turned to face me.

"Yeah?"

I gave him an appraising look. "Maybe we should lose the beret."

"Gotcha." He smiled and pushed off from the curb. As he gained speed, he pulled his beret off his head and stuffed it into his back pocket without slowing down.

I'd never been to Arcadia, but Hal clearly had. We made our way through Orion's mostly deserted streets to an industrial area of town. It was dark here, and the pavement was pitted with potholes. Just as I was about to suggest to Hal that we forget the whole go-to-the-club thing, he pointed, saying, "It's just up ahead."

A small crowd was milling around outside of a brick warehouse that didn't look very different from all the other warehouses around us except that this one had a neon-lit door while the others were dark. A black-and-white sign on the wall read, PUNK ROCK IS FOR LOSERS with today's date. At first I was like,

Why is punk rock for losers today only? But then I realized that was the name of the band. We paid a creepy-looking guy with a shaved head and a tattoo of a lizard circling his neck, then made our way down a dark, rickety staircase. Despite the huge warehouse we'd entered, the room we arrived in was small, maybe as big as the downstairs of my house. Still, the band was playing loudly enough to fill a major concert hall, and I could feel the music throbbing in each of my internal organs. Hal screamed something at me, but I just shook my head. He yelled again, and again I had no idea what he'd just said. He pointed at his eyes, then pointed around the room, and I realized he was going to look around. I nodded and gave him a thumbs-up, deciding I'd do the same.

It was almost as crowded as The Villa had been, and the search I did through the crowd was about as pointless as my earlier search. At one point I thought I saw this weird musician girl who's in our class at Endeavor, but then I looked again and I wasn't sure it was the same chick. The truth was that *everyone* at Arcadia looked enough like that girl that they could have been her or could have not been her—it wouldn't really have mattered. By the time I got back to where we'd separated, Hal was waiting for me.

He pressed his mouth up against my ear. "Want to leave?" he asked.

I nodded and started to follow him up the stairs when all of a sudden the fifty million cups of coffee I'd drunk caught up with me. For a brief second, I was afraid I might actually have an accident right there. I tugged on Hal's shirt.

"I'll meet you outside," I said. No way was I going to shout, *I have to pee* at the top of my lungs.

He cupped his ear and shook his head.

I pointed toward the exit and mouthed, *One minute*. Hal nodded.

It took me about five minutes just to find the bathroom, and if I hadn't had to pee so bad, I would have been sorry to find it at all. The floor was sticky and there wasn't any paper and the seat wasn't exactly sterile. Oh well, when you've gotta go, you've gotta go.

It wasn't until I'd zipped up my pants and turned to flush the toilet that I saw it. Written in bright silver pen that shone against the black of the tiles even in the dim light of the bathroom were five words, all in capital letters.

AMANDA VALENTINO, WHERE R U?

 chapter 31

Maybe if I'd had a good night's sleep I wouldn't have minded waking up in spite of the weather, but in my exhausted state, the freezing rain and gale-level winds made getting myself out of bed feel like a nearly impossible feat. And one glance at my face was enough to make me want to crawl back into bed and never emerge from it again—my skin was pasty white, almost gray, and there were creepy dark circles under my eyes, as if looking for Amanda were turning me into some kind of vampire.

After I'd seen the writing on the wall, I rushed out of the bathroom, sure I'd find something that explained the message. But nothing had changed—the music blared, the audience was full of strangers. There was no indication that Amanda had ever set foot in there.

Except that she had. Or someone who knew her had.

I raced upstairs to find Hal and told him what I'd seen, and he went back downstairs to the guy's bathroom. But there was nothing written on any of the stalls in there, and a second circuit he did of the club proved as fruitless as the first.

"At least we know someone else is looking for her," he said when he came upstairs to meet me.

"Yes, but who? And why?" Finding this tiny clue was almost more frustrating than not finding anything at all. I wanted to tear my hair out.

"I'm going to text Nia," said Hal. He took out his phone. "Damn, I'm gonna be late. Look, are you okay biking home alone?"

Biking home alone seemed like the least of my problems at this point, so I just told him not to worry about it and got on my bike, thinking that what I needed was a restful night of sleep to make sense of everything. Unfortunately, I had the exact opposite of a restful night, and now I was as exhausted and wired and confused as I'd been since this whole nightmare had started.

Which wasn't exactly a great way to start the day.

I'd mentioned to my dad that I had to be at school early, but he was still sleeping, so I just pulled my mom's slicker over what I was wearing and climbed on my bike. It was really cold out—any promises the air had held that spring was coming had been totally obliterated by the storm—but pedaling all the way to school was hard work, and by the time I pulled into the parking lot, I was sweating underneath my heavy sweater and down vest. I'd only been awake for an hour, and all I wanted was to have another shower and get back into bed.

The parking lot only had a few cars in it—usually there's a lot going on at Endeavor on the weekends, like rehearsals and yearbook meetings and practices, but apparently March was a slow month, or maybe it was too early in the morning for any non-punitive school activities. I saw Thornhill's car parked in its usual spot in the faculty parking lot, and again I couldn't help thinking about the letter that the three of us might or might not have seen in it. If ever there was a good day to break into the vice principal's car, it would be today, but no sooner had I had the thought than I pushed it out of my head. What were we supposed to do if we broke into the car and didn't find the letter—was his house going to be next?

Nia and Hal were already sitting in their seats from last week when I pushed open the door of the library. There were four other kids there, three guys and one girl, none of whom I recognized; I wondered what their crimes were in Thornhill's eyes. Nia and Hal and I made eye contact, but even though Thornhill wasn't sitting at his desk at the front of the room, I was too scared of his catching us talking when he walked in to say anything to them. One of the guys was sitting where I'd been last week, so I just picked another table in the back.

As I sat down, the clock hit nine. One of the girls shifted in her seat, but no one said anything about Thornhill's being late. Obviously he was in the building—I'd seen his car. I dropped my backpack onto the desk and opened up my bio book, but

I wasn't exactly in the right frame of mind to focus on mitochondria. I looked back at the clock—five past nine. Now two of the girls up at the front started whispering to each other. I was about to whisper Nia's name when the door to the library flew open and Mr. Richards, the head of the gym department, stalked into the room.

"No talking!" he bellowed, which was kind of unnecessary considering his arrival had caused insta-silence. He stood in front of the room.

"I have an announcement to make," he said. "Last night, Vice Principal Thornhill suffered an injury. He is currently in the ICU at Orion General."

Without realizing, I gasped.

"Oh my god," said one of the muttering girls.

"What happened? Is he going to be okay?" asked Nia, and I could tell from her shaking voice that she was as undone by Mr. Richards's news as I was.

Mr. Richards toyed with the bill of his baseball cap. "At this point, I have no information about his condition other than that he was brought to the hospital unconscious and, as of this morning, he had not regained consciousness."

"You mean he's in a *coma*?" said Nia.

"That's enough talking," snapped Mr. Richards. "There will be a schoolwide announcement Monday morning about his condition. I'm sure we'll know much more once the police have finalized their report."

The *police*? Why were the police involved? My mind was racing. Mr. Richards said Mr. Thornhill had suffered an injury?

What did that mean? Had he fallen? If so, why were the police involved? And if he'd just had an accident or fallen down or something, why had Mr. Richards said he'd *suffered an injury*?

Had the vice principal been attacked?

Suddenly freezing cold, I wrapped my arms around my chest, but it did nothing to ease the ice water that seemed to be running through my veins instead of blood.

"Mr. Richards," said Nia, as the gym teacher sat down and opened up a folder in front of him.

"What is it now?" Mr. Richards was still irritated, but he did look up.

"Um, I forgot my history book in my locker. Is it okay if I run and get it?"

"Mmmmm," he said. In light of his usual hard-assed behavior, I was surprised at how easily he assented. I wondered if he, too, was freaking out about Thornhill.

Nia shot out of her chair. Even though she was way closer to the front of the library than I was, she circled around her table and walked by mine. "Front door, two minutes," she hissed. She made her way past the table where Hal was sitting. I heard her clear her throat as she passed him but couldn't tell if she'd been able to tell him what she'd told me.

And then she was gone.

Just as I was wondering if I was supposed to deliver Nia's message to Hal, he said, "Mr. Richards, Nia must have forgotten, but she lent me the book she just went to get from her locker. Can I go tell her to get it from my locker?"

"Fine, fine." Mr. Richards brushed away Hal's question like

it was a pesky fly and kept his face buried in his folder.

And a second later, Hal was out the door, too.

I was still shaking from the news about Mr. Thornhill, and it made it hard to concentrate on finding a legitimate excuse to leave the room.

Mr. Richards, Hal and Nia are both *wrong. I'm the one with the book that Nia wants.*

Sure, Callie. Go join your friends.

A minute passed. Then another. I wracked my brain for a plausible reason to leave before settling on the tried and true.

"Mr. Richards?"

"What?" he asked, lifting his head in exasperation.

"May I please go to the bathroom?"

"Go!" he practically shouted.

I made my way up to the front of the room and past his desk, curious to see what was so interesting to him that our interruptions didn't make him suspicious. But the paper he was looking at just had a lot of *X*'s and *O*'s and lines with arrows, and I couldn't even figure out what it meant, much less why anyone would care about it.

The corridors were as deserted as they had been the previous week, but today there was the howling wind and rain smacking against the enormous windows to contend with. The sky was so dark it felt like evening, not morning, and I wished the lights were on in the hallways. By the time I got to Hal and Nia standing by the front door, I was so freaked out by the news about Thornhill and by the empty, darkened corridors that I was overwhelmed by relief just to see them standing there. Something about the way the morning had gone made it feel possible that they'd have disappeared off the face of the earth.

Anything could happen on a day like this.

Nia was sitting on the hall monitor's desk. As soon as she saw me, she leaped off. "We've got to get into his car *now*."

"Thornhill's attack has something to do with Amanda," said Hal. He was leaning against the wall, but even though his stance seemed casual, I could tell from his clenched fists that he was on edge.

"What?" I took a step back. "What did you hear?"

"Nothing," said Hal. "It's just a feeling."

I couldn't help being irritated. Hal had just scared the crap out of me for a *feeling* he had?

"Hal, no offense, but I think maybe you're being para-noid," I said. I pushed my own fears of the vice principal's having been attacked out of my mind. "For all we knew, he just tripped over his own computer cord and fell."

"Then explain why the police are involved," challenged Nia, following my own train of thought.

I thought of my dad and how much he disliked Thornhill for—as far as I could tell—no good reason. Maybe there were other parents out there whose kids' privileges he'd ended (like Heidi's) or who'd violated his strict code of ethics. Maybe violently assaulting the vice principal because he'd suspended your kid was a bit of an extreme reaction, but surely it could happen.

"Let's say he *was* attacked, and we don't know if that's

the case," I added quickly. "There's no reason to think it has something to do with Amanda. There are about eight hundred students at Endeavor. Even if only two percent of them get in trouble, and you know that's a low estimate, we're still talking about thirty-two parents who could have some reason to go after Thornhill."

"How do you do that?" asked Nia, looking at me like I'd just levitated.

"This wasn't some irate parent," said Hal, ignoring her question.

"What about when, what's his name, Don Marker's dad hit that other dad at the football game and the guy needed stitches," I continued. "There are some crazy people in this town." I didn't add that we'd probably been friends with one of the craziest: a girl who'd claimed to be our friend while lying to us with every word; a girl who simultaneously begged us to look for her and refused to be found.

"Look, guys, for our purposes, whether or not he was attacked by a parent is irrelevant," said Nia. "If he doesn't come out of his coma, the police or *someone* is going to search his car at some point. And when they do, they're going to find Amanda's letter."

"If there even *is* a letter," I pointed out.

Nia ignored me. "We have to know what she said to him. We have to know if he knows something about her. Especially now that he might . . . well, you know."

Neither Hal nor I said anything. Nia had a point. Even if Hal's theory was crazy, he and I had seen (or thought we'd seen) her note. And now that Thornhill was out of commission, someone else was going to get his (or her) hands on that note.

"Look, even if I *wanted* to get into his car," I said, "and I'm not saying I don't, how are we supposed to do it? I mean, did Amanda happen to give either of you a key to an old Honda?"

Smiling, Nia lifted her shirt. Her high-waisted vintage jeans were held up by a belt with a really weird looking metal tool hanging off them.

"Nope," she said. "Which is why I have this."

Outside, it was even colder and rainier than it had been, or maybe it just felt that way since I'd left the slicker inside at my chair. By the time we'd crossed the parking lot to Thornhill's car, my hair was plastered to my head and cold water had begun to trickle down the back of my neck. I wondered how we were going to explain our appearance to Mr. Richards when we traipsed back into the library, dripping water with every step.

Nia had assured us that her brother used this magic tool about once a month, which was how often he locked himself out of *his* Honda, but for several minutes she just stood there, sliding it back and forth between the car doorframe and the window while the three of us got more and more soaked. It occurred to me that if the police *did* want to search Thornhill's car, there was no reason for them not to do it today. And how, exactly, were we going to explain ourselves to them if they did show up? Not to mention any one of a million faculty members, students, or parents who could pull into the parking lot at any second and see that we were trying to jimmy open the car door of a school official.

Suddenly, as if my thinking of it had caused it to happen, a pair of headlights shone on the metal fence that encircles the Endeavor property, and there was the sound of a car slowing.

"Get down!" I shouted, and Hal and I, who had been leaning against the passenger side of the car while Nia worked on the driver's door, quickly raced around the car to huddle next to her.

"What was it?" asked Nia. Her eyes were huge, and I knew she was thinking about what Mr. and Mrs. Rivera would say if Chief Bragg suddenly showed up at their door with their handcuffed daughter.

Slowly a car pulled past us and into the circular driveway. We heard a kid's voice yell, "Bye, Mom!" and then a door slammed shut. A second later, the car pulled onto Ridgeway Drive.

"Oh my god," said Nia. She pressed her forehead against the side of the car.

"We've got to get this car door open," said Hal. "Is there something I can do?"

Nia shook her head slowly, not lifting it off the car. After a minute she stood up and slipped the thin piece of metal back between the doorframe and the window.

"My hands are shaking so much," she explained, but when Hal gestured to take over, she wouldn't let him. "You need to feel it go . . . just . . ." She was biting her lower lip and her eyes were half-closed in concentration. We waited, watching her, my body warm now from the adrenaline pumping through it.

She must have felt something because suddenly she opened her eyes and smiled. "Just like this!" And with that, she put her hand on the door handle and opened it.

I returned Nia's grin with one of my own. A second later, she'd popped open the automatic locks and the three of us scrambled into the car, immediately shutting the doors behind us. I was pretty sure that to anybody speeding by, the driving rain would make it impossible to see into the car's interior. And if the police *did* decide now was the time to check the VP's car for clues . . .

I put the idea out of my head. If I really wanted a distraction, I could calculate the odds, but I opted for good old-fashioned denial.

Just as it had been the day we washed it, Thornhill's car was a total mess on the inside. There were piles of papers and CDs everywhere, old coffee cups, textbooks, and even an ancient, rock-hard donut in a bag shoved under the backseat.

"At least nobody will suspect the car's been ransacked," said Nia. She was sitting in the driver's seat with her head down by the pedals, examining the floor. "We don't exactly have to worry about covering our tracks." Considering how much water we were dripping everywhere, I hoped she was right.

Hal was kneeling on the floor of the passenger seat and going through the pile of papers exactly where I'd thought I saw the note. "It was right here," he said, halfway through the pile. "That's where I thought I saw it."

Nia interrupted her search to watch Hal.

But even though he went through the pile twice, he didn't find the piece of purple notepaper or a purple envelope or anything else that looked like it could be a letter from Amanda.

"Crap," he said finally. "I was so sure it would be here." He beat his fists against the seat. "Crap, crap, crap."

I realized I'd been holding my breath, and I exhaled. "Look, just because we haven't found it yet doesn't mean it's not here. We have to keep looking."

To keep the faith, I turned around and began going through a pile of folders on the backseat next to me. They were the same kind of manila folders that had been in the file drawer back in Thornhill's office, but on each of the folders, there was just a row of numbers and letters on the tab where the student names had been on the ones in the file drawers. Even though I was pretty sure the folders had nothing to do with Amanda, the mysterious codes piqued my interest. I was about to open the top folder when suddenly Nia let out a shriek.

"Look!"

She was sitting in the driver's seat and holding out her hands toward the middle of the car. Lying across her palms was a purple envelope with a coyote sticker in the upper left-hand corner.

"Oh my god," I said, even though I am so not the type of person who says *Oh my god.*

Despite the fact that we were actually looking at it, the note felt unreal to me, as if it would evaporate if we tried to touch it. I wondered if Nia was thinking the same thing because she

284

didn't make a move to open the envelope. For a long minute, we all just sat there, staring at the purple paper.

Finally Hal said, "Open it." Nia, her hands shaking, flipped over the envelope and opened it. The back of the envelope was stained with water or coffee, and some of it had leaked onto the card Nia pulled out.

"It was under the plastic floor protector," said Nia, whether because she wanted to explain the stains or just to fill the silence I didn't know.

And then the card was out of the envelope and we were all looking at Amanda's familiar handwriting.

Underneath the quote, Amanda had scribbled something not in quotes. The writing was so small and messy that at first I couldn't read it. I reached over and took Nia's wrist, turning the card toward me. As I did, the letters formed themselves into three clear words.

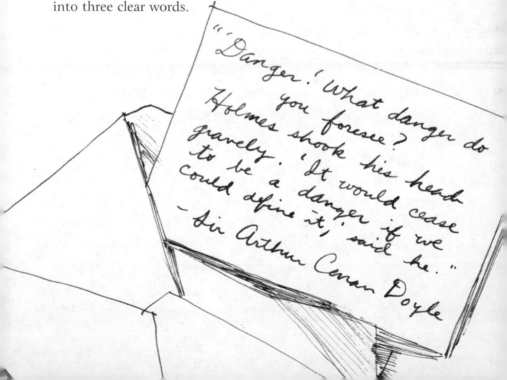

"'Danger! What danger do you foresee?'
Holmes shook his head gravely. 'It would cease to be a danger if we could define it,' said he."
— Sir Arthur Conan Doyle

Please help us .

I don't think I'd ever been so frightened in my entire life. I lifted my eyes from the paper and saw that Nia and Hal were both staring back at me. They looked as scared as I felt. For a second, nobody spoke, then suddenly we were all talking at once.

"Why would she ask Thornhill for help? She *hated* him," I started.

"How could he hide this?" asked Hal. "Why didn't he go to the police?"

"Why didn't he tell us he thought she was in trouble?" demanded Nia.

As if we'd spent our voices with those questions, we again slipped into silence.

"Do you think he thought it was some kind of joke?" I asked finally.

"A joke?" Hal's voice cracked on the second word.

I looked at Nia. To my surprise, her eyes were full of tears. "I'm really scared," she said. "I'm scared something happened to her."

I reached for her hand and held it. "Me too."

Nia reached over to Hal and took his hand with her free one. After a second he said, "Me too."

The only noise was the rain hammering at the roof; every few seconds, a gust of wind so strong it shook the car swept past. Nobody said anything, and nobody made a move to leave.

CHAPTER THIRTY-TWO

"Wow."

"I know."

"It's incredible."

"Seriously."

"I can't believe she did this—she's only twelve."

"I just hope it works."

We were sitting in front of Hal's computer, the three of us staring at the picture of one of Amanda's Oracle cards up on the screen. It seemed impossible that only a few hours had passed since we'd found Amanda's letter to Vice Principal Thornhill.

Someone knocked and simultaneously opened the door. Standing in the doorway was Cornelia.

"Hey," she said.

"This is amazing," I said. "We were just saying that we can't believe you set it up."

Cornelia shrugged, and I thought of all the times people expressed incredulity at my ability to add up a couple of numbers quickly. Even when they mean to be complimentary, sometimes it just makes you feel like a freak.

"I don't see why you don't just go to the police if you're worried about your friend," said Cornelia. She came up behind us and took a cookie out of the open box of Oreos next to Hal.

Nia and I looked at each other. We'd talked about this in the school bathroom while frantically drying ourselves under the hand dryer in the hopes that Mr. Richards wouldn't realize we'd been outside. Nia had pointed out that once we revealed to the police that almost everything Amanda had told us was a lie, they were bound to dismiss her as a nut and the three of us as a bunch of idiots who'd believed some crazy girl who'd claimed she was our friend.

Plus there was the money. What if she'd stolen it? And what if she'd given the school a fake address? How many ways had she possibly broken the law? Maybe their dismissing her as a kook was the *best-case* scenario. Maybe they'd want to find and arrest her.

"Um, hello!" Cornelia wiped some crumbs off her shirt. "I just asked a question."

Hal looked from me to Nia, and when neither of us spoke, he said simply, "It's complicated."

"When people tell you something's complicated, it just means they don't want to tell you about it," said Cornelia. She took another Oreo.

"Yeah, well," said Hal. "Deal with it. Now, how do we work this thing?"

Cornelia leaned over and hit two buttons on the keyboard. When she did, a picture of Amanda that she scanned in from Hal's sketchbook came up on the screen, along with a photograph of the exterior of Play It Again, Sam. There was writing on the screen with words like *edit* and *text* and small boxes drawn around everything.

"Look," she said. "This is how people will get in touch with you, and this is what you have to do to respond to them."

She started moving the arrow around the screen, revealing new empty boxes and typing into them as she went. A few times she went to the top of the screen and clicked onto another page with the heading "Our Stories" on it, all the while explaining what she was doing. But I couldn't concentrate on what she was saying, and it's not just because for a mathematician I'm a total Luddite. As I watched the pictures Hal had sketched flying past, along with photos of Thornhill's car, quotes from Amanda, and facts we knew about her, I thought again how crazy it was that we had *no* photographs of her entire face, only ones that caught her in profile or from the back or got a glimpse of her leg or shoe or bag. When we'd realized this, Nia had asked her brother to text the yearbook editor (who despite being a senior would, we knew, *immediately* return a text from Cisco Rivera) to get their photo of Amanda, only to discover she'd been absent on photo day.

A coincidence? I shuddered, shocked by how we'd stupidly lost (or she had purposely erased) all identifying images of Amanda Valentino. The words from her note ran through my head like a voiceover. *Danger! What danger do you foresee? Danger! What danger do you foresee?*

And then, as if I were reading aloud from the card, I found myself whispering the three words Amanda herself had written.

Nia must have heard me because she put her arm around my shoulder. "It's going to work. Somebody out there is going to know something."

I nodded.

"So that's basically it," said Cornelia. She hit another key and a new screen came up, one I hadn't seen before. "When you're ready, you just hit LAUNCH." She took another Oreo from the package.

"Thanks," said Nia.

"Yeah," I whispered. "Thanks."

"Sure," said Cornelia. "Happy to help." She headed across the room to the door.

"Hey," Nia called to her, "I have a question." Cornelia turned around. "How'd you come up with the name?"

Cornelia cocked her head to one side and looked up at the ceiling, absently licking at the filling of the cookie. "Well, like I'd expected, amanda.com and amandavalentino.com were taken. And then I remembered what you'd said about this being a major project and so I just . . ." She shrugged and bit into the cookie.

"Got it," said Nia. "Well, thanks again."

"No problem," said Cornelia.

When he heard the click of the door, Hal turned around on his chair to face us.

"So," he said. I could read the strain of the past week on his tired face.

"Speak now," Nia intoned. "Or forever hold your peace."

I felt the fear I'd been feeling all day sitting in my stomach like something I'd eaten. What if this didn't work? What if there was no one out there who knew anything about Amanda?

As if he could read my mind, Hal said, "I can't decide which I'm more scared of—that nobody will know anything about her, or that tons of people will."

"Well," said Nia, "we'll never know until we ask."

Her voice was casual, but when I looked down, I saw that her hands were shaking.

"So we're agreed?" said Hal. He looked at Nia. When she nodded, he turned to me. For a second, our eyes seemed to bore into one another's. I thought of all the gifts Amanda had given me—not just the money and the tattoo, but Hal and Nia and a sense that there was more to life than being one of Heidi Bragg's satellites. Looking for Amanda had already changed my life for the better. Was I really going to stop searching for her now, just when we'd realized she needed us? If Amanda had taught me one thing, it was how to be a friend. And if there was one thing Amanda needed now, it was her friends.

Without taking my eyes from Hal's, I nodded. "We're agreed."

Hal turned his chair back so he was facing the computer, then slid his hand over the mouse pad until the arrow on the screen sat on the LAUNCH icon.

"Ready or not . . . ," said Hal, and he clicked.

Almost before he'd hit the button, the screen changed to a single line of text with a small drawing of a clock on which the minute hand was racing around. *Please wait a moment while www. theamandaproject.com launches.*

A second later, the home page of The Amanda Project filled the screen. A single line of text appeared over Cornelia's design. *Your site has successfully launched.* The words only remained there briefly; then they disappeared and we were looking at a photo of Amanda—mostly the side of her face and her arm—with a brick wall in the background. *What happened to Amanda?* the screen demanded. And then it seemed to plead, *Will you help us find her?*

"No way to turn back now," said Hal.

"Seriously," said Nia.

But as we each put a hand on the back of Hal's chair and stood behind him, staring at the computer screen, I had the feeling that it wasn't just too late to turn back now.

Somehow I knew that it had always been too late to turn back.

THE NIGHT WE LAUNCHED THE WEBSITE, THIS POST
APPEARED. WE COULDN'T BELIEVE IT! RESPONSES FROM ALL
SORTS OF PEOPLE WE NEVER WOULD'VE IMAGINED. JUST LIKE
AMANDA SAID, ANSWERS COME FROM UNEXPECTED PLACES.

WE LOVED WHAT STACY HAD TO SAY, AND WE RUSHED IT IN AS
THE BOOK WAS GOING TO THE PRINTER.

—HAL, CALLIE & NIA

WHO IS THIS AMANDA TRULY?

Posted: 31 March 7:17pm

From the moment Amanda walked into my math class,
I knew she was no normal girl. From what I can tell
she seemed different to everyone. Her unusual fashion choices were the first glaringly obvious clues that
she certainly was not of this world. She sat diagonally
across from me, and, well, because of my own shyness,
I never actually spoke with her, but I observed her carefully. Call me creepy, but I like to study people. I guess
it's my fascination with psychology. She seemed rather
secretive. She kept a lot to herself, although she is far
from shy. She spoke to anybody and everybody.

From what I saw, she is intelligent, always participating and getting the answers right in class; she is secretive, from her shady background to her suspicious reasons for coming here; she is clearly hiding something. And I found her to be strangely enchanting. Most everyone around her seems to be drawn to her. I have yet to find someone who dislikes her that actually knows her. Though, perhaps, we don't—any of us—truly know her. With so much of herself hidden, who is this Amanda?

When Amanda went missing, I wasn't too surprised, considering from the beginning this girl gave off a vibe that screamed trouble. She is just too unusual for there not to be a mystery revolving around her.

So please, tell us all, what have you seen of Amanda? What have you spoken with her about? And most important of all, who is she? Do you know the answer, for I fear I fall far from it . . .

Yours truly, Stacy <3

CHARACTER NAME:	Stacy
CHARACTER SCREEN NAME:	Physics Nerd
MEMBER SINCE:	March 31, 2009
MY FAVORITE TUESDAY OUTFIT:	3-inch heels, skinny jeans, trendy colorful shirt, long necklace, dangly earrings, 2 rings, and a bracelet
THE BEST BREAKFAST:	Lucky Charms, bagel with strawberry cream cheese, cantaloupe, Eggo waffle, and a sunny-side down egg

---

ABOUT THE AUTHOR: Lisa Sturm is a 17-year-old high school senior in Texas. She spends most of her free time reading and hopes to one day be an author.

signal from afar

So, Callie did a good job of getting this story started, but I'll be telling you the next part of our search for Amanda in *Signal from Afar*. Amanda is still missing, obviously, and still sending us messages and leaving strange clues that we have to interpret, which we try our best to do, in those rare times we can agree. Nia? Callie? ME? We are about the oddest combo platter ever— we never expected to be friends, much less the only three people (well, with my sister, Cornelia, who just can't stay out of our business) who seem to be able to put together all these totally random pieces of Amanda's life. We're trying to follow her bread crumbs to find her, but now some weirdos are constantly warning us to give it up, which makes the whole thing take a turn for the . . . more mysterious. Anyway, keep checking out the website and sending us your ideas, and look out for book two.

See you online,
Hal

WWW.THEAMANDAPROJECT.COM

CORNELIA'S CODE

Hey, Guys!

Cornelia here. Have you ever seen someone and wondered if they know what you know? Or wondered how to let them know that you know that they know what you know, without actually saying it, just in case they don't know what you know? Luckily, I've come up with the perfect solution—datamatrix codes! They're BIG in Japan, which means they're headed this way. (Um, Pokémon? Sushi? Hello Kitty? Need I say more?)

I looove using new technology (duh), which is why I am SO excited for you guys to start using the codes to help Hal, Callie, and Nia find Amanda.

Basically, a datamatrix code is a bar code like the ones you're used to seeing in stores . . . only way cooler. You don't need a special scanner, just a phone with camera and internet connection. To read them, all you have to do is:

- Use your phone to download the 2D Bar Code reader software at http://theamandaproject.mobi/thereader
- Fire it up (it's usually under Applications)
- Snap a picture of the code using your phone's camera

And voilà! The browser on your phone will automatically unlock the magic programmed into the code—a secret website with video, messages, pictures, and more!

So, what's the secret in this code? You'll have to scan to find out. And remember— the next time you see a code it might be a message from me, or from Amanda, or from that new girl at school who wants to know if you know what she knows . . .

Over and out
— Cornelia B.

theamandaproject.mobi/cornelia